THE INCREDULITY OF FATHER BROWN

G. K. CHESTERTON

G. K. Chesterton was born in 1874, and educated at St Paul's School, where, despite his efforts to achieve honourable oblivion at the bottom of his class, he was singled out as a boy with distinct literary promise. He decided to follow art as a career, and studied at the Slade School, where, while 'attending or not attending to his studies', he met Ernest Hodder-Williams, who formed the fixed notion that Chesterton could write. At his request he reviewed a number of books for the *Bookman* and found himself launched on a profession he was to follow all his life. Probably his most famous stories are those of 'Father Brown', but he wrote much about every conceivable subject under or beyond the sun. The best accounts of his life are to be found in his own *Autobiography*, published soon after his death in 1936, and in Miss Maisie Ward's *Life* of him. Several of his books are available in Penguins.

Cover design by Romek Marber

G. K. CHESTERTON

THE INCREDULITY OF FATHER BROWN

*

PENGUIN BOOKS

Penguin Books Ltd, Harmondsworth, Middlesex
AUSTRALIA: Penguin Books Pty Ltd, 762 Whitehorse Road,
Mitcham, Victoria

———

First published by Cassell 1926
Published in Penguin Books 1958
Reprinted 1960, 1962, 1963

———

———

Made and printed in Great Britain
by Cox and Wyman Ltd,
London, Reading, and Fakenham
Set in Monotype Times

CONTENTS

★

ONE

The Resurrection of Father Brown

THERE was a brief period during which Father Brown enjoyed, or rather did not enjoy, something like fame. He was a nine days' wonder in the newspapers; he was even a common topic of controversy in the weekly reviews; his exploits were narrated eagerly and inaccurately in any number of clubs and drawing-rooms, especially in America. Incongruous and indeed incredible as it may seem to any one who knew him, his adventures as a detective were even made the subject of short stories appearing in magazines.

Strangely enough, this wandering limelight struck him in the most obscure, or at least the most remote, of his many places of residence. He had been sent out to officiate, as something between a missionary and a parish priest, in one of those sections of the northern coast of South America, where strips of country still cling insecurely to European powers, or are continually threatening to become independent republics, under the gigantic shadow of President Monroe. The population was red and brown with pink spots; that is, it was Spanish-American, and largely Spanish-American-Indian, but there was a considerable and increasing infiltration of Americans of the northern sort – Englishmen, Germans, and the rest. And the trouble seems to have begun when one of these visitors, very recently landed and very much annoyed at having lost one of his bags, approached the first building of which he came in sight – which happened to be the mission-house and chapel attached to it, in front of which ran a long veranda and a long row of stakes, up which were trained the black twisted vines, their square leaves red with autumn. Behind them, also in a row, a number of human beings sat almost as rigid as the stakes, and coloured in some fashion like the vines. For while their broad-brimmed hats were as black as their unblinking eyes, the complexions of many of them might have been made out of the dark red timber of those transatlantic forests. Many of them were smoking very long, thin black cigars; and in all that group the smoke was almost the only moving thing. The visitor would probably have described them as natives, though some of them were very proud of Spanish blood. But he was not one to draw any fine distinction between Spaniards and Red Indians, being rather disposed to dismiss people from the scene when once he had convicted them of being native to it.

He was a newspaper man from Kansas City, a lean, light-haired man with what Meredith called an adventurous nose; one could almost fancy it found its way by feeling its way and moved like the proboscis of an ant-eater. His name was Snaith, and his parents, after some obscure meditation, had called him Saul, a fact which he had the good feeling to conceal as far as possible. Indeed, he had ultimately compromised by calling himself Paul, though by no means for the same reason that had affected the Apostle of the Gentiles. On the contrary, so far as he had any views on such things, the name of the persecutor would have been more appropriate; for he regarded organized religion with the conventional contempt which can be learnt more easily from Ingersoll than from Voltaire. And this was, as it happened, the not very important side of his character which he turned towards the mission-station and the groups in front of the veranda. Something in their shameless repose and indifference inflamed his own fury of efficiency; and, as he could get no particular answer to his first questions, he began to do all the talking himself.

Standing out there in the strong sunshine, a spick-and-span figure in his Panama hat and neat clothes, his grip-sack held in a steely grip, he began to shout at the people in the shadow. He began to explain to them very loudly why they were lazy and filthy, and bestially ignorant and lower than the beasts that perish, in case this problem should have previously exercised their minds. In his opinion it was the deleterious influence of priests that had made them so miserably poor and so hopelessly oppressed that they were able to sit in the shade and smoke and do nothing.

'And a mighty soft crowd you must be at that,' he said, 'to be bullied by these stuck-up josses because they walk about in their mitres and their tiaras and their gold copes and other glad rags, looking down on everybody else like dirt – being bamboozled by crowns and canopies and sacred umbrellas like a kid at a panto-mime; just because a pompous old High Priest of Mumbo-Jumbo looks as if he was the lord of the earth. What about you? What do you look like, you poor simps? I tell you, that's why you're way-back in barbarism and can't read or write and –'

At this point the High Priest of Mumbo-Jumbo came in an undignified hurry out of the door of the mission-house, not look-ing very like a lord of the earth, but rather like a bundle of black second-hand clothes buttoned round a short bolster in the sem-blance of a guy. He was not wearing his tiara, supposing him to possess one, but a shabby broad hat not very dissimilar from those of the Spanish Indians, and it was thrust to the back of his head with a gesture of botheration. He seemed just about to speak to the motionless natives when he caught sight of the stranger and said quickly:

'Oh, can I be of any assistance? Would you like to come inside?'

Mr Paul Snaith came inside; and it was the beginning of a considerable increase of that journalist's information on many things. Presumably his journalistic instinct was stronger than his prejudices, as, indeed, it often is in clever journalists; and he asked a good many questions, the answers to which interested and surprised him. He discovered that the Indians could read and write, for the simple reason that the priest had taught them; but that they did not read or write any more than they could help, from a natural preference for more direct communications. He learned that these strange people, who sat about in heaps on the veranda without stirring a hair, could work quite hard on their own patches of land; especially those of them who were more than half Spanish; and he learned with still more astonishment that they all had patches of land that were really their own. That much was part of a stubborn tradition that seemed quite native to natives. But in that also the priest had played a certain part, and by doing so had taken perhaps what was his first and last part in politics, if it was only local politics. There had recently swept through that region one of those fevers of atheist and almost anarchist Radicalism which break out periodically in countries of the Latin culture, generally beginning in a secret society and generally ending in a civil war and in very little else. The local leader of the iconoclastic party was a certain Alvarez, a rather picturesque adventurer of Portuguese nationality but, as his enemies said, of partly Negro origin, the head of any number of lodges and temples of initiation of the sort that in such places clothe even atheism with something mystical. The leader on the more conservative side was a much more commonplace person, a very wealthy man named Mendoza, the owner of many factories and quite respectable, but not very exciting. It was the general opinion that the cause of law and order would have been entirely lost if it had not adopted a more popular policy of its own, in the form of securing land for the peasants; and this movement had mainly originated from the little mission-station of Father Brown.

While he was talking to the journalist, Mendoza, the Conservative leader, came in. He was a stout, dark man, with a bald head like a pear and a round body also like a pear; he was smoking a very fragrant cigar, but he threw it away, perhaps a little theatrically, when he came into the presence of the priest, as if he had been entering church; and bowed with a curve that in so corpulent a gentleman seemed quite improbable. He was always exceedingly serious in his social gestures, especially towards religious institutions. He was one of those laymen who are much more ecclesiastical than ecclesiastics. It embarrassed Father Brown a good deal, especially when carried thus into private life.

'I think I am an anti-clerical,' Father Brown would say with a faint smile; 'but there wouldn't be half so much clericalism if they would only leave things to the clerics.'

'Why Mr Mendoza,' exclaimed the journalist with a new animation, 'I think we have met before. Weren't you at the Trade Congress in Mexico last year?'

The heavy eyelids of Mr Mendoza showed a flutter of recognition, and he smiled in his slow way. 'I remember.'

'Pretty big business done there in an hour or two,' said Snaith with relish. 'Made a good deal of difference to you, too, I guess.'

'I have been very fortunate,' said Mendoza modestly.

'Don't you believe it!' cried the enthusiastic Snaith. 'Good fortune comes to the people who know when to catch hold; and you caught hold good and sure. But I hope I'm not interrupting your business?'

'Not at all,' said the other. 'I often have the honour of calling on the padre for a little talk. Merely for a little talk.'

It seemed as if this familiarity between Father Brown and a successful and even famous man of business completed the reconciliation between the priest and the practical Mr Snaith. He felt, it might be supposed, a new respectability clothe the station and the mission, and was ready to overlook such occasional reminders of the existence of religion as a chapel and a presbytery can seldom wholly avoid. He became quite enthusiastic about the priest's programme – at least on its secular and social side – and announced himself ready at any moment to act in the capacity of a live wire for its communication to the world at large. And it was at this point that Father Brown began to find the journalist rather more troublesome in his sympathy than in his hostility.

Mr Paul Snaith set out vigorously to feature Father Brown. He sent long and loud eulogies on him across the continent to his newspaper in the Middle West. He took snapshots of the unfortunate cleric in the most commonplace occupations, and exhibited them in gigantic photographs in the gigantic Sunday papers of the United States. He turned his sayings into slogans, and was continually presenting the world with 'A message' from the reverend gentleman in South America. Any stock less strong and strenuously receptive than the American race would have become very much bored with Father Brown. As it was, he received handsome and eager offers to go on a lecturing tour in the States; and when he declined, the terms were raised with expressions of respectful wonder. A series of stories about him, like the stories of Sherlock Holmes, were, by the instrumentality of Mr Snaith, planned out and put before the hero with requests for his assistance and encouragement. As the priest found they had started, he could offer no suggestion except that they should stop. And this in turn was taken by Mr Snaith as the text for a discussion on whether Father Brown should disappear temporarily over a cliff, in the manner of Dr Watson's hero. To all these demands the priest had patiently to reply in writing, saying that he would consent on such terms to the temporary cessation of the stories and begging that a considerable interval might occur before they began again. The notes he wrote grew shorter and shorter; and as he wrote the last of them, he sighed.

Needless to say, this strange boom in the North reacted on the little outpost in the South where he had expected to live in so lonely an exile. The considerable English and American population already on the spot began to be proud of possessing so widely advertised a person. American tourists, of the sort who land with a loud demand for Westminister Abbey, landed on that distant coast with a loud demand for Father Brown. They were within measurable distance of running excursion trains named after him, and bringing crowds to see him as if he were a public monument. He was especially troubled by the active and ambitious new traders and shopkeepers of the place, who were perpetually pestering him to try their wares and to give them testimonials. Even if the testimonials were not forthcoming, they would prolong the correspondence for the purpose of collecting autographs. As he was a good-natured person they got a good deal of what they wanted out of him; and it was in answer to a particular request from a Frankfort wine-merchant named Eckstein that he wrote hastily a few words on a card, which were to prove a terrible turning-point in his life.

Eckstein was a fussy little man with fuzzy hair and pince-nez, who was wildly anxious that the priest should not only try some of his celebrated medicinal port, but should let him know where and when he would drink it, in acknowledging its receipt. The priest was not particularly surprised at the request, for he was long past surprise at the lunacies of advertisement. So he scribbled something down and turned to other business which seemed a little more sensible. He was again interrupted, by a note from no less a person than his political enemy Alvarez, asking him to come to a conference at which it was hoped that a compromise on an outstanding question might be reached; and suggesting an appointment that evening at a café just outside the walls of the little town. To this also he sent a message of acceptance by the rather florid and military messenger who was waiting for it; and then, having an hour or two before him, sat down to attempt to get through a little of his own legitimate business. At the end of the time he poured himself out a glass of Mr Eckstein's remarkable wine and, glancing at the clock with a humorous expression, drank it and went out into the night.

Strong moonlight lay on the little Spanish town, so that when he came to the picturesque gateway, with its rather rococo arch and the fantastic fringe of palms beyond it, it looked rather like a scene in a Spanish opera. One long leaf of palm with jagged edges, black against the moon, hung down on the other side of the arch, visible through the archway, and had something of the look of the jaw of a black crocodile. The fancy would not have lingered in his imagination but for something else that caught his naturally alert eye. The air was deathly still, and there was not a stir of wind; but he distinctly saw the pendent palm-leaf move.

He looked around him and realized that he was alone. He had left behind the last houses, which were mostly closed and shuttered, and was walking between two long blank walls built of large and shapeless but flattened stones, tufted here and there with the queer prickly weeds of that region – walls which ran parallel all the way to the gateway. He could not see the lights of the café outside the gate; probably it was too far away. Nothing could be seen under the arch but a wider expanse of large-flagged pavement, pale in the moon, with the straggling prickly pear here and there. He had a strong sense of the smell of evil; he felt queer physical oppression; but he did not think of stopping. His courage, which was considerable, was perhaps even less strong a part of him than his curiosity. All his life he had been led by an intellectual hunger for the truth, even of trifles. He often controlled it in the name of proportion; but it was always there. He walked straight through the gateway, and on the other side a man sprang like a monkey out of the tree-top and struck at him with a knife. At the same moment another man came crawling swiftly along the wall and, whirling a cudgel round his head, brought it down. Father Brown turned, staggered, and sank in a heap, but as he sank there dawned on his round face an expression of mild and immense surprise.

There was living in the same little town at this time another young American, particularly different from Mr Paul Snaith. His name was John Adams Race, and he was an electrical engineer, employed by Mendoza to fit out the old town with all the new conveniences. He was a figure far less familiar in satire and international gossip than that of the American journalist. Yet, as a matter of fact, America contains a million men of the moral type of Race to one of the moral type of Snaith. He was exceptional in being exceptionally good at his job, but in every other way he was very simple. He had begun life as a druggist's assistant in a Western village, and risen by sheer work and merit; but he still regarded his home town as the natural heart of the habitable world. He had been taught a very Puritan, or purely Evangelical, sort of Christianity from the Family Bible at his mother's knee; and in so far as he had time to have any religion, that was still his religion. Amid all the dazzling lights of the latest and even wildest discoveries, when he was at the very edge and extreme of experiment, working miracles of light and sound like a god creating new stars and solar systems, he never for a moment doubted that the things 'back home' were the best things in the world; his mother and the Family Bible and the quiet and quaint morality of his village. He had as serious and noble a sense of the sacredness of his mother as if he had been a frivolous Frenchman. He was quite sure the Bible religion was really the right thing; only he vaguely missed it wherever he went in the modern world. He could hardly be expected to sympathize with the religious externals of Catholic countries; and in a dislike of mitres and croziers he sympathized with Mr Snaith, though not in so cocksure a fashion. He had no liking for the public bowings and scrapings of Mendoza and certainly no temptation to the masonic mysticism of the atheist Alvarez. Perhaps all that semi-tropical life was too coloured for him, shot with Indian red and Spanish gold. Anyhow, when he said there was nothing to touch his home town, he was not boasting. He really meant that there was somewhere something plain and unpretentious and touching, which he really respected more than anything else in the world. Such being the mental attitude of John Adams Race in a South American station, there had been growing on him for some time a curious feeling, which contradicted all his prejudices and for which he could not account. For the truth was this: that the only thing he had ever met in his travels that in the least reminded him of the old wood-pile and the provincial proprieties and the Bible on his mother's knee was (for some inscrutable reason) the round face and black clumsy umbrella of Father Brown.

He found himself insensibly watching that commonplace and even comic black figure as it went bustling about; watching it with an almost morbid fascination, as if it were a walking riddle or contradiction. He had found something he could not help liking in the heart of everything he hated; it was as if he had been horribly tormented by lesser demons and then found that the Devil was quite an ordinary person.

Thus it happened that, looking out of his window on that moonlit night, he saw the Devil go by, the demon of unaccountable blamelessness, in his broad black hat and long black coat, shuffling along the street towards the gateway, and saw it with an interest which he could not himself understand. He wondered where the priest was going, and what he was really up to; and remained gazing out into the moonlit street long after the little black figure had passed. And then he saw something else that intrigued him further. Two other men whom he recognized passed across his window as across a lighted stage. A sort of blue limelight of the moon ran in a spectral halo round the big bush of hair that stood erect on the head of little Eckstein, the wine-seller, and it outlined a taller and darker figure with an eagle profile and a queer old-fashioned and very top-heavy black hat, which seemed to make the whole outline still more bizarre, like a shape in a shadow pantomime. Race rebuked himself for allowing the moon to play such tricks with his fancy; for on a second glance he recognized the black Spanish sidewhiskers and high-featured face of Dr Calderon, a worthy medical man of the town, whom he had once found attending professionally on Mendoza. Still, there was something in the way the men were whispering to each other and peering up the street that struck him as peculiar. On a sudden impulse he leapt over the low window-sill and himself went bareheaded up the road, following their trail. He saw them disappear under the dark archway, and a moment after there came a dreadful cry from beyond; curiously loud and piercing, and all the more blood-curdling to Race because it said something very distinctly in some tongue that he did not know.

The next moment there was a rushing of feet, more cries, and then a confused roar of rage or grief that shook the turrets and tall palm trees of the place; there was a movement in the mob that had gathered, as if they were sweeping backwards through the gateway. And then the dark archway resounded with a new voice, this time intelligible to him and falling with the note of doom, as someone shouted through the gateway:

'Father Brown is dead!'

He never knew what prop gave way in his mind, or why something on which he had been counting suddenly failed him; but he ran towards the gateway and was just in time to meet his countryman, the journalist Snaith, coming out of the dark entrance, deadly pale and snapping his fingers nervously.

'It's quite true,' said Snaith, with something which for him approached to reverence. 'He's a goner. The doctor's been looking at him, and there's no hope. Some of these damned Dagos clubbed him as he came through the gate – God knows why. It'll be a great loss to the place.'

Race did not or perhaps could not reply, but ran on under the arch to the scene beyond. The small black figure lay where it had fallen on the wilderness of wide stones starred here and there with green thorn; and the great crowd was being kept back, chiefly by the mere gestures of one gigantic figure in the foreground. For there were many there who swayed hither and thither at the mere movement of his hand, as if he had been a magician.

Alvarez, the dictator and demagogue, was a tall, swaggering figure, always rather flamboyantly clad, and on this occasion he wore a green uniform with embroideries like silver snakes crawling all over it, with an order round his neck hung on a very vivid maroon ribbon. His close curling hair was already grey, and in contrast his complexion, which his friends called olive and his foes octoroon, looked almost literally golden, as if it were a mask moulded in gold. But his large-featured face, which was powerful and humorous, was at this moment properly grave and grim. He had been waiting, he explained, for Father Brown at the café when he had heard a rustle and a fall and, coming out, had found the corpse lying on the flagstones.

'I know what some of you are thinking,' he said, looking round proudly, 'and if you are afraid of me – as you are – I will say it for you. I am an atheist; I have no god to call on for those who will not take my word. But I tell you in the name of every root of honour that may be left to a soldier and a man, that I had no part in this. If I had the men here that did it, I would rejoice to hang them on that tree.'

'Naturally we are glad to hear you say so,' said old Mendoza stiffly and solemnly, standing by the body of his fallen coadjutor. 'This blow has been too appalling for us to say what else we feel at present. I suggest that it will be more decent and proper if we remove my friend's body and break up this irregular meeting. I understand,' he added gravely to the doctor, 'that there is unfortunately no doubt.'

'There is no doubt,' said Dr Calderon.

John Race went back to his lodgings sad and with a singular sense of emptiness. It seemed impossible that he should miss a man whom he never knew. He learned that the funeral was to take place next day; for all felt that the crisis should be past as quickly as possible, for fear of riots that were hourly growing more probable. When Snaith had seen the row of Red Indians sitting on the veranda, they might have been a row of ancient Aztec images carved in red wood. But he had not seen them as they were when they heard that the priest was dead.

Indeed they would certainly have risen in revolution and lynched the republican leader, if they had not been immediately blocked by the direct necessity of behaving respectfully to the coffin of their own religious leader. The actual assassins, whom it would have been most natural to lynch, seemed to have vanished into thin air. Nobody knew their names; and nobody would ever know whether the dying man had even seen their faces. That strange look of surprise that was apparently his last look on earth might have been the recognition of their faces. Alvarez repeated violently that it was no work of his, and attended the funeral, walking behind the coffin in his splendid silver and green uniform with a sort of bravado of reverence.

Behind the veranda a flight of stone steps scaled a very steep green bank, fenced by a cactus-hedge, and up this the coffin was laboriously lifted to the ground above, and placed temporarily at the foot of the great gaunt crucifix that dominated the road and guarded the consecrated ground. Below in the road were great seas of people lamenting and telling their beads – an orphan population that had lost a father. Despite all these symbols that were provocative enough to him, Alvarez behaved with restraint and respect; and all would have gone well – as Race told himself – had the others only let him alone.

Race told himself bitterly that old Mendoza had always looked like an old fool and had now very conspicuously and completely behaved like an old fool. By a custom common in simpler societies, the coffin was left open and the face uncovered, bringing the pathos to the point of agony for all those simple people. This, being consonant to tradition, need have done no harm; but some officious person had added to it the custom of the French free-thinkers, of having speeches by the graveside. Mendoza proceeded to make a speech – a rather long speech, and the longer it was, the longer and lower sank John Race's spirits and sympathies with the religious ritual involved. A list of saintly attributes, apparently of the most antiquated sort, was rolled out with the dilatory dullness of an after-dinner speaker who does not know how to sit down. That was bad enough; but Mendoza had also the ineffable stupidity to start reproaching and even taunting his political opponents. In three minutes he had succeeded in making a scene, and a very extraordinary scene it was.

'We may well ask,' he said, looking around him pompously;

'we may well ask where such virtues can be found among those who have madly abandoned the creed of their fathers. It is when we have atheists among us, atheist leaders, nay sometimes even atheist rulers, that we find their infamous philosophy bearing fruit in crimes like this. If we ask who murdered this holy man, we shall assuredly find –'

Africa of the forests looked out of the eyes of Alvarez the hybrid adventurer; and Race fancied he could see suddenly that the man was after all a barbarian, who could not control himself to the end; one might guess that all his 'illuminated' transcendentalism had a touch of Voodoo. Anyhow, Mendoza could not continue, for Alvarez had sprung up and was shouting back at him and shouting him down, with infinitely superior lungs.

'Who murdered him?' he roared. 'Your God murdered him! His own God murdered him! According to you, he murders all his faithful and foolish servants – as he murdered *that* one,' and he made a violent gesture, not towards the coffin but the crucifix. Seeming to control himself a little, he went on in a tone still angry but more argumentative: 'I don't believe it, but you do. Isn't it better to have no God than one that robs you in this fashion? I, at least, am not afraid to say that there is none. There is no power in all this blind and brainless universe that can hear your prayer or return your friend. Though you beg Heaven to raise him, he will not rise. Though I dare Heaven to raise him, he will not rise. Here and now I will put it to the test – I defy the God who is not there to waken the man who sleeps for ever.'

There was a shock of silence, and the demagogue had made his sensation.

'We might have known,' cried Mendoza in a thick gobbling voice, 'when we allowed such men as you –'

A new voice cut into his speech; a high and shrill voice with a Yankee accent.

'Stop! Stop!' cried Snaith the journalist; 'something's up! I swear I saw him move.'

He went racing up the steps and rushed to the coffin, while the mob below swayed with indescribable frenzies. The next moment he had turned a face of amazement over his shoulder and made a signal with his finger to Dr Calderon, who hastened forward to confer with him. When the two men stepped away again from the coffin, all could see that the position of the head had altered. A roar of excitement rose from the crowd and seemed to stop suddenly, as if cut off in mid-air; for the priest in the coffin gave a groan and raised himself on one elbow, looking with bleared and blinking eyes at the crowd.

John Adams Race, who had hitherto known only miracles of science, never found himself able in after-years to describe the topsy-turvydom of the next few days. He seemed to have burst out of the world of time and space, and to be living in the impossible. In half an hour the whole of that town and district had been transformed into something never known for a thousand years; a medieval people turned to a mob of monks by a staggering miracle; a Greek city where the god had descended among men. Thousands prostrated themselves in the road; hundreds took vows on the spot; and even the outsiders, like the two Americans, were able to think and speak of nothing but the prodigy. Alvarez himself was shaken, as well he might be; and sat down, with his head upon his hands.

And in the midst of all this tornado of beatitude was a little man struggling to be heard. His voice was small and faint, and the noise was deafening. He made weak little gestures that seemed more those of irritation than anything else. He came to the edge of the parapet above the crowd, waving it to be quiet, with movements rather like the flap of the short wings of a penguin. There was something a little more like a lull in the noise; and then Father Brown for the first time reached the utmost stretch of the indignation that he could launch against his children.

'Oh, you *silly* people,' he said in a high and quavering voice; 'Oh, you silly, *silly* people.'

Then he suddenly seemed to pull himself together, made a bolt for the steps with his more normal gait, and began hurriedly to descend.

'Where are you going, Father?' said Mendoza, with more than his usual veneration.

'To the telegraph office,' said Father Brown hastily. 'What?

No; of course it's not a miracle. Why should there be a miracle? Miracles are not so cheap as all that.'

And he came tumbling down the steps, the people flinging themselves before him to implore his blessing.

'Bless you, bless you,' said Father Brown hastily. 'God bless you all and give you more sense.'

And he scuttled away with extraordinary rapidity to the telegraph office, where he wired to his Bishop's secretary: 'There is some mad story about a miracle here; hope his lordship not give authority. Nothing in it.'

As he turned away from his effort, he tottered a little with the reaction, and John Race caught him by the arm.

'Let me see you home,' he said; 'you deserve more than these people are giving you.'

John Race and the priest were seated in the presbytery; the table was still piled up with the papers with which the latter had been wrestling the day before; the bottle of wine and the emptied wine-glass still stood where he had left them.

'And now,' said Father Brown almost grimly, 'I can begin to think.'

'I shouldn't think too hard just yet,' said the American. 'You must be wanting a rest. Besides, what are you going to think about?'

'I have pretty often had the task of investigating murders, as it happens,' said Father Brown. 'Now I have got to investigate my own murder.'

'If I were you,' said Race, 'I should take a little wine first.'

Father Brown stood up and filled himself another glass, lifted it, looked thoughtfully into vacancy, and put it down again. Then he sat down once more and said:

'Do you know what I felt like when I died? You may not believe it, but my feeling was one of overwhelming astonishment.'

'Well,' answered Race, 'I suppose you were astonished at being knocked on the head.'

Father Brown leaned over to him and said in a low voice,

'I was astonished at not being knocked on the head.'

21

Race looked at him for a moment as if he thought the knock on the head had been only too effective; but he only said: 'What do you mean?'

'I mean that when that man brought his bludgeon down with a great swipe, it stopped at my head and did not even touch it. In the same way, the other fellow made as if to strike me with a knife, but he never gave me a scratch. It was just like play-acting. I think it was. But then followed the extraordinary thing.'

He looked thoughtfully at the papers on the table for a moment and then went on:

'Though I had not even been touched with knife or stick, I began to feel my legs doubling up under me and my very life failing. I knew I was being struck down by something, but it was not by those weapons. Do you know what I think it was?'

And he pointed to the wine on the table.

Race picked up the wine-glass and looked at it and smelt it.

'I think you are right,' he said. 'I began as a druggist and studied chemistry. I couldn't say for certain without an analysis, but I think there's something very unusual in this stuff. There are drugs by which the Asiatics produce a temporary sleep that looks like death.'

'Quite so,' said the priest calmly. 'The whole of this miracle was faked, for some reason or other. That funeral scene was staged – and timed. I think it is part of that raving madness of publicity that has got hold of Snaith; but I can hardly believe he would go quite so far, merely for that. After all, it's one thing to make copy out of me and run me as a sort of sham Sherlock Holmes, and –'

Even as the priest spoke his face altered. His blinking eyelids shut suddenly and he stood up as if he were choking. Then he put one wavering hand as if groping his way towards the door.

'Where are you going?' asked the other in some wonder.

'If you ask me,' said Father Brown, who was quite white, 'I was going to pray. Or rather, to praise.'

'I'm not sure I understand. What is the matter with you?'

'I was going to praise God for having so strangely and so incredibly saved me – saved me by an inch.'

'Of course,' said Race, 'I am not of your religion; but believe me, I have religion enough to understand that. Of course, you would thank God for saving you from death.'

'No,' said the priest. 'Not from death. From disgrace.'

The other sat staring; and the priest's next words broke out of him with a sort of cry.

'And if it had only been my disgrace! But it was the disgrace of all I stand for; the disgrace of the Faith that they went about to encompass. What it might have been! The most huge and horrible scandal ever launched against us since the last lie was choked in the throat of Titus Oates.'

'What on earth are you talking about?' demanded his companion.

'Well, I had better tell you at once,' said the priest; and sitting down, he went on more composedly: 'It came to me in a flash when I happened to mention Snaith and Sherlock Holmes. Now I happen to remember what I wrote about his absurd scheme; it was the natural thing to write, and yet I think they had ingeniously manoeuvred me into writing just those words. They were something like "I am ready to die and come to life again like Sherlock Holmes, if that is the best way." And the moment I thought of that, I realized that I had been made to write all sorts of things of that kind, all pointing to the same idea. I wrote, as if to an accomplice, saying that I would drink the drugged wine at a particular time. Now, don't you see?'

Racc sprang to his feet still staring: 'Yes,' he said, 'I think I began to see.'

'*They* would have boomed the miracle. Then *they* would have bust up the miracle. And what is the worst, they would have proved that *I* was in the conspiracy. It would have been *our* sham miracle. That's all there is to it; and about as near hell as you and I will ever be, I hope.'

Then he said, after a pause, in quite a mild voice:

'They certainly would have got quite a lot of good copy out of me.'

Race looked at the table and said darkly: 'How many of these brutes were in it?'

Father Brown shook his head. 'More than I like to think of,' he said; 'but I hope some of them were only tools. Alvarez might think that all's fair in war, perhaps; he has a queer mind. I'm very much afraid that Mendoza is an old hypocrite; I never trusted him, and he hated my action in an industrial matter. But all that will wait; I have only got to thank God for the escape. And especially that I wired at once to the Bishop.'

John Race appeared to be very thoughtful.

'You've told me a lot I didn't know,' he said at last, 'and I feel inclined to tell you the only thing you don't know. I can imagine how those fellows calculated well enough. They thought any man alive, waking up in a coffin to find himself canonized like a saint, and made into a walking miracle for everyone to admire, would be swept along with his worshippers and accept the crown of glory that fell on him out the sky. And I reckon their calculation was pretty practical psychology, as men go. I've seen all sorts of men in all sorts of places; and I tell you frankly I don't believe there's one man in a thousand who could wake up like that with all his wits about him; and while he was still almost talking in his sleep, would have the sanity and the simplicity and the humility to –'

He was much surprised to find himself moved, and his level voice wavering.

Father Brown was gazing abstractedly, and in a rather cockeyed fashion, at the bottle on the table. 'Look here,' he said, 'what about a bottle of real wine?'

TWO

The Arrow of Heaven

IT is to be feared that about a hundred detective stories have begun with the discovery that an American millionaire has been murdered; an event which is, for some reason, treated as a sort of calamity. This story, I am happy to say, has to begin with a murdered millionaire; in one sense, indeed, it has to begin with three murdered millionaires, which some may regard as an *embarras de richesse*. But it was chiefly this coincidence or continuity of criminal policy that took the whole affair out of the ordinary run of criminal cases and made it the extraordinary problem that it was.

It was very generally said that they had all fallen victims to some vendetta or curse attaching to the possession of a relic of great value both intrinsically and historically: a sort of chalice inlaid with precious stones and commonly called the Coptic Cup. Its origin was obscure, but its use was conjectured to be religious; and some attributed the fate that followed its possessors to the fanaticism of some Oriental Christian horrified at its passing through such materialistic hands. But the mysterious slayer, whether or no he was such a fanatic, was already a figure of lurid and sensational interest in the world of journalism and gossip. The nameless being was provided with a name, or a nickname. But it is only with the story of the third victim that we are now concerned; for it was only in this case that a certain Father Brown, who is the subject of these sketches, had an opportunity of making his presence felt.

When Father Brown first stepped off an Atlantic liner on to American soil, he discovered as many other Englishman has done, that he was a much more important person than he had ever supposed. His short figure, his short-sighted and undistinguished countenance, his rather rusty-black clerical clothes, could pass through any crowd in his own country without being noticed as anything unusual, except perhaps unusually insignificant. But

America has a genius for the encouragement of fame; and his appearance in one or two curious criminal problems, together with his long association with Flambeau, the ex-criminal and detective, had consolidated a reputation in America out of what was little more than a rumour in England. His round face was blank with surprise when he found himself held up on the quay by a group of journalists, as by a gang of brigands, who asked him questions about all the subjects on which he was least likely to regard himself as an authority, such as the details of female dress and the criminal statistics of the country that he had only that moment clapped his eyes on. Perhaps it was the contrast with the black embattled solidarity of this group that made more vivid another figure that stood apart from it, equally black against the burning white daylight of that brilliant place and season, but entirely solitary; a tall, rather yellow-faced man in great goggles, who arrested him with a gesture when the journalists had finished and said: 'Excuse me, but maybe you are looking for Captain Wain.'

Some apology may be made for Father Brown; for he himself would have been sincerely apologetic. It must be remembered that he had never seen America before, and more especially that he had never seen that sort of tortoise-shell spectacles before; for the fashion at this time had not spread to England. His first sensation was that of gazing at some goggling sea-monster with a faint suggestion of a diver's helmet. Otherwise the man was exquisitely dressed; and to Brown, in his innocence, the spectacles seemed the queerest disfigurement for a dandy. It was as if a dandy had adorned himself with a wooden leg as an extra touch of elegance. The question also embarrassed him. An American aviator of the name of Wain, a friend of some friends of his own in France, was indeed one of a long list of people he had some hope of seeing during his American visit; but he had never expected to hear of him so soon.

'I beg your pardon,' he said doubtfully, 'are you Captain Wain? Do you -- do you know him?'

'Well, I'm pretty confident I'm not Captain Wain,' said the man in goggles, with a face of wood. 'I was pretty clear about that when I saw him waiting for you over there in the car. But the other question's a bit more problematical. I reckon I know Wain and his uncle, and old man Merton, too. I know old man Merton, but old man Merton don't know me. And he thinks he has the advantage, and I think I have the advantage. See?'

Father Brown did not quite see. He blinked at the glittering seascape and the pinnacles of the city, and then at the man in goggles. It was not only the masking of the man's eyes that produced the impression of something impenetrable. Something in his yellow face was almost Asiatic, even Chinese; and his conversation seemed to consist of stratified layers of irony. He was a type to be found here and there in that hearty and sociable population; he was the inscrutable American.

'My name's Drage,' he said, 'Norman Drage, and I'm an American citizen, which explains everything. At least I imagine your friend Wain would like to explain the rest; so we'll postpone The Fourth of July till another date.'

Father Brown was dragged in a somewhat dazed condition towards a car at some little distance, in which a young man with tufts of untidy yellow hair and a rather harassed and haggard expression, hailed him from afar and presented himself as Peter Wain. Before he knew where he was he was stowed in the car and travelling with considerable speed through and beyond the city. He was unused to the impetuous practicality of such American action, and felt about as bewildered as if a chariot drawn by dragons had carried him away into fairyland. It was under these disconcerting conditions that he heard for the first time, in long monologues from Wain, and short sentences from Drage, the story of the Coptic Cup and the two crimes already connected with it.

It seemed that Wain had an uncle named Crake who had a partner named Merton, who was number three in the series of rich business men to whom the cup had belonged. The first of them, Titus P. Trant, the Copper King, had received threatening letters from somebody signing himself Daniel Doom. The name was presumably a pseudonym, but it had come to stand for a very public if not a very popular character; for somebody as well known as Robin Hood and Jack the Ripper combined. For it soon became clear that the writer of the threatening letter did not confine himself to threatening. Anyhow, the upshot was that old Trant was found one morning with his head in his own lily-pond, and there was not the shadow of a clue. The cup was, fortunately, safe in the bank; and it passed with the rest of Trant's property to his cousin, Brian Horder, who was also a man of great wealth and who was also threatened by the nameless enemy. Brian Horder was picked up dead at the foot of a cliff outside his sea-side residence, at which there was a burglary, this time on a large scale. For though the cup apparently again escaped, enough bonds and securities were stolen to leave Horder's financial affairs in confusion.

'Brian Horder's widow,' explained Wain, 'had to sell most of his valuables, I believe, and Brander Merton must have purchased the cup at that time, for he had it when I first knew him. But you can guess for yourself that it's not a very comfortable thing to have.'

'Has Mr Merton ever had any of the threatening letters?' asked Father Brown, after a pause.

'I imagine he has,' said Mr Drage; and something in his voice made the priest look at him curiously, until he realized that the man in goggles was laughing silently, in a fashion that gave the newcomer something of a chill.

'I'm pretty sure he has,' said Peter Wain, frowning. 'I've not seen the letters, only his secretary sees any of his letters, for he is pretty reticent about business matters, as big business men have to be. But I've seen him real upset and annoyed with letters; and letters that he tore up, too, before even his secretary saw them. The secretary himself is getting nervous and says he is sure some-body is laying for the old man; and the long and the short of it is, that we'd be very grateful for a little advice in the matter. Every-body knows your great reputation, Father Brown, and the secretary asked me to see if you'd mind coming straight out to the Merton house at once.'

'Oh, I see,' said Father Brown, on whom the meaning of this apparent kidnapping began to dawn at last. 'But, really, I don't see that I can do any more than you can. You're on the spot, and must have a hundred times more data for a scientific conclusion than a chance visitor.'

'Yes,' said Mr Drage dryly; 'our conclusions are much too scientific to be true. I reckon if anything hit a man like Titus P. Trant, it just came out of the sky without waiting for any scientific explanation. What they call a bolt from the blue.'

'You can't possibly mean,' cried Wain, 'that it was supernatural!'

But it was by no means easy at any time to discover what Mr Drage could possibly mean; except that if he said somebody was a real smart man, he very probably meant he was a fool. Mr Drage maintained an Oriental immobility until the car stopped, a little while after, at what was obviously their destination. It was rather a singular place. They had been driving through a thinly-wooded country that opened into a wide plain, and just in front of them was a building consisting of a single wall or very high fence, round, like a Roman camp, and having rather the appearance of an aerodrome. The barrier did not look like wood or stone, and closer inspection proved it to be of metal.

They all alighted from the car, and one small door in the wall was slid open with considerable caution, after manipulations resembling the opening of a safe. But, much to Father Brown's surprise, the man called Norman Drage showed no disposition to enter, but took leave of them with sinister gaiety.

'I won't come in,' he said. 'It 'ud be too much pleasurable excitement for old man Merton, I reckon. He loves the sight of me so much that he'd die of joy.'

And he strode away, while Father Brown, with increasing wonder, was admitted through the steel door which instantly clicked behind him. Inside was a large and elaborate garden of gay and varied colours, but entirely without any trees or tall shrubs or flowers. In the centre of it rose a house of handsome and even striking architecture, but so high and narrow as rather to resemble a tower. The burning sunlight gleamed on glass roofing here and there at the top, but there seemed to be no windows at all in the lower part of it. Over everything was that spotless and sparkling cleanliness that seemed so native to the clear American air. When they came inside the portal, they stood amid resplendent marble and metals and enamels of brilliant colours, but there was no staircase. Nothing but a single shaft for a lift went up the centre between the solid walls, and the approach to it was guarded by heavy, powerful men like plain-clothes policemen.

'Pretty elaborate protection, I know,' said Wain. 'Maybe it makes you smile a little, Father Brown, to find Merton has to live in a fortress like this without even a tree in the garden for anyone to hide behind. But you don't know what sort of proposition we're up against in this country. And perhaps you don't know just what the name of Brander Merton means. He's a quiet-looking man enough, and anybody might pass him in the street; not that they get much chance nowadays, for he can only go out now and then in a closed car. But if anything happened to Brander Merton there'd be earthquakes from Alaska to the Cannibal Islands. I fancy there was never a king or emperor who had such power over the nations as he has. After all, I suppose if you'd been asked to visit the tsar, or the king of England, you'd have had the curiosity to go. You mayn't care much for tsars or millionaires; but it just means that power like that is always interesting. And I hope it's not against your principles to visit a modern sort of emperor like Merton.'

'Not at all,' said Father Brown, quietly. 'It is my duty to visit prisoners and all miserable men in captivity.'

There was a silence, and the young man frowned with a strange and almost shifty look on his lean face. Then he said, abruptly:

'Well, you've got to remember it isn't only common crooks or the Black Hand that's against him. This Daniel Doom is pretty much like the devil. Look how he dropped Trant in his own gardens and Horder outside his house, and got away with it.'

The top floor of the mansion, inside the enormously thick walls, consisted of two rooms; an outer room which they entered, and an inner room that was the great millionaire's sanctum. They entered the outer room just as two other visitors were coming out of the inner one. One was hailed by Peter Wain as his uncle – a small but very stalwart and active man with a shaven head that looked bald, and a brown face that looked almost too brown to have ever been white. This was old Crake, commonly called Hickory Crake in reminiscence of the more famous Old Hickory, because of his fame in the last Red Indian wars. His companion was a singular contrast – a very dapper gentleman with dark hair like a black varnish and a broad, black ribbon to his monocle: Barnard Blake, who was old Merton's lawyer and had been discussing with the partners the business of the firm. The four men met in the middle of the outer room and paused for a little polite conversation, in the act of respectively going and coming. And through all goings and comings another figure sat at the back of the room near the inner door, massive and motionless in the half-light from the inner window; a man with a Negro face and enormous shoulders. This was what the humorous self-criticism of America playfully calls the Bad Man; whom his friends might call a bodyguard and his enemies a bravo.

This man never moved or stirred to greet anybody; but the sight of him in the outer room seemed to move Peter Wain to his first nervous query.

'Is anybody with the chief?' he asked.

'Don't get rattled, Peter,' chuckled his uncle. 'Wilton the secretary is with him, and I hope that's enough for anybody. I don't believe Wilton ever sleeps for watching Merton. He is better than twenty bodyguards. And he's quick and quiet as an Indian.'

'Well, you ought to know,' said his nephew, laughing. 'I remember the Red Indian tricks you used to teach me when I was a boy and liked to read Red Indian stories. But in my Red Indian stories Red Indians seemed always to have the worst of it.'

'They didn't in real life,' said the old frontiersman grimly.

'Indeed?' inquired the bland Mr Blake. 'I should have thought they could do very little against our firearms.'

'I've seen an Indian stand under a hundred guns with nothing but a little scalping-knife and kill a white man standing on the top of a fort,' said Crake.

'Why, what did he do with it?' asked the other.

'Threw it,' replied Crake, 'threw it in a flash before a shot could be fired. I don't know where he learnt the trick.'

'Well, I hope you didn't learn it,' said his nephew, laughing.

'It seems to me,' said Father Brown, thoughtfully, 'that the story might have a moral.'

While they were speaking Mr Wilton, the secretary, had come out of the inner room and stood waiting; a pale, fair-haired man with a square chin and steady eyes with a look like a dog's; it was not difficult to believe that he had the single-eye of a watchdog.

He only said, 'Mr Merton can see you in about ten minutes,' but it served for a signal to break up the gossiping group. Old Crake said he must be off, and his nephew went out with him and his legal companion, leaving Father Brown for the moment alone with his secretary; for the negroid giant at the other end of the room could hardly be felt as if he were human or alive; he sat so motionless with his broad back to them, staring towards the inner room.

'Arrangements rather elaborate here, I'm afraid,' said the secretary. 'You've probably heard all about this Daniel Doom, and why it isn't safe to leave the boss very much alone.'

'But he is alone just now, isn't he?' said Father Brown.

The secretary looked at him with grave, grey eyes.

'For fifteen minutes,' he said. 'For fifteen minutes out of the twenty-four hours. That is all the real solitude he has; and that he insists on, for a pretty remarkable reason.'

'And what is the reason?' inquired the visitor.

Wilton, the secretary, continued his steady gaze, but his mouth, that had been merely grave, became grim.

'The Coptic Cup,' he said. 'Perhaps you've forgotten the Coptic Cup; but he hasn't forgotten that or anything else. He doesn't trust any of us about the Coptic Cup. It's locked up somewhere and somehow in that room so that only he can find it; and he won't take it out till we're all out of the way. So we have to risk that quarter of an hour while he sits and worships it; I reckon it's the only worshipping he does. Not that there's any risk really; for I've turned all this place into a trap I don't believe the devil himself could get into – or at any rate, get out of. If this infernal Daniel Doom pays us a visit, he'll stay to dinner and a good bit later, by God! I sit here on hot bricks for the fifteen minutes, and the instant I heard a shot or a sound of struggle I'd press this button and an electrocuting current would run in a ring round that garden wall, so that it 'ud be death to cross or climb it. Of course, there couldn't be a shot, for this is the only way in; and the only window he sits at is away up on the top of a tower as smooth as a greasy pole. But, anyhow, we're all armed here, of course; and if Doom did get into that room he'd be dead before he got out.'

Father Brown was blinking at the carpet in a brown study. Then he said suddenly, with something like a jerk:

'I hope you won't mind my mentioning it, but a kind of a notion came into my head just this minute. It's about you.'

'Indeed,' remarked Wilton, 'and what about me?'

'I think you are a man of one idea,' said Father Brown, 'and you will forgive me for saying that it seems to be even more the idea of catching Daniel Doom than of defending Brander Merton.'

Wilton started a little and continued to stare at his companion; then very slowly his grim mouth took on a rather curious smile.

'How did you – what makes you think that?' he asked.

'You said that if you heard a shot you could instantly electrocute the escaping enemy,' remarked the priest. 'I suppose it occurred to you that the shot might be fatal to your employer before the shock was fatal to his foe. I don't mean that you wouldn't protect Mr Merton if you could, but it seems to come rather second in your thoughts. The arrangements are very elaborate, as you say, and you seem to have elaborated them. But they seem even more designed to catch a murderer than to save a man.'

'Father Brown,' said the secretary, who had recovered his quiet tone, 'you're very smart, but there's something more to you than smartness. Somehow you're the sort of man to whom one wants to tell the truth; and besides, you'll probably hear it, anyhow, for in one way it's a joke against me already. They all say I'm a monomaniac about running down this big crook, and perhaps I am. But I'll tell you one thing that none of them know. My full name is John Wilton Horder.' Father Brown nodded as if he were completely enlightened, but the other went on.

'This fellow who calls himself Doom killed my father and uncle and ruined my mother. When Merton wanted a secretary I took the job, because I thought that where the cup was the criminal might sooner or later be. But I didn't know who the criminal was and could only wait for him; and I meant to serve Merton faithfully.'

'I understand,' said Father Brown gently; 'and, by the way, isn't it time that we attended on him?'

'Why, yes,' answered Wilton, again starting a little out of his brooding so that the priest concluded that his vindictive mania had again absorbed him for a moment. 'Go in now by all means.'

Father Brown walked straight into the inner room. No sound of greetings followed, but only a dead silence; and a moment after the priest reappeared in the doorway.

At the same moment the silent bodyguard sitting near the door moved suddenly; and it was as if a huge piece of furniture had come to life. It seemed as though something in the very attitude of the priest had been a signal; for his head was against the light from the inner window and his face was in shadow.

'I suppose you will press that button,' he said with a sort of sigh.

Wilton seemed to awake from his savage brooding with a bound and leapt up with a catch in his voice.

'There was no shot,' he cried.

'Well,' said Father Brown, 'it depends what you mean by a shot.'

Wilton rushed forward, and they plunged into the inner room together. It was a comparatively small room and simply though elegantly furnished. Opposite to them one wide window stood open, over-looking the garden and the wooded plain. Close up against the window stood a chair and a small table, as if the captive desired as much air and light as was allowed him during his brief luxury of loneliness.

On the little table under the window stood the Coptic Cup; its owner had evidently been looking at it in the best light. It was well worth looking at, for that white and brilliant daylight turned its precious stones to many-coloured flames so that it might have been a model of the Holy Grail. It was well worth looking at; but Brander Merton was not looking at it. For his head had fallen back over his chair, his mane of white hair hanging towards the floor, and his spike of grizzled beard thrust up towards the ceiling, and out of his throat stood a long, brown-painted arrow with red feathers at the other end.

'A silent shot,' said Father Brown, in a low voice; 'I was just wondering about those new inventions for silencing firearms. But this is a very old invention, and quite as silent.'

Then, after a moment, he added: 'I'm afraid he is dead. What are you going to do?'

The pale secretary roused himself with abrupt resolution. 'I'm going to press that button, of course,' he said, 'and if that doesn't do for Daniel Doom, I'm going to hunt him through the world till I find him.'

'Take care it doesn't do for any of our friends,' observed Father Brown; 'they can hardly be far off; we'd better call them.'

'That lot know all about the wall,' answered Wilton. 'None of them will try to climb it, unless one of them . . . is in a great hurry.'

Father Brown went to the window by which the arrow had evidently entered and looked out. The garden, with its flat flower-beds, lay far below like a delicately coloured map of the world. The whole vista seemed so vast and empty, the tower seemed set so far up in the sky that as he stared out a strange phrase came back to his memory.

'A bolt from the blue,' he said. 'What was that somebody said about a bolt from the blue and death coming out of the sky? Look how far away everything looks; it seems extraordinary that an arrow could come so far, unless it were an arrow from heaven.'

Wilton had returned, but did not reply, and the priest went on as in soliloquy.

'One thinks of aviation. We must ask young Wain . . . about aviation.'

'There's a lot of it round here,' said the secretary.

'Case of very old or very new weapons,' observed Father Brown. 'Some would be quite familiar to his old uncle, I suppose; we must ask him about arrows. This looks rather like a Red

Indian arrow. I don't know where the Red Indian shot it from; but you remember the story the old man told. I said it had a moral.'

'If it had a moral,' said Wilton warmly, 'it was only that a real Red Indian might shoot a thing farther than you'd fancy. It's nonsense your suggesting a parallel.'

'I don't think you've got the moral quite right,' said Father Brown.

Although the little priest appeared to melt into the millions of New York next day, without any apparent attempt to be anything but a number in a numbered street, he was, in fact, unobtrusively busy for the next fortnight with the commission that had been given him, for he was filled with profound fear about a possible miscarriage of justice. Without having any particular air of singling them out from his other new acquaintances, he found it easy to fall into talk with the two or three men recently involved in the mystery; and with old Hickory Crake especially he had a curious and interesting conversation. It took place on a seat in Central Park, where the veteran sat with his bony hands and hatchet face resting on the oddly-shaped head of a walking-stick of dark red wood, possibly modelled on a tomahawk.

'Well, it may be a long shot,' he said, wagging his head, 'but I wouldn't advise you to be too positive about how far an Indian arrow could go. I've known some bow-shots that seemed to go straighter than any bullets, and hit the mark to amazement, considering how long they had been travelling. Of course, you practically never hear now of a Red Indian with a bow and arrows, still less of a Red Indian hanging about here. But if by any chance there were one of the old Indian marksmen, with one of the old Indian bows, hiding in those trees hundreds of yards beyond the Merton outer wall – why, then I wouldn't put it past the noble savage to be able to send an arrow over the wall and into the top window of Merton's house; no, nor into Merton, either. I've seen things quite as wonderful as that done in the old days.'

'No doubt,' said the priest, 'you have done things quite as wonderful, as well as seen them.'

Old Crake chuckled, and then said gruffly: 'Oh, that's all ancient history.'

'Some people have a way of studying ancient history,' the priest said. 'I suppose we may take it there is nothing in your old record to make people talk unpleasantly about this affair.'

'What do you mean?' demanded Crake, his eyes shifting sharply for the first time, in his red, wooden face, that was rather like the head of a tomahawk.

'Well, since you were so well acquainted with all the arts and crafts of the Redskin –' began Father Brown slowly.

Crake had had a hunched and almost shrunken appearance as he sat with his chin propped on its queer-shaped crutch. But the next instant he stood erect in the path like a fighting bravo with the crutch clutched like a cudgel.

'What?' he cried – in something like a raucous screech – 'wnat the hell! Are you standing up to me to tell me I might happen to have murdered my own brother-in-law?'

From a dozen seats dotted about the path people looked towards the disputants, as they stood facing each other in the middle of the path, the bald-headed energetic little man brandishing his outlandish stick like a club, and the black, dumpy figure of the little cleric looking at him without moving a muscle, save for his blinking eyelids. For a moment it looked as if the black, dumpy figure would be knocked on the head, and laid out with true Red Indian promptitude and dispatch; and the large form of an Irish policeman could be seen heaving up in the distance and bearing down on the group. But the priest only said, quite placidly, like one answering an ordinary query:

'I have formed certain conclusions about it, but I do not think I will mention them till I make my report.'

Whether under the influence of the footsteps of the policeman or of the eyes of the priest, old Hickory tucked his stick under his arm and put his hat on again, grunting. The priest bade him a placid good morning, and passed in an unhurried fashion out of the park, making his way to the lounge of the hotel where he knew that young Wain was to be found. The young man sprang up with a greeting; he looked even more haggard and harassed

THE INCREDULITY OF FATHER BROWN

than before, as if some worry were eating him away; and the priest had a suspicion that his young friend had recently been engaged, with only too conspicuous success, in evading the last Amendment to the American Constitution. But at the first word about his hobby or favourite science he was vigilant and concentrated enough. For Father Brown had asked, in an idle and conversational fashion, whether much flying was done in that district, and had told how he had at first mistaken Mr Merton's circular wall for an aerodrome.

'It's a wonder you didn't see any while we were there,' answered Captain Wain. 'Sometimes they're as thick as flies; that open plain is a great place for them, and I shouldn't wonder if it were the chief breeding-ground, so to speak, for my sort of birds in the future. I've flown a good deal there myself, of course, and I know most of the fellows about here who flew in the war; but there are a whole lot of people taking to it out there now whom I never heard of in my life. I suppose it will be like motoring soon, and every man in the States will have one.'

'Being endowed by his Creator,' said Father Brown with a smile, 'with the right to life, liberty, and the pursuit of motoring – not to mention aviation. So I suppose we may take it that one strange aeroplane passing over that house, at certain times, wouldn't be noticed much.'

'No,' replied the young man; 'I don't suppose it would.'

'Or even if the man were known,' went on the other, 'I suppose he might get hold of a machine that wouldn't be recognized as his. If you, for instance, flew in the ordinary way, Mr Merton and his friends might recognize the rig-out, perhaps; but you might pass pretty near that window on a different pattern of plane, or whatever you call it; near enough for practical purposes.'

'Well, yes,' began the young man, almost automatically, and then ceased, and remained staring at the cleric with an open mouth and eyes standing out of his head.

'My God!' he said, in a low voice; 'my God!'

Then he rose from the lounge seat, pale and shaking from head to foot and still staring at the priest.

'Are you mad?' he said; 'are you raving mad?'

38

There was a silence and then he spoke again in a swift hissing fashion. 'You positively come here to suggest –'

'No; only to collect suggestions,' said Father Brown, rising. 'I may have formed some conclusions provisionally, but I had better reserve them for the present.'

And then saluting the other with the same stiff civility, he passed out of the hotel to continue his curious peregrinations.

By the dusk of that day they had led him down the dingy streets and steps that straggled and tumbled towards the river in the oldest and most irregular part of the city. Immediately under the coloured lantern that marked the entrance to a rather low Chinese restaurant he encountered a figure he had seen before, though by no means presenting itself to the eye as he had seen it.

Mr Norman Drage still confronted the world grimly behind his great goggles, which seemed somehow to cover his face like a dark mask of glass. But except for the goggles, his appearance had undergone a strange transformation in the month that had elapsed since the murder. He had then, as Father Brown had noted, been dressed up to the nines – up to that point, indeed, where there begins to be too fine a distinction between the dandy and the dummy outside a tailor's shop. But now all those externals were mysteriously altered for the worse; as if the tailor's dummy had been turned into a scarecrow. His top hat still existed, but it was battered and shabby; his clothes were dilapidated; his watch-chain and minor ornaments were gone. Father Brown, however, addressed him as if they had met yesterday, and made no demur to sitting down with him on a bench in the cheap eating-house whither he was bound. It was not he, however, who began the conversation.

'Well?' growled Drage; 'and have you succeeded in avenging your holy and sainted millionaire? We know all millionaires are holy and sainted; you can find it all in the papers next day, about how they lived by the light of the Family Bible they read at their mother's knee. Gee! if they'd only read out some of the things there are in the Family Bible, the mother might have been startled some. And the millionaire, too, I reckon. The old Book's full of a lot of grand fierce old notions they don't grow nowadays;

sort of wisdom of the Stone Age and buried under the Pyramids. Suppose somebody had flung old man Merton from the top of that tower of his, and let him be eaten by dogs at the bottom, it would be no worse than what happened to Jezebel. Wasn't Agag hacked into little pieces, for all he went walking delicately? Merton walked delicately all his life, damn him – until he got too delicate to walk at all. But the shaft of the Lord found him out, as it might have done in the old Book, and struck him dead on the top of his tower to be a spectacle to the people.'

'The shaft was material, at least,' said his companion.

'The Pyramids are mighty material, and they hold down the dead kings all right,' grinned the man in the goggles. 'I think there's a lot to be said for these old material religions. There's old carvings that have lasted for thousands of years, showing their gods and emperors with bended bows; with hands that look as if they could really bend bows of stone. Material, perhaps – but what materials! Don't you sometimes stand staring at those old Eastern patterns and things, till you have a hunch that old Lord God is still driving like a dark Apollo, and shooting black rays of death?'

'If he is,' replied Father Brown, 'I might call him by another name. But I doubt whether Merton died by a dark ray or even a stone arrow.'

'I guess you think he's St Sebastian,' sneered Drage, 'killed with an arrow. A millionaire must be a martyr. How do you know he didn't deserve it? You don't know much about your millionaire, I fancy. Well, let me tell you he deserved it a hundred times over.'

'Well,' asked Father Brown gently, 'why didn't you murder him?'

'You want to know why I didn't?' said the other, staring. 'Well, you're a nice sort of clergyman.'

'Not at all,' said the other, as if waving away a compliment.

'I suppose it's your way of saying I did,' snarled Drage. 'Well, prove it, that's all. As for him, I reckon he was no loss.'

'Yes, he was,' said Father Brown, sharply. 'He was a loss to you. That's why you didn't kill him.'

And he walked out of the room, leaving the man in goggles gaping after him.

It was nearly a month later that Father Brown revisited the house where the third millionaire had suffered from the vendetta of Daniel Doom. A sort of council was held of the persons most interested. Old Crake sat at the head of the table with his nephew on his right hand, the lawyer on his left; the big man with the African features, whose name appeared to be Harris, was ponderously present, if only as a material witness; a red-haired, sharp-nosed individual addressed as Dixon seemed to be the representative of Pinkerton's or some such private agency; and Father Brown slipped unobtrusively into an empty seat beside him.

Every newspaper in the world was full of the catastrophe of the colossus of finance, of the great organizer of the Big Business that bestrides the modern world; but from the tiny group that had been nearest to him at the very instant of his death very little could be learned. The uncle, nephew, and attendant solicitor declared they were well outside the outer wall before the alarm was raised; and inquiries of the official guardians at both barriers brought answers that were rather confused, but on the whole confirmatory. Only one other complication seemed to call for consideration. It seemed that round about the time of the death, before or after, a stranger had been found hanging mysteriously round the entrance and asking to see Mr Merton. The servants had some difficulty in understanding what he meant, for his language was very obscure; but it was afterwards considered to be also very suspicious, since he had said something about a wicked man being destroyed by a word out of the sky.

Peter Wain leaned forward, the eyes bright in his haggard face, and said:

'I'll bet on that, anyhow. Norman Drage.'

'And who in the world is Norman Drage?' asked his uncle.

'That's what I want to know,' replied the young man. 'I practically asked him, but he has got a wonderful trick of twisting every straight question crooked; it's like lunging at a fencer. He hooked on to me with hints about the flying-ship of the future; but I never trusted him much.'

'But what sort of a man is he?' asked Crake.

'He's a mystagogue,' said Father Brown, with innocent promptitude. 'There are quite a lot of them about; the sort of men about town who hint to you in Paris cafés and cabarets that they've lifted the veil of Isis or know the secret of Stonehenge. In a case like this they're sure to have some sort of mystical explanations.'

The smooth, dark head of Mr Barnard Blake, the lawyer, was inclined politely towards the speaker, but his smile was faintly hostile.

'I should hardly have thought, sir,' he said, 'that you had any quarrel with mystical explanations.'

'On the contrary,' replied Father Brown, blinking amiably at him. 'That's just why I can quarrel with 'em. Any sham lawyer could bamboozle me, but he couldn't bamboozle you; because you're a lawyer yourself. Any fool could dress up as a Red Indian and I'd swallow him whole as the only original Hiawatha; but Mr Crake would see through him at once. A swindler could pretend to me that he knew all about aeroplanes, but not to Captain Wain. And it's just the same with the other, don't you see? It's just because I have picked up a little about mystics that I have no use for mystagogues. Real mystics don't hide mysteries, they reveal them. They set a thing up in broad daylight, and when you've seen it it's still a mystery. But the mystagogues hide a thing in darkness and secrecy, and when you find it, it's a platitude. But in the case of Drage, I admit he had also another and more practical notion in talking about fire from heaven or bolts from the blue.'

'And what was his notion?' asked Wain. 'I think it wants watching whatever it is.'

'Well,' replied the priest, slowly, 'he wanted us to think the murders were miracles because . . . well, because he knew they weren't.'

'Ah,' said Wain, with a sort of hiss, 'I was waiting for that. In plain words, he is the criminal.'

'In plain words, he is the criminal who didn't commit the crime,' answered Father Brown calmly.

'Is that your conception of plain words?' inquired Blake politely.

42

'You'll be saying I'm the mystagogue now,' said Father Brown somewhat abashed, but with a broad smile, 'but it was really quite accidental. Drage didn't commit the crime – I mean this crime. His only crime was blackmailing somebody, and he hung about here to do it; but he wasn't likely to want the secret to be public property or the whole business to be cut short by death. We can talk about him afterwards. Just at the moment, I only want him cleared out of the way.'

'Out of the way of what?' asked the other.

'Out of the way of the truth,' replied the priest, looking at him tranquilly, with level eyelids.

'Do you mean,' faltered the other, 'that you know the truth?'

'I rather think so,' said Father Brown modestly.

There was an abrupt silence, after which Crake cried out suddenly and irrelevantly in a rasping voice:

'Why, where is that secretary fellow? Wilton! He ought to be here.'

'I am in communication with Mr Wilton,' said Father Brown gravely; 'in fact, I asked him to ring me up here in a few minutes from now. I may say that we've worked the thing out together, in a manner of speaking.'

'If you're working together, I suppose it's all right,' grumbled Crake. 'I know he was always a sort of bloodhound on the trail of this vanishing crook, so perhaps it was well to hunt in couples with him. But if you know the truth about this, where the devil did you get it from?'

'I got it from you,' answered the priest, quietly, and continued to gaze mildly at the glaring veteran. 'I mean I made the first guess from a hint in a story of yours about an Indian who threw a knife and hit a man on the top of a fortress.'

'You've said that several times,' said Wain, with a puzzled air; 'but I can't see any inference, except that his murderer threw an arrow and hit a man on the top of a house very like a fortress. But of course the arrow wasn't thrown but shot, and would go much farther. Certainly it went uncommonly far; but I don't see how it brings us any farther.'

'I'm afraid you missed the point of the story,' said Father

Brown. 'It isn't that if one thing can go far another can go farther. It is that the wrong use of a tool can cut both ways. The men on Crake's fort thought of a knife as a thing for a hand-to-hand fight and forgot that it could be a missile like a javelin. Some other people I know thought of a thing as a missile like a javelin and forgot that, after all, it could be used hand-to-hand as a spear. In short, the moral of the story is that since a dagger can be turned into an arrow, so can an arrow be turned into a dagger.'

They were all looking at him now; but he continued in the same casual and unconscious tone:

'Naturally we wondered and worried a good deal about who shot that arrow through the window and whether it came from far away, and so on. But the truth is that nobody shot the arrow at all. It never came in at the window at all.'

'Then how did it come there?' asked the swarthy lawyer, with a rather lowering face.

'Somebody brought it with him, I suppose,' said Father Brown; 'it wouldn't be hard to carry or conceal. Somebody had it in his hand as he stood with Merton in Merton's own room. Somebody thrust it into Merton's throat like a poignard, and then had the highly intelligent idea of placing the whole thing at such a place and angle that we all assumed in a flash that it had flown in at the window like a bird.'

'Somebody,' said old Crake, in a voice as heavy as stone.

The telephone bell rang with a strident and horrible clamour of insistence. It was in the adjoining room, and Father Brown had darted there before anybody else could move.

'What the devil is it all about?' cried Peter Wain, who seemed all shaken and distracted.

'He said he expected to be rung up by Wilton, the secretary,' replied his uncle in the same dead voice.

'I suppose it is Wilton?' observed the lawyer, like one speaking to fill up a silence. But nobody answered the question until Father Brown reappeared suddenly and silently in the room, bringing the answer.

'Gentlemen,' he said, when he had resumed his seat, 'it was you who asked me to look into the truth about this puzzle; and having found the truth, I must tell it, without any pretence of softening the shock. I'm afraid anybody who pokes his nose into things like this can't afford to be a respecter of persons.'

'I suppose,' said Crake, breaking the silence that followed, 'that means that some of us are accused, or suspected.'

'All of us are suspected,' answered Father Brown. 'I may be suspected myself, for I found the body.'

'Of course we're suspected,' snapped Wain. 'Father Brown kindly explained to me how I could have besieged the tower in a flying-machine.'

'No,' replied the priest, with a smile; 'you described to me how you could have done it. That was just the interesting part of it.'

'He seemed to think it likely,' growled Crake, 'that I killed him myself with a Red Indian arrow.'

'I thought it most unlikely,' said Father Brown, making rather a wry face. 'I'm sorry if I did wrong, but I couldn't think of any other way of testing the matter. I can hardly think of anything more improbable than the notion that Captain Wain went careering in a huge machine past the window, at the very moment of the murder, and nobody noticed it; unless, perhaps, it were the notion that a respectable old gentleman should play at Red Indians with a bow and arrow behind the bushes, to kill somebody he could have killed in twenty much simpler ways. But I had to find out if they had had anything to do with it; and so I had to accuse them in order to prove their innocence.'

'And how have you proved their innocence?' asked Blake the lawyer, leaning forward eagerly.

'Only by the agitation they showed when they were accused,' answered the other.

'What do you mean, exactly?'

'If you will permit me to say so,' remarked Father Brown, composedly enough, 'I did undoubtedly think it my duty to suspect them and everybody else. I did suspect Mr Crake and I did suspect Captain Wain, in the sense that I considered the possibility or probability of their guilt. I told them I had formed conclusions about it; and I will now tell them what those conclusions were. I was sure they were innocent, because of the manner and the moment in which they passed from unconsciousness to indignation. So long as they never thought they were accused, they went on giving me materials to support the accusation. They practically explained to me how they might have committed the crime. Then they suddenly realized with a shock and a shout of rage that they were accused; they realized it long after they might well have expected to be accused, but long before I had accused them. Now no guilty person could possibly do that. He might be snappy and suspicious from the first; or he might simulate unconsciousness and innocence up to the end. But he wouldn't begin by making things worse for himself and then give a great jump and begin furiously denying the notion he had himself helped to suggest. That could only come by his having really failed to realize what he was suggesting. The self-consciousness of a murderer would always be at least morbidly vivid enough to prevent him first forgetting his relation with the thing and then remembering to deny it. So I ruled you both out and others for other reasons I needn't discuss now. For instance, there was the secretary –

'But I'm not talking about that just now. Look here, I've just heard from Wilton on the phone, and he's given me permission to tell you some rather serious news. Now I suppose you all know by this time who Wilton was, and what he was after.'

'I know he was after Daniel Doom and wouldn't be happy till he got him,' answered Peter Wain; 'and I've heard the story that he's the son of old Horder, and that's why he's the avenger of blood. Anyhow, he's certainly looking for the man called Doom.'

'Well,' said Father Brown, 'he has found him.'

Peter Wain sprang to his feet in excitement.

'The murderer!' he cried. 'Is the murderer in the lock-up already?'

'No,' said Father Brown, gravely; 'I said the news was serious, and it's more serious than that. I'm afraid poor Wilton has taken a terrible responsibility. I'm afraid he's going to put a terrible responsibility on us. He hunted the criminal down, and just when he had him cornered at last – well, he has taken the law into his own hands.'

'You mean that Daniel Doom –' began the lawyer.

'I mean that Daniel Doom is dead,' said the priest. 'There was some sort of wild struggle, and Wilton killed him.'

'Serve him right,' growled Mr Hickory Crake.

'Can't blame Wilton for downing a crook like that, especially considering the feud,' assented Wain; 'it was like stepping on a viper.'

'I don't agree with you,' said Father Brown. 'I suppose we all talk romantic stuff at random in defence of lynching and lawlessness; but I have a suspicion that if we lose our laws and liberties we shall regret it. Besides, it seems to me illogical to say there is something to be said for Wilton committing murder, without even inquiring whether there was anything to be said for Doom committing it. I rather doubt whether Doom was merely a vulgar assassin; he may have been a sort of outlaw with a mania about the cup, demanding it with threats and only killing after a struggle; both victims were thrown down just outside their houses. The objection to Wilton's way of doing it is that we shall never hear Doom's side of the case.'

'Oh, I've no patience with all this sentimental whitewashing of worthless, murderous blackguards,' cried Wain, heatedly. 'If Wilton croaked the criminal he did a jolly good day's work, and there's an end of it.'

'Quite so, quite so,' said his uncle, nodding vigorously.

Father Brown's face had a yet heavier gravity as he looked slowly round the semicircle of faces.

'Is that really what you all think?' he asked. Even as he did so he realized that he was an Englishman and an exile. He realized that he was among foreigners, even if he was among friends. Around that ring of foreigners ran a restless fire that was not native to his own breed; the fiercer spirit of the western nation that can rebel and lynch, and above all, combine. He knew that they had already combined.

'Well,' said Father Brown, with a sigh, 'I am to understand, then, that you do definitely condone this unfortunate man's crime, or act of private justice, or whatever you call it. In that case it will not hurt him if I tell you a little more about it.'

He rose suddenly to his feet; and though they saw no meaning in his movement, it seemed in some way to change or chill the very air in the room.

'Wilton killed Doom in a rather curious way,' he began.

'How did Wilton kill him?' asked Crake, abruptly.

'With an arrow,' said Father Brown.

Twilight was gathering in the long room, and daylight dwindling to a gleam from the great window in the inner room, where the great millionaire had died. Almost automatically the eyes of the group turned slowly towards it, but as yet there was no sound. Then the voice of Crake came cracked and high and senile in a sort of crowing gabble.

'What you mean? What you mean? Brander Merton killed by an arrow. This crook killed by an arrow –'

'By the same arrow,' said the priest, 'and at the same moment.'

Again there was a sort of strangled and yet swollen and bursting silence, and young Wain began: 'You mean –'

'I mean that your friend Merton was Daniel Doom,' said Father Brown firmly; 'and the only Daniel Doom you'll ever find. Your friend Merton was always crazy after that Coptic Cup that he used to worship like an idol every day; and in his wild youth he had really killed two men to get it, though I still think the deaths may have been in a sense accidents of the robbery. Anyhow, he had it; and that man Drage knew the story and was blackmailing him. But Wilton was after him for a very different purpose; I fancy he only discovered the truth when he'd got into this house. But anyhow, it was in this house, and in that room, that this hunt ended, and he slew the slayer of his father.'

For a long time nobody answered. Then old Crake could be heard drumming with his fingers on the table and muttering: 'Brander must have been mad. He must have been mad.'

'But, good Lord!' burst out Peter Wain; 'what are we to do? What are we to say? Oh, it's all quite different! What about the papers and the big business people? Brander Merton is a thing like the President or the Pope of Rome.'

'I certainly think it is rather different,' began Barnard Blake, the lawyer, in a low voice. 'The difference involves a whole –'

Father Brown struck the table so that the glasses on it rang; and they could almost fancy a ghostly echo from the mysterious chalice that still stood in the room beyond.

'No!' he cried, in a voice like a pistol-shot. 'There shall be no difference. I gave you your chance of pitying the poor devil when you thought he was a common criminal. You wouldn't listen then; you were all for private vengeance then. You were all for letting him be butchered like a wild beast without a hearing or a public trial, and said he had only got his deserts. Very well then, if Daniel Doom has got his deserts, Brander Merton has got his deserts. If that was good enough for Doom, by all that is holy it is good enough for Merton. Take your wild justice or our dull legality; but in the name of Almighty God, let there be an equal lawlessness or an equal law.'

Nobody answered except the lawyer, and he answered with something like a snarl:

'What will the police say if we tell them we mean to condone a crime?'

'What will they say if I tell them you did condone it?' replied Father Brown. 'Your respect for the law comes rather late, Mr Barnard Blake.'

After a pause he resumed in a milder tone: 'I, for one, am ready to tell the truth if the proper authorities ask me; and the rest of you can do as you like. But as a fact, it will make very little difference. Wilton only rang me up to tell me that I was now free to lay his confession before you; for when you heard it, he would be beyond pursuit.'

He walked slowly into the inner room and stood there by the little table beside which the millionaire had died. The Coptic Cup still stood in the same place, and he remained there for a space staring at its cluster of all the colours of the rainbow, and beyond it into a blue abyss of sky.

THREE

The Oracle of the Dog

'Yes,' said Father Brown, 'I always like a dog, so long as he isn't spelt backwards.'

Those who are quick in talking are not always quick in listening. Sometimes even their brilliancy produces a sort of stupidity. Father Brown's friend and companion was a young man with a stream of ideas and stories, an enthusiastic young man named Fiennes, with eager blue eyes and blond hair that seemed to be brushed back, not merely with a hair-brush but with the wind of the world as he rushed through it. But he stopped in the torrent of his talk in a momentary bewilderment before he saw the priest's very simple meaning.

'You mean that people make too much of them?' he said. 'Well, I don't know. They're marvellous creatures. Sometimes I think they know a lot more than we do.'

Father Brown said nothing, but continued to stroke the head of the big retriever in a half-abstracted but apparently soothing fashion.

'Why,' said Fiennes, warming again to his monologue, 'there was a dog in the case I've come to see you about: what they call the "Invisible Murder Case", you know. It's a strange story, but from my point of view the dog is about the strangest thing in it. Of course, there's the mystery of the crime itself, and how old Druce can have been killed by somebody else when he was all alone in the summer-house –'

The hand stroking the dog stopped for a moment in its rhythmic movement, and Father Brown said calmly: 'Oh, it was a summer-house, was it?'

'I thought you'd read all about it in the papers,' answered Fiennes. 'Stop a minute; I believe I've got a cutting that will give you all the particulars.' He produced a strip of newspaper from his pocket and handed it to the priest, who began to read it, holding it close to his blinking eyes with one hand while the other continued its half-conscious caresses of the dog. It looked like the parable of a man not letting his right hand know what his left hand did.

Many mystery stories, about men murdered behind locked doors and windows, and murderers escaping without means of entrance and exit, have come true in the course of the extraordinary events at Cranston on the coast of Yorkshire, where Colonel Druce was found stabbed from behind by a dagger that has entirely disappeared from the scene, and apparently even from the neighbourhood.

The summer-house in which he died was indeed accessible at one entrance, the ordinary doorway which looked down the central walk of the garden towards the house. But, by a combination of events almost to be called a coincidence, it appears that both the path and the entrance were watched during the crucial time, and there is a chain of witnesses who confirm each other. The summer-house stands at the extreme end of the garden, where there is no exit or entrance of any kind. The central garden path is a lane between two ranks of tall delphiniums, planted so close that any stray step off the path would leave its traces; and both path and plants run right up to the very mouth of the summer-house, so that no straying from that straight path could fail to be observed, and no other mode of entrance can be imagined.

Patrick Floyd, secretary of the murdered man, testified that he had been in a position to overlook the whole garden from the time when Colonel Druce last appeared alive in the doorway to the time when he was found dead; as he, Floyd, had been on the top of a step-ladder clipping the garden hedge. Janet Druce, the dead man's daughter, confirmed this, saying that she had sat on the terrace of the house throughout that time and had seen Floyd at his work. Touching some part of the time, this is again supported by Donald Druce, her brother – who overlooked the garden – standing at his bedroom window in his dressing-gown, for he had risen late. Lastly, the account is consistent with that given by Dr Valentine, a neighbour, who called for a time to talk with Miss Druce on the terrace, and by the Colonel's solicitor, Mr Aubrey Traill, who was apparently the last to see the murdered man alive – presumably with the exception of the murderer.

All are agreed that the course of events was as follows: About half past three in the afternoon, Miss Druce went down the path to ask her father when he would like tea; but he said he did not want any and was waiting to see Traill, his lawyer, who was to be sent to him in the summer-house. The girl then came away and met Traill coming down the path; she directed him to her father and he went in as directed. About half an hour afterwards he came out again, the Colonel coming with him to the door and showing himself to all appearance in health and even high spirits. He had been somewhat annoyed earlier in the day by his son's irregular hours, but seemed to recover his temper in a perfectly normal fashion, and had been rather markedly genial in receiving other visitors, including two of his nephews, who came over for the day. But as these were out walking during the whole period of the tragedy, they had no evidence to give. It is said, indeed, that the Colonel was not on very good terms with Dr Valentine, but that gentleman only had a brief interview with the daughter of the house, to whom he is supposed to be paying serious attentions.

Traill, the solicitor, says he left the Colonel entirely alone in the summer-house, and this is confirmed by Floyd's bird's-eye view of the garden, which showed nobody else passing the only entrance. Ten minutes later, Miss Druce again went down the garden and had not reached the end of the path when she saw her father, who was conspicuous by his white linen coat, lying in a heap on the floor. She uttered a scream which brought others to the spot, and on entering the place they found the Colonel lying dead beside his basket-chair, which was also upset. Dr Valentine, who was still in the immediate neighbourhood, testified that the wound was made by some sort of stiletto, entering under the shoulder-blade and piercing the heart. The police have searched the neighbourhood for such a weapon, but no trace of it can be found.

'So Colonel Druce wore a white coat, did he?' said Father Brown as he put down the paper.

'Trick he learnt in the tropics,' replied Fiennes, with some wonder. 'He'd had some queer adventures there, by his own account; and I fancy his dislike of Valentine was connected with the doctor coming from the tropics, too. But it's all an infernal puzzle. The account there is pretty accurate; I didn't see the tragedy, in the sense of the discovery; I was out walking with the young nephews and the dog – the dog I wanted to tell you about. But I saw the stage set for it as described; the straight lane between the blue flowers right up to the dark entrance, and the lawyer going down it in his blacks and his silk hat, and the red head of the secretary showing high above the green hedge as he worked on it with his shears. Nobody could have mistaken that red head at any distance; and if people say they saw it there all the time, you may be sure they did. This red-haired secretary, Floyd, is quite a character; a breathless bounding sort of fellow, always doing everybody's work as he was doing the gardener's. I think he is an American; he's certainly got the American view of life – what they call the view-point, bless 'em.'

'What about the lawyer?' asked Father Brown.

There was a silence and then Fiennes spoke quite slowly for him. 'Traill struck me as a singular man. In his fine black clothes he was almost foppish, yet you can hardly call him fashionable. For he wore a pair of long, luxuriant black whiskers such as haven't been seen since Victorian times. He had rather a fine grave face and a fine grave manner, but every now and then he seemed to remember to smile. And when he showed his white teeth he seemed to lose a little of his dignity, and there was something faintly fawning about him. It may have been only embarrassment, for he would also fidget with his cravat and his tie-pin, which were at once handsome and unusual, like himself. If I could think of anybody – but what's the good, when the whole thing's impossible? Nobody knows who did it. Nobody knows how it could be done. At least there's only one exception I'd make, and that's why I really mentioned the whole thing. The dog knows.'

Father Brown sighed and then said absently: 'You were there as a friend of young Donald, weren't you? He didn't go on your walk with you?'

'No,' replied Fiennes smiling, 'The young scoundrel had gone to bed that morning and got up that afternoon. I went with his cousins, two young officers from India, and our conversation was trivial enough. I remember the elder, whose name I think is Herbert Druce and who is an authority on horse-breeding, talked about nothing but a mare he had bought and the moral character of the man who sold her; while his brother Harry seemed to be brooding on his bad luck at Monte Carlo. I only mention it to show you, in the light of what happened on our walk, that there was nothing psychic about us. The dog was the only mystic in our company.'

'What sort of a dog was he?' asked the priest.

'Same breed as that one,' answered Fiennes. 'That's what started me off on the story, your saying you didn't believe in believing in a dog. He's a big black retriever, named Nox, and a suggestive name, too; for I think what he did a darker mystery than the murder. You know Druce's house and garden are by the sea; we walked about a mile from it along the sands and then turned back, going the other way. We passed a rather curious rock called the Rock of Fortune, famous in the neighbourhood because it's one of those examples of one stone barely balanced on another, so that a touch would knock it over. It is not really very high but the hanging outline of it makes it look a little wild and sinister; at least it made it look so to me, for I don't imagine my jolly young companions were afflicted with the picturesque. But it may be that I was beginning to feel an atmosphere; for just then the question arose of whether it was time to go back to tea, and even then I think I had a premonition that time counted for a good deal in the business. Neither Herbert Druce nor I had a watch, so we called out to his brother, who was some paces behind, having stopped to light his pipe under the hedge. Hence it happened that he shouted out the hour, which was twenty past four, in his big voice through the growing twilight; and somehow the loudness of it made it sound like the proclamation of something tremendous. His unconsciousness seemed to make it all the more so; but that was always the way with omens; and particular ticks of the clock were really very ominous things that afternoon. According to Dr Valentine's testimony, poor Druce had actually died just about half past four.

'Well, they said we needn't go home for ten minutes, and we walked a little farther along the sands, doing nothing in particular – throwing stones for the dog and throwing sticks into the sea for him to swim after. But to me the twilight seemed to grow oddly oppressive, and the very shadow of the top-heavy Rock of Fortune lay on me like a load. And then the curious thing happened. Nox had just brought back Herbert's walking-stick out of the sea and his brother had thrown his in also. The dog swam out again, but just about what must have been the stroke of the half-hour, he stopped swimming. He came back again on to the shore and stood in front of us. Then he suddenly threw up his head and sent up a howl or wail of woe – if ever I heard one in the world.

'"What the devil's the matter with the dog?"asked Herbert; but none of us could answer. There was a long silence after the brute's wailing and whining died away on the desolate shore; and then the silence was broken. As I live, it was broken by a faint and far-off shriek, like the shriek of a woman from beyond the hedges inland. We didn't know what it was then; but we knew after-wards. It was the cry the girl gave when she first saw the body of her father.'

'You went back, I suppose,' said Father Brown patiently. 'What happened then?'

'I'll tell you what happened then,' said Fiennes with a grim emphasis. 'When we got back into that garden the first thing we saw was Traill, the lawyer; I can see him now with his black hat and black whiskers relieved against the perspective of the blue flowers stretching down to the summer-house, with the sunset and the strange outline of the Rock of Fortune in the distance. His face and figure were in shadow against the sunset; but I swear the white teeth were showing in his head and he was smiling.

'The moment Nox saw that man the dog dashed forward and stood in the middle of the path barking at him madly, murder-ously, volleying out curses that were almost verbal in their dreadful distinctness of hatred. And the man doubled up and fled along the path between the flowers.'

Father Brown sprang to his feet with a startling impatience.

'So the dog denounced him, did he?' he cried. 'The oracle of the dog condemned him. Did you see what birds were flying, and are you sure whether they were on the right hand or the left? Did you consult the augurs about the sacrifices? Surely you didn't omit to cut open the dog and examine his entrails. That is the sort of scientific test you heathen humanitarians seem to trust when you are thinking of taking away the life and honour of a man.'

Fiennes sat gaping for an instant before he found breath to say: 'Why, what's the matter with you? What have I done now?'

A sort of anxiety came back into the priest's eyes – the anxiety of a man who has run against a post in the dark and wonders for a moment whether he has hurt it.

'I'm most awfully sorry,' he said with sincere distress. 'I beg your pardon for being so rude; pray forgive me.'

Fiennes looked at him curiously. 'I sometimes think you are more of a mystery than any of the mysteries,' he said. 'But anyhow, if you don't believe in the mystery of the dog, at least you can't get over the mystery of the man. You can't deny that at the very moment when the beast came back from the sea and bellowed, his master's soul was driven out of his body by the blow of some unseen power that no mortal man can trace or even imagine. And as for the lawyer – I don't go only by the dog – there are other curious details, too. He struck me as a smooth, smiling, equivocal sort of person; and one of his tricks seemed like a sort of hint. You know the doctor and the police were on the spot very quickly; Valentine was brought back when walking away from the house, and he telephoned instantly. That, with the secluded house, small numbers, and enclosed space, made it pretty possible to search everybody who could have been near; and everybody was thoroughly searched – for a weapon. The whole house, garden, and shore were combed for a weapon. The disappearance of the dagger is almost as crazy as the disappearance of the man.'

'The disappearance of the dagger,' said Father Brown, nodding. He seemed to have become suddenly attentive.

'Well,' continued Fiennes, 'I told you that man Traill had a trick of fidgeting with his tie and tie-pin – especially his tie-pin. His pin, like himself, was at once showy and old-fashioned. It had one of those stones with concentric coloured rings that look like an eye; and his own concentration on it got on my nerves, as if he had been a Cyclops with one eye in the middle of his body. But the pin was not only large but long; and it occurred to me that his anxiety about its adjustment was because it was even longer than it looked; as long as a stiletto in fact.'

Father Brown nodded thoughtfully. 'Was any other instrument ever suggested?' he asked.

'There was another suggestion,' answered Fiennes, 'from one

of the young Druces – the cousins, I mean. Neither Herbert nor Harry Druce would have struck one at first as likely to be of assistance in scientific detection; but while Herbert was really the traditional type of heavy Dragoon, caring for nothing but horses and being an ornament to the Horse Guards, his younger brother Harry had been in the Indian Police and knew something about such things. Indeed, in his own way he was quite clever; and I rather fancy he had been too clever; I mean he had left the police through breaking some red-tape regulations and taking some sort of risk and responsibility of his own. Anyhow, he was in some sense a detective out of work, and threw himself into this business with more than the ardour of an amateur. And it was with him that I had an argument about the weapon – an argument that led to something new. It began by his countering my description of the dog barking at Traill; and he said that a dog at his worst didn't bark, but growled.'

'He was quite right there,' observed the priest.

'This young fellow went on to say that, if it came to that, he'd heard Nox growling at other people before then; and among others at Floyd, the secretary. I retorted that his own argument answered itself; for the crime couldn't be brought home to two or three people, and least of all to Floyd, who was as innocent as a harum-scarum schoolboy, and had been seen by everybody all the time perched above the garden hedge with his fan of red hair as conspicuous as a scarlet cockatoo. "I know there's difficulties anyhow," said my colleague; "but I wish you'd come with me down the garden a minute. I want to show you something I don't think any one else has seen." This was on the very day of the discovery, and the garden was just as it had been. The step-ladder was still standing by the hedge, and just under the hedge my guide stopped and disentangled something from the deep grass. It was the sheers used for clipping the hedge, and on the point of one of them was a smear of blood.'

There was a short silence, and then Father Brown said suddenly, 'What was the lawyer there for?'

'He told us the Colonel sent for him to alter his will,' answered Fiennes. 'And, by the way, there was another thing about the business of the will that I ought to mention. You see, the will wasn't actually signed in the summer-house that afternoon.'

'I suppose not,' said Father Brown; 'there would have to be two witnesses.'

'The lawyer actually came down the day before and it was signed then; but he was sent for again next day because the old man had a doubt about one of the witnesses and had to be re-assured.'

'Who were the witnesses?' asked Father Brown.

'That's just the point,' replied his informant eagerly, 'the witnesses were Floyd, the secretary, and this Dr Valentine, the foreign sort of surgeon or whatever he is; and the two had a quarrel. Now I'm bound to say that the secretary is something of a busybody. He's one of those hot and headlong people whose warmth of temperament has unfortunately turned mostly to pugnacity and bristling suspicion; to distrusting people instead of to trusting them. That sort of red-haired red-hot fellow is always either universally credulous or universally incredulous; and sometimes both. He was not only a Jack-of-all-trades, but he knew better than all tradesmen. He not only knew everything, but he warned everybody against everybody. All that must be taken into account in his suspicions about Valentine; but in that particular case there seems to have been something behind it. He said the name of Valentine was not really Valentine. He said he had seen him elsewhere known by the name of De Villon. He said it would invalidate the will; of course he was kind enough to explain to the lawyer what the law was on that point. They were both in a frightful wax.'

Father Brown laughed. 'People often are when they are to witness a will,' he said; 'for one thing, it means that they can't have any legacy under it. But what did Dr Valentine say? No doubt the universal secretary knew more about the doctor's name than the doctor did. But even the doctor might have some information about his own name.'

Fiennes paused a moment before he replied.

'Dr Valentine took it in a curious way. Dr Valentine is a curious man. His appearance is rather striking but very foreign. He is young but wears a beard cut square; and his face is very pale, dreadfully pale and dreadfully serious. His eyes have a sort of ache in them, as if he ought to wear glasses, or had given himself a headache with thinking; but he is quite handsome and always very formally dressed, with a top hat and a dark coat and a little red rosette. His manner is rather cold and haughty, and he has a way of staring at you which is very disconcerting. When thus charged with having changed his name, he merely stared like a sphinx and then said with a little laugh that he supposed Americans had no names to change. At that I think the Colonel also got into a fuss and said all sorts of angry things to the doctor; all the more angry because of the doctor's pretensions to a future place in his family. But I shouldn't have thought much of that but for a few words that I happened to hear later, early in the afternoon of the tragedy. I don't want to make a lot of them, for they weren't the sort of words on which one would like, in the ordinary way, to play the eavesdropper. As I was passing out towards the front gate with my two companions and the dog, I heard voices which told me that Dr Valentine and Miss Druce had withdrawn for a moment in the shadow of the house, in an angle behind a row of flowering plants, and were talking to each other in passionate whisperings – sometimes almost like hissings; for it was something of a lovers' quarrel as well as a lovers' tryst. Nobody repeats the sort of things they said for the most part; but in an unfortunate business like this I'm bound to say that there was repeated more than once a phrase about killing somebody. In fact, the girl seemed to be begging him not to kill somebody, or saying that no provocation could justify killing anybody; which seems an unusual sort of talk to address to a gentleman who has dropped in to tea.'

'Do you know,' asked the priest, 'whether Dr Valentine seemed to be very angry after the scene with the secretary and the Colonel – I mean about witnessing the will?'

'By all accounts,' replied the other, 'he wasn't half so angry as the secretary was. It was the secretary who went away raging after witnessing the will.'

'And now,' said Father Brown, 'what about the will itself?'

'The Colonel was a very wealthy man, and his will was important. Traill wouldn't tell us the alteration at that stage, but I have since heard only this morning in fact – that most of the money was transferred from the son to the daughter. I told you that Druce was wild with my friend Donald over his dissipated hours.'

'The question of motive has been rather over-shadowed by the question of method,' observed Father Brown thoughtfully. 'At that moment, apparently, Miss Druce was the immediate gainer by the death.'

'Good God! What a cold-blooded way of talking,' cried Fiennes, staring at him. 'You don't really mean to hint that she –'

'Is she going to marry that Dr Valentine?' asked the other.

'Some people are against it,' answered his friend. 'But he is liked and respected in the place and is a skilled and devoted surgeon.'

'So devoted a surgeon,' said Father Brown, 'that he had surgical instruments with him when he went to call on the young lady at teatime. For he must have used a lancet or something, and he never seems to have gone home.'

Fiennes sprang to his feet and looked at him in a heat of inquiry. 'You suggest he might have used the very same lancet –'

Father Brown shook his head. 'All these suggestions are fancies just now,' he said. 'The problem is not who did it or what did it, but how it was done. We might find many men and even many tools – pins and shears and lancets. But how did a man get into the room? How did even a pin get into it?'

He was staring reflectively at the ceiling as he spoke, but as he said the last words his eye cocked in an alert fashion as if he had suddenly seen a curious fly on the ceiling.

'Well, what would you do about it?' asked the young man. 'You have a lot of experience; what would you advise now?'

'I'm afraid I'm not much use,' said Father Brown with a sigh. 'I can't suggest very much without having ever been near the place or the people. For the moment you can only go on with local inquiries. I gather that your friend from the Indian Police is more or less in charge of your inquiry down there. I should run down and see how he is getting on. See what he's been doing in the way of amateur detection. There may be news already.'

As his guests, the biped and the quadruped, disappeared, Father Brown took up his pen and went back to his interrupted occupation of planning a course of lectures on the Encyclical *Rerum Novarum*. The subject was a large one and he had to recast it more than once, so that he was somewhat similarly employed some two days later when the big black dog again came bounding into the room and sprawled all over him with enthusiasm and excitement. The master who followed the dog shared the excitement if not the enthusiasm. He had been excited in a less pleasant fashion, for his blue eyes seemed to start from his head and his eager face was even a little pale.

'You told me,' he said abruptly and without preface, 'to find out what Harry Druce was doing. Do you know what he's done?'

The priest did not reply, and the young man went on in jerky tones:

'I'll tell you what he's done. He's killed himself.'

Father Brown's lips moved only faintly, and there was nothing practical about what he was saying – nothing that has anything to do with this story or this world.

'You give me the creeps sometimes,' said Fiennes. 'Did you – did you expect this?'

'I thought it possible,' said Father Brown; 'that was why I asked you to go and see what he was doing. I hoped you might not be too late.'

'It was I who found him,' said Fiennes rather huskily. 'It was the ugliest and most uncanny thing I ever knew. I went down that old garden again, and I knew there was something new and unnatural about it besides the murder. The flowers still tossed about in blue masses on each side of the black entrance into the old grey summer-house; but to me the blue flowers looked like blue devils dancing before some dark cavern of the underworld. I looked all round, everything seemed to be in its ordinary place. But the queer notion grew on me that there was something wrong with the very shape of the sky. And then I saw what it was. The Rock of Fortune always rose in the background beyond the garden hedge and against the sea. The Rock of Fortune was gone.'

Father Brown had lifted his head and was listening intently.

'It was as if a mountain had walked away out of a landscape or a moon fallen from the sky; though I knew, of course, that a touch at any time would have tipped the thing over. Something possessed me and I rushed down that garden path like the wind and went crashing through that hedge as if it were a spider's web. It was a thin hedge really, though its undisturbed trimness had made it serve all the purposes of a wall. On the shore I found the loose rock fallen from its pedestal; and poor Harry Druce lay like a wreck underneath it. One arm was thrown round it in a sort of embrace as if he had pulled it down on himself; and on the broad brown sands beside it, in large crazy lettering, he had scrawled the words: "The Rock of Fortune falls on the Fool". '

'It was the Colonel's will that did that,' observed Father Brown. 'The young man had staked everything on profiting himself by Donald's disgrace, especially when his uncle sent for him on the same day as the lawyer, and welcomed him with so much warmth. Otherwise he was done; he'd lost his police job; he was beggared at Monte Carlo. And he killed himself when he found he'd killed his kinsman for nothing.'

'Here, stop a minute!' cried the staring Fiennes. 'You're going too fast for me.'

'Talking about the will, by the way,' continued Father Brown calmly, 'before I forget it, or we go on to bigger things, there was a simple explanation, I think, of all that business about the doctor's name. I rather fancy I have heard both names before somewhere. The doctor is really a French nobleman with the title of the Marquis de Villon. But he is also an ardent Republican and has abandoned his title and fallen back on the forgotten family surname. "With your Citizen Riquetti you have puzzled Europe for ten days." '

'What is that?' asked the young man blankly.

'Never mind,' said the priest. 'Nine times out of ten it is a rascally thing to change one's name; but this was a piece of fine fanaticism. That's the point of his sarcasm about Americans having no names – that is, no titles. Now in England the Marquis of Hartington is never called Mr Hartington; but in France the Marquis de Villon is called M. de Villon. So it might well look like a change of name. As for the talk about killing, I fancy that also was a point of French etiquette. The doctor was talking about challenging Floyd to a duel, and the girl was trying to dissuade him.'

'Oh, I *see*,' cried Fiennes slowly. 'Now I understand what she meant.'

'And what is that about?' asked his companion, smiling.

'Well,' said the young man, 'it was something that happened to me just before I found that poor fellow's body; only the catastrophe drove it out of my head. I suppose it's hard to remember a little romantic idyll when you've just come on top of a tragedy. But as I went down the lanes leading to the Colonel's old place I met his daughter walking with Dr Valentine. She was in mourning, of course, and he always wore black as if he were going to a funeral; but I can't say that their faces were very funereal. Never have I seen two people looking in their own way more respectably radiant and cheerful. They stopped and saluted me, and then she told me they were married and living in a little house on the outskirts of the town, where the doctor was continuing his practice. This rather surprised me, because I knew that her old father's will had left her his property; and I hinted at it delicately by saying I was going along to her father's old place and had half expected to meet her there. But she only laughed and said: "Oh, we've given up all that. My husband doesn't like heiresses." And I discovered with some astonishment they really had insisted on restoring the property to poor Donald; so I hope he's had a healthy shock and will treat it sensibly. There was never much really the matter with him; he was very young and his father was not very wise. But it was in connexion with that that she said something I didn't understand at the time; but now I'm sure it must be as you say. She said with a sort of sudden and splendid arrogance that was entirely altruistic:

' "I hope it'll stop that red-haired fool from fussing any more about the will. Does he think my husband, who has given up a crest and a coronet as old as the Crusades for his principles,

would kill an old man in a summer-house for a legacy like that?"
Then she laughed again and said, "My husband isn't killing anybody except in the way of business. Why, he didn't even ask his friends to call on the secretary." Now, of course, I see what she meant.'

'I see part of what she meant, of course,' said Father Brown. 'What did she mean exactly by the secretary fussing about the will?'

Fiennes smiled as he answered, 'I wish you knew the secretary, Father Brown. It would be a joy to you to watch him make things hum, as he calls it. He made the house of mourning hum. He filled the funeral with all the snap and zip of the brightest sporting event. There was no holding him, after something had really happened. I've told you how he used to oversee the gardener as he did the garden, and how he instructed the lawyer in the law. Needless to say, he also instructed the surgeon in the practice of surgery; and as the surgeon was Dr Valentine, you may be sure it ended in accusing him of something worse than bad surgery. The secretary got it fixed in his red head that the doctor had committed the crime, and when the police arrived he was perfectly sublime. Need I say that he became, on the spot, the greatest of all amateur detectives? Sherlock Holmes never towered over Scotland Yard with more Titanic intellectual pride and scorn than Colonel Druce's private secretary over the police investigating Colonel Druce's death. I tell you it was a joy to see him. He strode about with an abstracted air, tossing his scarlet crest of hair and giving curt impatient replies. Of course it was his demeanour during these days that made Druce's daughter so wild with him. Of course he had a theory. It's just the sort of theory a man would have in a book; and Floyd is the sort of man who ought to be in a book. He'd be better fun and less bother in a book.'

'What was his theory?' asked the other.

'Oh, it was full of pep,' replied Fiennes gloomily. 'It would have been glorious copy if it could have held together for ten minutes longer. He said the Colonel was still alive when they found him in the summer-house, and the doctor killed him with the surgical instrument on pretence of cutting the clothes.'

'I see,' said the priest. 'I suppose he was lying flat on his face on the mud floor as a form of siesta.'

'It's wonderful what hustle will do,' continued his informant. 'I believe Floyd would have got his great theory into the papers at any rate, and perhaps had the doctor arrested, when all these things were blown sky high as if by dynamite by the discovery of that dead body lying under the Rock of Fortune. And that's what we come back to after all. I suppose the suicide is almost a confession. But nobody will ever know the whole story.'

There was a silence, and then the priest said modestly: 'I rather think I know the whole story.'

Fiennes stared. 'But look here,' he cried; 'how do you come to know the whole story, or to be sure it's the true story? You've been sitting here a hundred miles away writing a sermon; do you mean to tell me you really know what happened already? If you've really come to the end, where in the world do you begin? What started you off with your own story?'

Father Brown jumped up with a very unusual excitement and his first exclamation was like an explosion.

'The dog!' he cried. 'The dog, of course! You had the whole story in your hands in the business of the dog on the beach, if you'd only noticed the dog properly.'

Fiennes stared still more. 'But you told me before that my feelings about the dog were all nonsense, and the dog had nothing to do with it.'

'The dog had everything to do with it,' said Father Brown, 'as you'd have found out if you'd only treated the dog as a dog, and not as God Almighty judging the souls of men.'

He paused in an embarrassed way for a moment, and then said, with a rather pathetic air of apology: 'The truth is, I happen to be awfully fond of dogs. And it seemed to me that in all this lurid halo of dog superstitions nobody was really thinking about the poor dog at all. To begin with a small point, about his barking at the lawyer or growling at the secretary. You asked how I could guess things a hundred miles away; but honestly it's mostly to your credit, for you described people so well that I know the types. A man like Traill, who frowns usually and smiles suddenly, a man who fiddles with things, especially at his throat, is a nervous, easily embarrassed man. I shouldn't wonder if Floyd, the efficient secretary, is nervy and jumpy, too; those Yankee hustlers often are. Otherwise he wouldn't have cut his fingers on the shears and dropped them when he heard Janet Druce scream.

'Now dogs hate nervous people. I don't know whether they make the dog nervous, too; or whether, being after all a brute, he is a bit of a bully; or whether his canine vanity (which is colossal) is simply offended at not being liked. But anyhow there was nothing in poor Nox protesting against those people, except that he disliked them for being afraid of him. Now I know you're awfully clever, and nobody of sense sneers at cleverness. But I sometimes fancy, for instance, that you are too clever to understand animals. Sometimes you are too clever to understand men, especially when they act almost as simply as animals. Animals are very literal; they live in a world of truisms. Take this case: a dog barks at a man and a man runs away from a dog. Now you do not seem to be quite simple enough to see the fact: that the dog barked because he disliked the man and the man fled because he was frightened of the dog. They had no other motives and they needed none; but you must read psychological mysteries into it and suppose the dog had super-normal vision, and was a mysterious mouthpiece of doom. You must suppose the man was running away, not from the dog but from the hangman. And yet, if you come to think if it, all this deeper psychology is exceedingly improbable. If the dog really could completely and consciously realize the murderer of his master he wouldn't stand yapping as he might at a curate at a tea-party; he's much more likely to fly at his throat. And on the other hand, do you really think a man who had hardened his heart to murder an old friend and then walk about smiling at the old friend's family, under the eyes of his old friend's daughter and post-mortem doctor – do you think a man like that would be doubled up by mere remorse because a dog barked? He might feel the tragic irony of it; it might shake his soul, like any other tragic trifle. But he wouldn't rush madly the length of a garden to escape from the only witness whom he knew to be unable to talk. People have a panic like that when they are frightened, not of tragic ironies, but of teeth. The whole thing is simpler than you can understand.

'But when we come to that business by the seashore, things are much more interesting. As you stated them, they were much more puzzling. I didn't understand that tale of the dog going in and out of the water; it didn't seem to me a doggy thing to do. If Nox had been very much upset about something else, he might possibly have refused to go after the stick at all. He'd probably go off nosing in whatever direction he suspected the mischief. But when once a dog is actually chasing a thing, a stone or a stick or a rabbit, my experience is that he won't stop for anything but the most peremptory command, and not always for that. That he should turn round because his mood changed seems to me unthinkable.'

'But he did turn round,' insisted Fiennes; 'and came back without the stick.'

'He came back without the stick for the best reason in the world,' replied the priest. 'He came back because he couldn't find it. He whined because he couldn't find it. That's the sort of thing a dog really does whine about. A dog is a devil of a ritualist. He is as particular about the precise routine of a game as a child about the precise repetition of a fairy-tale. In this case something had gone wrong with the game. He came back to complain seriously of the conduct of the stick. Never had such a thing happened before. Never had an eminent and distinguished dog been so treated by a rotten old walking-stick.'

'Why, what had the walking-stick done?' inquired the young man.

'It had sunk,' said Father Brown.

Fiennes said nothing, but continued to stare; and it was the priest who continued:

'It had sunk because it was not really a stick, but a rod of steel with a very thin shell of cane and a sharp point. In other words, it was a sword stick. I suppose a murderer never gets rid of a bloody weapon so oddly and yet so naturally as by throwing it into the sea for a retriever.'

'I begin to see what you mean,' admitted Fiennes; 'but even if a sword-stick was used, I have no guess of how it was used.'

'I had a sort of guess,' said Father Brown, 'right at the beginning when you said the word summer-house. And another when you said that Druce wore a white coat. As long as everybody was looking for a short dagger, nobody thought of it; but if we admit a rather long blade like a rapier, it's not so impossible.'

He was leaning back, looking at the ceiling, and began like one going back to his own first thoughts and fundamentals.

'All that discussion about detective stories like the Yellow Room, about a man found dead in sealed chambers which no one could enter, does not apply to the present case, because it is a summer-house. When we talk of a Yellow Room, or any room, we imply walls that are really homogeneous and impenetrable. But a summer-house is not made like that; it is often made, as it was in this case, of closely interlaced but separate boughs and strips of wood, in which there are chinks here and there. There was one of them just behind Druce's back as he sat in his chair up against the wall. But just as the room was a summer-house, so the chair was a basket-chair. That also was a lattice of loopholes. Lastly, the summer-house was close up under the hedge; and you have just told me that it was really a thin hedge. A man standing outside it could easily see, amid a network of twigs and branches and canes, one white spot of the Colonel's coat as plain as the white of a target.

'Now, you left the geography a little vague; but it was possible to put two and two together. You said the Rock of Fortune was not really high; but you also said it could be seen dominating the garden like a mountain-peak. In other words, it was very near the end of the garden, though your walk had taken you a long way round to it. Also, it isn't likely the young lady really howled so as to be heard half a mile. She gave an ordinary involuntary cry, and yet you heard it on the shore. And among other interesting things that you told me, may I remind you that you said Harry Druce had fallen behind to light his pipe under a hedge.'

Fiennes shuddered slightly. 'You mean he drew his blade there and sent it through the hedge at the white spot. But surely it was a

very odd chance and a very sudden choice. Besides, he couldn't
be certain the old man's money had passed to him, and as a fact it
hadn't.'

Father Brown's face became animated.

'You misunderstand the man's character,' he said, as if he himself had known the man all his life. 'A curious but not unknown
type of character. If he had really *known* the money would come
to him, I seriously believe he wouldn't have done it. He would
have seen it as the dirty thing it was.'

'Isn't that rather paradoxical?' asked the other.

'This man was a gambler,' said the priest, 'and a man in disgrace for having taken risks and anticipated orders. It was
probably for something pretty unscrupulous, for every imperial
police is more like a Russian secret police than we like to think.
But he had gone beyond the line and failed. Now, the temptation
of that type of man is to do a mad thing precisely because the risk
will be wonderful in retrospect. He wants to say, "Nobody but I
could have seized that chance or seen that it was then or never.
What a wild and wonderful guess it was, when I put all those
things together; Donald in disgrace; and the lawyer being sent
for; and Herbert and I sent for at the same time – and then nothing more but the way the old man grinned at me and shook hands.
Anybody would say I was mad to risk it; but that is how fortunes
are made, by the man mad enough to have a little foresight." In
short, it is the vanity of guessing. It is the megalomania of the
gambler. The more incongruous the coincidence, the more instan-
taneous the decision, the more likely he is to snatch the chance.
The accident, the very triviality of the white speck and the hole in
the hedge intoxicated him like a vision of the world's desire.
Nobody clever enough to see such a combination of accidents
could be cowardly enough not to use them! That is how the devil
talks to the gambler. But the devil himself would hardly have
induced that unhappy man to go down in a dull, deliberate way
and kill an old uncle from whom he'd always had expectations. It
would be too respectable.'

He paused a moment, and then went on with a certain quiet
emphasis.

'And now try to call up the scene, even as you saw it yourself. As he stood there, dizzy with his diabolical opportunity, he looked up and saw that strange outline that might have been the image of his own tottering soul; the one great crag poised perilously on the other like a pyramid on its point, and remembered that it was called the Rock of Fortune. Can you guess how such a man at such a moment would read such a signal? I think it strung him up to action and even to vigilance. He who would be a tower must not fear to be a toppling tower. Anyhow, he acted; his next difficulty was to cover his tracks. To be found with a sword-stick, let alone a blood-stained sword-stick, would be fatal in the search that was certain to follow. If he left it anywhere, it would be found and probably traced. Even if he threw it into the sea the action might be noticed, and thought noticeable – unless indeed he could think of some more natural way of covering the action. As you know, he did think of one, and a very good one. Being the only one of you with a watch, he told you it was not yet time to return, strolled a little farther, and started the game of throwing in sticks for the retriever. But how his eyes must have rolled darkly over all that desolate sea-shore before they alighted on the dog!'

Fiennes nodded, gazing thoughtfully into space. His mind seemed to have drifted back to a less practical part of the narrative.

'It's queer,' he said, 'that the dog really was in the story after all.'

'The dog could almost have told you the story, if he could talk,' said the priest. 'All I complain of is that because he couldn't talk you made up his story for him, and made him talk with the tongues of men and angels. It's part of something I've noticed more and more in the modern world, appearing in all sorts of newspaper rumours and conversational catchwords; something that's arbitrary without being authoritative. People readily swallow the untested claims of this, that, or the other. It's drowning all your old rationalism and scepticism, it's coming in like a sea; and the name of it is superstition.' He stood up abruptly, his face heavy with a sort of frown, and went on talking almost as if he were alone. 'It's the first effect of not believing in God that you lose your common sense and can't see things as they are. Anything that anybody talks about, and says there's a good deal in it, extends itself indefinitely like a vista in a nightmare. And a dog is an omen, and a cat is a mystery, and a pig is a mascot, and a beetle is a scarab, calling up all the menagerie of polytheism from Egypt and old India; Dog Anubis and great green-eyed Pasht and all the holy howling Bulls of Bashan; reeling back to the bestial gods of the beginning, escaping into elephants and snakes and crocodiles; and all because you are frightened of four words: "He was made Man".'

The young man got up with a little embarrassment, almost as if he had overheard a soliloquy. He called to the dog and left the room with vague but breezy farewells. But he had to call the dog twice, for the dog had remained behind quite motionless for a moment, looking up steadily at Father Brown as the wolf looked at St Francis.

FOUR

The Miracle of Moon Crescent

MOON CRESCENT was meant in a sense to be as romantic as its name; and the things that happened there were romantic enough in their way. At least it had been an expression of that genuine element of sentiment – historic and almost heroic – which manages to remain side by side with commercialism in the elder cities on the eastern coast of America. It was originally a curve of classical architecture really recalling that eighteenth-century atmosphere in which men like Washington and Jefferson had seemed to be all the more republicans for being aristocrats. Travellers faced with the recurrent query of what they thought of our city were understood to be specially answerable for what they thought of our Moon Crescent. The very contrasts that confuse its original harmony were characteristic of its survival. At one extremity or horn of the crescent its last windows looked over an enclosure like a strip of a gentleman's park, with trees and hedges as formal as a Queen Anne garden. But immediately round the corner, the other windows, even of the same rooms, or rather 'apartments', looked out on the blank, unsightly wall of a huge warehouse attached to some ugly industry. The apartments of Moon Crescent itself were at that end remodelled on the monotonous pattern of an American hotel, and rose to a height, which, though lower than the colossal warehouse, would have been called a skyscraper in London. But the colonnade that ran round the whole frontage upon the street had a grey and weather-stained stateliness suggesting that the ghosts of the Fathers of the Republic might still be walking to and fro in it. The insides of the rooms, however, were as neat and new as the last New York fittings could make them, especially at the northern end between the neat garden and the blank warehouse wall. They were a system of very small flats, as we should say in England, each consisting of a sitting-room, bedroom, and bathroom, as identical as the hundred cells of a hive. In one of these the celebrated Warren Wynd sat at his desk sorting

letters and scattering orders with wonderful rapidity and exactitude. He could only be compared to a tidy whirlwind.

Warren Wynd was a very little man with loose grey hair and a
pointed beard, seemingly frail but fierily active. He had very
wonderful eyes, brighter than stars and stronger than magnets,
which nobody who had ever seen them could easily forget. And
indeed in his work as a reformer and regulator of many good
works he had shown at least that he had a pair of eyes in his head.
All sorts of stories and even legends were told of the miraculous
rapidity with which he could form a sound judgement, especially
of human character. It was said that he selected the wife who
worked with him so long in so charitable a fashion, by picking her
out of a whole regiment of women in uniform marching past at
some official celebration, some said of the Girl Guides and some
of the Women Police. Another story was told of how three tramps,
indistinguishable from each other in their community of filth and
rags, had presented themselves before him asking for charity.
Without a moment's hesitation he had sent one of them to a
particular hospital devoted to a certain nervous disorder, had
recommended the second to an inebriates' home, and had engaged the third at a handsome salary as his own private servant,
a position which he filled successfully for years afterwards. There
were, of course, the inevitable anecdotes of his prompt criticisms
and curt repartees when brought in contact with Roosevelt, with
Henry Ford, and with Mrs Asquith and all other persons with
whom an American public man ought to have a historic interview, if only in the newspapers. Certainly he was not likely to be
overawed by such personages; and at the moment here in
question he continued very calmly his centrifugal whirl of papers,
though the man confronting him was a personage of almost equal
importance.

Silas T. Vandam, the millionaire and oil magnate, was a lean
man with a long, yellow face and blue-black hair, colours which
were the less conspicuous yet somehow the more sinister because
his face and figure showed dark against the window and the white
warehouse wall outside it; he was buttoned up tight in an elegant
overcoat with strips of astrakhan. The eager face and brilliant

eyes of Wynd, on the other hand, were in the full light from the other window over-looking the little garden, for his chair and desk stood facing it; and though the face was preoccupied, it did not seem unduly preoccupied about the millionaire. Wynd's valet or personal servant, a big, powerful man with flat fair hair, was standing behind his master's desk holding a sheaf of letters; and Wynd's private secretary, a neat, red-haired youth with a sharp face, had his hand already on the door handle, as if guessing some purpose or obeying some gesture of his employer. The room was not only neat, but austere to the point of emptiness; for Wynd, with characteristic thoroughness, had rented the whole floor above, and turned it into a loft or storeroom, where all his other papers and possessions were stacked in boxes and corded bales.

'Give these to the floor-clerk, Wilson,' said Wynd to the servant holding the letters, 'and then get me the pamphlet on the Minneapolis Night Clubs; you'll find it in the bundle marked 'G'. I shall want it in half an hour, but don't disturb me till then. Well, Mr Vandam, I think your proposition sounds very promising; but I can't give a final answer till I've seen the report. It ought to reach me to-morrow afternoon, and I'll phone you at once. I'm sorry I can't say anything more definite just now.'

Mr Vandam seemed to feel that this was something like a polite dismissal; and his sallow, saturnine face suggested that he found a certain irony in the fact.

'Well, I suppose I must be going,' he said.

'Very good of you to call, Mr Vandam,' said Wynd, politely; 'you will excuse my not coming out, as I've something here I must fix at once. Fenner,' he added to the secretary, 'show Mr Vandam to his car, and don't come back again for half an hour. I've something here I want to work out by myself; after that I shall want you.'

The three men went out into the hallway together, closing the door behind them. The big servant, Wilson, was turning down the hallway in the direction of the floor-clerk, and the other two moving in the opposite direction towards the lift; for Wynd's apartment was high up on the fourteenth floor. They had hardly gone a yard from the closed door when they became conscious that the corridor was filled with a marching and even magnificent figure. The man was very tall and broad-shouldered, his bulk being the more conspicuous for being clad in white, or a light grey that looked like it, with a very wide white panama hat and an almost equally wide fringe or halo of almost equally white hair. Set in this aureole his face was strong and handsome, like that of a Roman emperor, save that there was something more than boyish, something a little childish, about the brightness of his eyes and the beatitude of his smile.

'Mr Warren Wynd in?' he asked, in hearty tones.

'Mr Warren Wynd is engaged,' said Fenner; 'he must not be disturbed on any account. I may say I am his secretary and can take any message.'

'Mr Warren Wynd is not at home to the Pope or the Crowned Heads,' said Vandam, the oil magnate, with sour satire. 'Mr Warren Wynd is mighty particular. I went in there to hand him over a trifle of twenty thousand dollars on certain conditions, and he told me to call again like as if I was a call-boy.'

'It's a fine thing to be a boy,' said the stranger, 'and a finer to have a call; and I've got a call he's just got to listen to. It's a call of the great good country out West, where the real American is being made while you're all snoring. Just tell him that Art Alboin of Oklahoma City has come to convert him.'

'I tell you nobody can see him,' said the red-haired secretary sharply. 'He has given orders that he is not to be disturbed for half an hour.'

'You folks down East are all against being disturbed,' said the breezy Mr Alboin, 'but I calculate there's a big breeze getting up in the West that will have to disturb you. He's been figuring out how much money must go to this and that stuffy old religion; but I tell you any scheme that leaves out the new Great Spirit movement in Texas and Oklahoma, is leaving out the religion of the future.'

'Oh; I've sized up those religions of the future,' said the millionaire, contemptuously. 'I've been through them with a tooth-comb and they're as mangy as yellow dogs. There was that woman called herself Sophia: ought to have called herself Sapphira, I reckon. Just a plum fraud. Strings tied to all the tables and tambourines. Then there were the Invisible Life bunch; said they could vanish when they liked, and they did vanish, too, and a hundred thousand of my dollars vanished with them. I knew Jupiter Jesus out in Denver; saw him for weeks on end; and he was just a common crook. So was the Patagonian Prophet; you bet he's made a bolt for Patagonia. No, I'm through with all that; from now on I only believe what I see. I believe they call it being an atheist.'

'I guess you got me wrong,' said the man from Oklahoma, almost eagerly. 'I guess I'm as much of an atheist as you are. No supernatural or superstitious stuff in our movement; just plain science. The only real right science is just health, and the only real right health is just breathing. Fill your lungs with the wide air of the prairie and you could blow all your old eastern cities into the sea. You could just puff away their biggest men like thistledown. That's what we do in the new movement out home: we breathe. We don't pray; we breathe.'

'Well, I suppose you do,' said the secretary, wearily. He had a keen, intelligent face which could hardly conceal the weariness; but he had listened to the two monologues with the admirable patience and politeness (so much in contrast with the legends of impatience and insolence) with which such monologues are listened to in America.

'Nothing supernatural,' continued Alboin, 'just the great natural fact behind all the supernatural fancies. What did the Jews want with a God except to breathe into man's nostrils the breath of life? We do the breathing into our own nostrils out in Oklahoma. What's the meaning of the very word Spirit? It's just the Greek for breathing exercises. Life, progress, prophecy; it's all breath.'

' Some would allow it's all wind,' said Vandam; 'but I'm glad you've got rid of the divinity stunt, anyhow.'

The keen face of the secretary, rather pale against his red hair, showed a flicker of some odd feeling suggestive of a secret bitterness.

'I'm not glad,' he said, 'I'm just sure. You seem to like being atheists; so you may be just believing what you like to believe. But I wish to God there were a God; and there ain't. It's just my luck.'

Without a sound or stir they all became almost creepily conscious at this moment that the group, halted outside Wynd's door, had silently grown from three figures to four. How long the fourth figure had stood there none of the earnest disputants could tell, but he had every appearance of waiting respectfully and even timidly for the opportunity to say something urgent. But to their nervous sensibility he seemed to have sprung up suddenly and silently like a mushroom. And indeed, he looked rather like a big, black mushroom, for he was quite short and his small, stumpy figure was eclipsed by his big, black clerical hat; the resemblance might have been more complete if mushrooms were in the habit of carrying umbrellas, even of a shabby and shapeless sort.

Fenner, the secretary, was conscious of a curious additional surprise at recognizing the figure of a priest; but when the priest turned up a round face under the round hat and innocently asked for Mr Warren Wynd, he gave the regular negative answer rather more curtly than before. But the priest stood his ground.

'I do really want to see Mr Wynd,' he said. 'It seems odd, but that's exactly what I do want to do. I don't want to speak to him. I just want to see him. I just want to see if he's there to be seen.'

'Well, I tell you he's there and can't be seen,' said Fenner, with increasing annoyance. 'What do you mean by saying you want to see if he's there to be seen? Of course he's there. We all left him there five minutes ago, and we've stood outside this door ever since.'

'Well, I want to see if he's all right,' said the priest.

'Why?' demanded the secretary, in exasperation.

'Because I have a serious, I might say solemn, reason,' said the cleric, gravely, 'for doubting whether he is all right.'

'Oh, Lord!' cried Vandam, in a sort of fury; 'not more superstitions.'

'I see I shall have to give my reasons,' observed the little cleric, gravely. 'I suppose I can't expect you even to let me look through the crack of a door till I tell you the whole story.'

He was silent a moment as in reflection, and then went on

without noticing the wondering faces around him. 'I was walking outside along the front of the colonnade when I saw a very ragged man running hard round the corner at the end of the crescent. He came pounding along the pavement towards me, revealing a great raw-boned figure and a face I knew. It was the face of a wild Irish fellow I once helped a little; I will not tell you his name. When he saw me he staggered, calling me by mine and saying, "Saints alive, it's Father Brown; you're the only man whose face could frighten me to-day." I knew he meant he'd been doing some wild thing or other, and I don't think my face frightened him much, for he was soon telling me about it. And a very strange thing it was. He asked me if I knew Warren Wynd, and I said no, though I knew he lived near the top of these flats. He said, "That's a man who thinks he's a saint of God; but if he knew what I was saying of him he should be ready to hang himself." And he repeated hysterically more than once, "Yes, ready to hang himself." I asked him if he'd done any harm to Wynd, and his answer was rather a queer one. He said: "I took a pistol and I loaded it with neither shot nor slug, but only with a curse." As far as I could make out, all he had done was to go down that little alley between this building and the big warehouse, with an old pistol loaded with a blank charge, and merely fire it against the wall, as if that would bring down the building. "But as I did it," he said, "I cursed him with the great curse, that the justice of God should take him by the hair and the vengeance of hell by the heels, and he should be torn asunder like Judas and the world know him no more." Well, it doesn't matter now what else I said to the poor, crazy fellow; he went away quieted down a little, and I went round to the back of the building to inspect. And sure enough, in the little alley at the foot of this wall there lay a rusty antiquated pistol; I know enough about pistols to know it had been loaded only with a little powder; there were the black marks of powder and smoke on the wall, and even the mark of the muzzle, but not even a dent of any bullet. He had left no trace of destruction; he had left no trace of anything, except those black marks and that black curse he had hurled into heaven. So I came back here to ask for this Warren Wynd and find out if he's all right.'

Fenner the secretary laughed. 'I can soon settle that difficulty for you. I assure you he's quite all right; we left him writing at his desk only a few minutes ago. He was alone in his flat; it's a hundred feet up from the street, and so placed that no shot could have reached him, even if your friend hadn't fired blank. There's no other entrance to this place but this door, and we've been standing outside it ever since.'

'All the same,' said Father Brown, gravely, 'I should like to look in and see.'

'Well, you can't,' retorted the other. 'Good Lord, you don't tell me you think anything of the curse.'

'You forget,' said the millionaire, with a slight sneer, 'the reverend gentleman's whole business is blessings and cursings. Come, sir, if he's been cursed to hell, why don't you bless him back again? What's the good of your blessings if they can't beat an Irish larrykin's curse.'

'Does anybody believe such things now?' protested the Westerner.

'Father Brown believes a good number of things, I take it,' said Vandam, whose temper was suffering from the past snub and the present bickering. 'Father Brown believes a hermit crossed a river on a crocodile conjured out of nowhere, and then he told the crocodile to die, and it sure did. Father Brown believes that some blessed saint or other died, and had his dead body turned into three dead bodies, to be served out to three parishes that were all bent on figuring as his home-town. Father Brown believes that a saint hung his cloak on a sunbeam, and another used his for a boat to cross the Atlantic. Father Brown believes the holy donkey had six legs and the house of Loretto flew through the air. He believes in hundreds of stone virgins winking and weeping all day long. It's nothing to him to believe that a man might escape through the keyhole or vanish out of a locked room. I reckon he doesnt take much stock of the laws of nature.'

'Anyhow, I have to take stock in the laws of Warren Wynd,' said the secretary, wearily, 'and it's his rule that he's to be left alone when he says so. Wilson will tell you just the same,' for the large servant who had been sent for the pamphlet, passed placidly down the corridor even as he spoke, carrying the pamphlet, but serenely passing the door. 'He'll go and sit on the bench by the floor-clerk and twiddle his thumbs till he's wanted; but he won't go in before then; and nor will I. I reckon we both know which side our bread is buttered, and it'd take a good many of Father Brown's saint and angels to make us forget it.'

'As for saints and angels –' began the priest.

'It's all nonsense,' repeated Fenner. 'I don't want to say anything offensive, but that sort of thing may be very well for crypts and cloisters and all sorts of moonshiny places. But ghosts can't get through a closed door in an American hotel.'

'But men can open a door, even in an American hotel,' replied Father Brown, patiently. 'And it seems to me the simplest thing would be to open it.'

'It would be simple enough to lose me my job,' answered the secretary, 'and Warren Wynd doesn't like his secretaries so simple as that. Not simple enough to believe in the sort of fairy tales you seem to believe in.'

'Well,' said the priest gravely, 'it is true enough that I believe in a good many things that you probably don't. But it would take a considerable time to explain all the things I believe in, and all the reasons I have for thinking I'm right. It would take about two seconds to open that door and prove I am wrong.'

Something in the phrase seemed to please the more wild and restless spirit of the man from the West.

'I'll allow I'd love to prove you wrong,' said Alboin, striding suddenly past them, 'and I will.'

He threw open the door of the flat and looked in. The first glimpse showed that Warren Wynd's chair was empty. The second glance showed that his room was empty also.

Fenner, electrified with energy in his turn, dashed past the other into the apartment.

'He's in his bedroom,' he said curtly, 'he must be.'

As he disappeared into the inner chamber the other men stood in the empty outer room staring about them. The severity and simplicity of its fittings, which had already been noted, returned on them with a rigid challenge. Certainly in this room there was no question of hiding a mouse, let alone a man. There were no curtains and, what is rare in American arrangements, no cupboards. Even the desk was no more than a plain table with a shallow drawer and a tilted lid. The chairs were hard and high-backed skeletons. A moment after the secretary reappeared at the inner door, having searched the two inner rooms. A staring negation stood in his eyes, and his mouth seemed to move in a mechanical detachment from it as he said sharply: 'He didn't come out through here?'

Somehow the others did not even think it necessary to answer that negation in the negative. Their minds had come up against something like the blank wall of the warehouse that stared in at the opposite window, gradually turning from white to grey as dusk slowly descended with the advancing afternoon. Vandam walked over to the window-sill against which he had leant half an hour before and looked out of the open window. There was no pipe or fire-escape, no shelf or foothold of any kind on the sheer fall to the little by-street below, there was nothing on the similar expanse of wall that rose many stories above. There was even less variation on the other side of the street; there was nothing whatever but the wearisome expanse of whitewashed wall. He peered downwards, as if expecting to see the vanished philanthropist lying in a suicidal wreck on the path. He could see nothing but one small dark object which, though diminished by distance, might well be the pistol that the priest had found lying there. Meanwhile, Fenner had walked to the other window, which looked out from a wall equally blank and inaccessible, but looking out over a small ornamental park instead of a side street. Here a clump of trees interrupted the actual view of the ground; but they reached but a little way up the huge human cliff. Both turned back into the room and faced each other in the gathering twilight where the last silver gleams of daylight on the shiny tops of desks and tables were rapidly turning grey. As if the twilight itself irritated him, Fenner touched the switch and the scene sprang into the startling distinctness of electric light.

'As you said just now,' said Vandam grimly, 'there's no shot from down there could hit him, even if there was a shot in the gun.

But even if he was hit with a bullet he wouldn't have just burst like a bubble.'

The secretary, who was paler than ever, glanced irritably at the bilious visage of the millionaire.

'What's got you started on those morbid notions? Who's talking about bullets and bubbles? Why shouldn't he be alive?'

'Why not indeed?' replied Vandam smoothly. 'If you'll tell me where he is, I'll tell you how he got there.'

After a pause the secretary muttered, rather sulkily: 'I suppose you're right. We're right up against the very thing we were talking about. It'd be a queer thing if you or I ever came to think there was anything in cursing. But who could have harmed Wynd shut up in here?'

Mr Alboin, of Oklahoma, had been standing rather astraddle in the middle of the room, his white, hairy halo as well as his round eyes seeming to radiate astonishment. At this point he said, abstractedly, with something of the irrelevant impudence of an *enfant terrible:*

'You didn't cotton to him much, did you, Mr Vandam?'

Mr Vandam's long yellow face seemed to grow longer as it grew more sinister, while he smiled and answered quietly:

'If it comes to these coincidences, it was you, I think, who said that a wind from the West would blow away our big men like thistledown.'

'I know I said it would,' said the Westerner, with candour; 'but all the same, how the devil could it?'

The silence was broken by Fenner saying with an abruptness amounting to violence:

'There's only one thing to say about this affair. It simply hasn't happened. It can't have happened.'

'Oh, yes,' said Father Brown out of the corner; 'it has happened all right.'

They all jumped; for the truth was they had all forgotten the insignificant little man who had originally induced them to open the door. And the recovery of memory went with a sharp reversal of mood; it came back to them with a rush that they had all dismissed him as a superstitious dreamer for even hinting at the very thing that had since happened before their eyes.

'Snakes!' cried the impetuous Westerner, like one speaking before he could stop himself; 'suppose there were something in it, after all!'

'I must confess,' said Fenner, frowning at the table, 'that his reverence's anticipations were apparently well founded. I don't know whether he has anything else to tell us.'

'He might possibly tell us,' said Vandam, sardonically, 'what the devil we are to do now.'

The little priest seemed to accept the position in a modest, but matter-of-fact manner. 'The only thing I can think of,' he said, 'is first to tell the authorities of this place, and then to see if there were any more traces of my man who let off the pistol. He vanished round the other end of the Crescent where the little garden is. There are seats there, and it's a favourite place for tramps.'

Direct consultations with the headquarters of the hotel, leading to indirect consultations with the authorities of the police, occupied them for a considerable time; and it was already nightfall when they went out under the long, classical curve of the colonnade. The crescent looked as cold and hollow as the moon after which it was named, and the moon itself was rising luminous but spectral behind the black tree-tops when they turned the corner by the little public garden. Night veiled much of what was merely urban and artificial about the place; and as they melted into the shadows of the trees they had a strange feeling of having suddenly travelled many hundred miles from their homes. When they had walked in silence for a little, Alboin, who had something elemental about him, suddenly exploded.

'I give up,' he cried; 'I hand in my checks. I never thought I should come to such things; but what happens when the things come to you? I beg your pardon, Father Brown; I reckon I'll just come across, so far as you and your fairy-tales are concerned. After this, it's me for the fairy-tales. Why, you said yourself, Mr Vandam, that you're an atheist and only believe what you see. Well, what was it you did see? Or rather, what was it you didn't see?'

'I know,' said Vandam and nodded in a gloomy fashion.

'Oh, it's partly all this moon and trees that get on one's nerves,' said Fenner obstinately. 'Trees always look queer by moonlight, with their branches crawling about. Look at that –'

'Yes,' said Father Brown, standing still and peering at the moon through a tangle of trees. 'That's a very queer branch up there.'

When he spoke again he only said:

'I thought it was a broken branch.'

But this time there was a catch in his voice that unaccountably turned his hearers cold. Something that looked rather like a dead branch was certainly dependent in a limp fashion from the tree that showed dark against the moon; but it was not a dead branch. When they came close to it to see what it was Fenner sprang away again with a ringing oath. Then he ran in again and loosened a rope from the neck of the dingy little body dangling with drooping plumes of grey hair. Somehow he knew that the body was a dead body before he managed to take it down from the tree. A very long coil of rope was wrapped round and round the branches, and a comparatively short length of it hung from the fork of the branch to the body. A long garden tub was rolled a yard or so from under the feet, like the stool kicked away from the feet of a suicide.

'Oh, my God!' said Alboin, so that it seemed as much a prayer as an oath. 'What was it that man said about him? – "If he knew, he would be ready to hang himself." Wasn't that what he said, Father Brown?'

'Yes,' said Father Brown.

'Well,' said Vandam in a hollow voice, 'I never thought to see or say such a thing. But what can one say except that the curse has worked?'

Fenner was standing with hands covering his face; and the priest laid a hand on his arm and said, gently, 'Were you very fond of him?'

The secretary dropped his hands and his white face was ghastly under the moon.

'I hated him like hell,' he said; 'and if he died by a curse it might have been mine.'

The pressure of the priest's hand on his arm tightened; and the priest said, with an earnestness he had hardly yet shown:

'It wasn't your curse; pray be comforted.'

The police of the district had considerable difficulty in dealing with the four witnesses who were involved in the case. All of them were reputable, and even reliable people in the ordinary sense; and one of them was a person of considerable power and importance: Silas Vandam of the Oil Trust. The first police-officer who tried to express scepticism about his story struck sparks from the steel of that magnate's mind very rapidly indeed.

'Don't you talk to me about sticking to the facts,' said the millionaire with asperity. 'I've stuck to a good many facts before you were born and a few of the facts have stuck to me. I'll give you the facts all right if you've got the sense to take 'em down correctly.'

The policeman in question was youthful and subordinate, and had a hazy idea that the millionaire was too political to be treated as an ordinary citizen; so he passed him and his companions on to a more stolid superior, one Inspector Collins, a grizzled man with a grimly comfortable way of talking; as one who was genial but would stand no nonsense.

'Well, well,' he said, looking at the three figures before him with twinkling eyes, 'this seems to be a funny sort of a tale.'

Father Brown had already gone about his daily business; but Silas Vandam had suspended even the gigantic business of the markets for an hour or so to testify to his remarkable experience. Fenner's business as secretary had ceased in a sense with his employer's life; and the great Art Alboin, having no business in New York or anywhere else, except the spreading of the Breath of Life religion or the Great Spirit, had nothing to draw him away at the moment from the immediate affair. So they stood in a row in the inspector's office, prepared to corroborate each other.

'Now I'd better tell you to start with,' said the inspector cheerfully, 'that it's no good for anybody to come to me with any miraculous stuff. I'm a practical man and a policeman, and that sort of thing is all very well for priests and parsons. This priest of yours seems to have got you all worked up about some story of a dreadful death and judgement; but I'm going to leave him and his religion out of it altogether. If Wynd came out of that room, somebody let him out. And if Wynd was found hanging on that tree, somebody hung him there.'

'Quite so,' said Fenner; 'but as our evidence is that nobody let him out, the question is how could anybody have hung him there?'

'How could anybody have a nose on his face?' asked the inspector. 'He had a nose on his face, and he had a noose round his neck. Those are facts; and, as I say, I'm a practical man and go by the facts. It can't have been done by a miracle, so it must have been done by a man.'

Alboin had been standing rather in the background; and indeed his broad figure seemed to form a natural background to the leaner and more vivacious men in front of him. His white head was bowed with a certain abstraction; but as the inspector said the last sentence, he lifted it, shaking his hoary mane in a leonine fashion, and looking dazed but awakened. He moved forward into the centre of the group, and they had a vague feeling that he was even vaster than before. They had been only too prone to take him for a fool or a mountebank; but he was not altogether wrong when he said that there was in him a certain depth of lungs and life, like a west wind stored up in its strength, which might some day puff lighter things away.

'So you're a practical man, Mr Collins,' he said, in a voice at once soft and heavy. 'It must be the second or third time you've mentioned in this little conversation that you are a practical man; so I can't be mistaken about that. And a very interesting little fact it is for anybody engaged in writing your life, letters, and table-talk, with portrait at the age of five, daguerreotype of your grandmother and views of the old home-town; and I'm sure your biographer won't forget to mention it along with the fact that you had a pug nose with a pimple on it, and were nearly too fat to walk. And as you're a practical man, perhaps you would just go on practising till you've brought Warren Wynd to life again, and found out exactly how a practical man gets through a deal door. But I think you've got it wrong. You're not a practical man. You're a practical joke; that's what you are. The Almighty was having a bit of fun with us when he thought of you.'

With a characteristic sense of drama he went sailing towards the door before the astonished inspector could reply; and no after-recriminations could rob him of a certain appearance of triumph.

'I think you were perfectly right,' said Fenner. 'If those are practical men, give me priests.'

Another attempt was made to reach an official version of the event when the authorities fully realized who were the backers of the story, and what were the implications of it. Already it had broken out in the Press in its most sensationally and even shamelessly psychic form. Interviews with Vandam on his marvellous adventure, articles about Father Brown and his mystical intuitions, soon led those who feel responsible for guiding the public, to wish to guide it into a wiser channel. Next time the inconvenient witnesses were approached in a more indirect and tactful manner. They were told, almost in an airy fashion, that Professor Vair was very much interested in such abnormal experiences; was especially interested in their own astonishing case. Professor Vair was a psychologist of great distinction; he had been known to take a detached interest in criminology; it was only some little time afterwards that they discovered that he was in any way connected with the police.

Professor Vair was a courteous gentleman, quietly dressed in pale grey clothes, with an artistic tie and a fair, pointed beard; he looked more like a landscape painter to anyone not acquainted with a certain special type of don. He had an air not only of courtesy, but of frankness.

'Yes, yes, I know,' he said smiling; 'I can guess what you must have gone through. The police do not shine in inquiries of a psychic sort, do they? Of course, dear old Collins said he only wanted the facts. What an absurd blunder! In a case of this kind we emphatically do *not* only want the facts. It is even more essential to have the fancies.'

'Do you mean,' asked Vandam gravely, 'that all that we call the facts were merely fancies?'

'Not at all,' said the professor; 'I only mean that the police are stupid in thinking they can leave out the psychological element in these things. Well, of course, the psychological element is everything in everything, though it is only just beginning to be understood. To begin with, take the element called personality. Now I have heard of this priest, Father Brown, before; and he is one of the most remarkable men of our time. Men of that sort carry a sort of atmosphere with them; and nobody knows how much his nerves and even his very senses are affected by it for the time being. People are hypnotized – yes, hypnotized; for hypnotism, like everything else, is a matter of degree; it enters slightly into all daily conversation: it is not necessarily conducted by a man in evening-dress on a platform in a public hall. Father Brown's religion has always understood the psychology of atmospheres, and knows how to appeal to everything simultaneously; even, for instance, to the sense of smell. It understands those curious effects produced by music on animals and human beings; it can –'

'Hang it,' protested Fenner, 'you don't think he walked down the corridor carrying a church organ?'

'He knows better than to do that,' said Professor Vair laughing. 'He knows how to concentrate the essence of all these spiritual sounds and sights, and even smells, in a few restrained gestures; in an art or school of manners. He could contrive so to concentrate your minds on the supernatural by his mere presence, that natural things slipped off your minds to left and right unnoticed. Now you know,' he proceeded with a return to cheerful good sense, 'that the more we study it the more queer the whole question of human evidence becomes. There is not one man in twenty who really observes things at all. There is not one man in a hundred who observes them with real precision; certainly not one in a hundred who can first observe, then remember, and finally describe. Scientific experiments have been made again and again showing that men under strain have thought a door was shut when it was open, or open when it was shut. Men have differed about the number of doors or windows in a wall just in front of them. They have suffered optical illusions in broad daylight. They have done this even without the hypnotic effect of personality; but here we have a very powerful and persuasive personality bent upon fixing only one picture on your minds; the picture of the wild Irish rebel shaking his pistol at the sky and firing that vain volley, whose echoes were the thunders of heaven.'

'Professor,' cried Fenner, 'I'd swear on my deathbed that door never opened.'

'Recent experiments,' went on the professor, quietly, 'have suggested that our consciousness is not continuous, but is a succession of very rapid impressions like a cinema; it is possible that somebody or something may, so to speak, slip in or out between the scenes. It acts only in the instant while the curtain is down. Probably the patter of conjurors and all forms of sleight of hand depend on what we may call these black flashes of blindness between the flashes of sight. Now this priest and preacher of transcendental notions had filled you with a transcendental imagery; the image of the Celt like a Titan shaking the tower with his curse. Probably he accompanied it with some slight but compelling gesture, pointing your eyes and minds in the direction of the unknown destroyer below. Or perhaps something else happened, or somebody else passed by.'

'Wilson, the servant,' grunted Alboin, 'went down the hallway to wait on the bench, but I guess he didn't distract us much.'

'You never know how much,' replied Vair; 'it might have been that or more likely your eyes following some gesture of the priest as he told his tale of magic. It was in one of those black flashes that Mr Warren Wynd slipped out of his door and went to his death. That is the most probable explanation. It is an illustration of the new discovery. The mind is not a continuous line, but rather a dotted line.'

'Very dotted,' said Fenner feebly. 'Not to say dotty.'

'You don't really believe,' asked Vair, 'that your employer was shut up in a room like a box?'

'It's better than believing that I ought to be shut up in a room like a padded cell,' answered Fenner. 'That's what I complain of in your suggestions, professor. I'd as soon believe in a priest who believes in a miracle, as disbelieve in any man having any right to believe in a fact. The priest tells me that a man can appeal to a God I know nothing about to avenge him by the laws of some higher justice that I know nothing about. There's nothing for me to say except that I know nothing about it. But, at least, if the poor Paddy's prayer and pistol could be heard in a higher world, that higher world might act in some way that seems odd to us. But you ask me to disbelieve the facts of this world as they appear to my own five wits. According to you, a whole procession of Irishmen carrying blunderbusses may have walked through this room while we were talking, so long as they took care to tread on the blind spots in our minds. Miracles of the monkish sort, like materializing a crocodile or hanging a cloak on a sunbeam, seem quite sane compared to you.'

'Oh, well,' said Professor Vair, rather curtly, 'if you are resolved to believe in your priest and his miraculous Irishman I can say no more. I'm afraid you have not had an opportunity of studying psychology.'

'No,' said Fenner dryly; 'but I've had an opportunity of studying psychologists.'

And, bowing politely, he led his deputation out of the room and did not speak till he got into the street; then he addressed them rather explosively.

'Raving lunatics!' cried Fenner in a fume. 'What the devil do they think is to happen to the world if nobody knows whether he's seen anything or not? I wish I'd blown his silly head off with a blank charge, and then explained that I did it in a blind flash. Father Brown's miracle may be miraculous or no, but he said it would happen and it did happen. All these blasted cranks can do is to see a thing happen and then say it didn't. Look here, I think we owe it to the padre to testify to his little demonstration. We're all sane, solid men who never believed in anything. We weren't drunk. We weren't devout. It simply happened just as he said it would.'

'I quite agree,' said the millionaire. 'It may be the beginning of mighty big things in the spiritual line; but anyhow, the man who's in the spiritual line himself, Father Brown, has certainly scored over this business.'

A few days afterwards Father Brown received a very polite note signed Silas T. Vandam, and asking him if he would attend at a stated hour at the apartment which was the scene of the disappearance, in order to take steps for the establishment of that marvellous occurrence. The occurrence itself had already begun to break out in the newspapers, and was being taken up everywhere by the enthusiasts of occultism. Father Brown saw the flaring posters inscribed 'Suicide of Vanishing Man', and 'Man's Curse Hangs Philanthropist', as he passed towards Moon Crescent and mounted the steps on the way to the elevator. He found the little group much as he left it, Vandam, Alboin, and the secretary; but there was an entirely new respectfulness and even reverence in their tone towards himself. They were standing by Wynd's desk, on which lay a large paper and writing materials, as they turned to greet him.

'Father Brown,' said the spokesman, who was the white-haired Westerner, somewhat sobered with his responsibility, 'we asked you here in the first place to offer our apologies and our thanks. We recognize that it was you that spotted the spiritual manifestation from the first. We were hard-shell sceptics, all of us; but we realize now that a man must break that shell to get at the great things behind the world. You stand for those things; you stand for the super-normal explanation of things; and we have to hand it to you. And in the second place, we feel that this document would not be complete without your signature. We are notifying the exact facts to the Psychical Research Society, because the newspaper accounts are not what you might call exact. We've stated how the curse was spoken out in the street; how the man was sealed up here in a room like a box; how the curse dissolved him straight into thin air, and in some unthinkable way materialized him as a suicide hoisted on a gallows. That's all we can say about it; but all that we know, and have seen with our own eyes. And as you were the first to believe in the miracle, we all feel that you ought to be the first to sign.'

'No, really,' said Father Brown, in embarrassment. 'I don't think I should like to do that.'

'You mean you'd rather not sign first?'

'I mean I'd rather not sign at all,' said Father Brown, modestly. 'You see, it doesn't quite do for a man in my position to joke about miracles.'

'But it was you who said it was a miracle,' said Alboin, staring.

'I'm so sorry,' said Father Brown; 'I'm afraid there's some mistake. I don't think I ever said it was a miracle. All I said was that it might happen. What you said was that it couldn't happen, because it would be a miracle if it did. And then it did. And so you said it was a miracle. But I never said a word about miracles or magic, or anything of the sort from beginning to end.'

'But I thought you believed in miracles,' broke out the secretary.

'Yes,' answered Father Brown, 'I believe in miracles. I believe in man-eating tigers, but I don't see them running about everywhere. If I want any miracles, I know where to get them.'

'I can't understand your taking this line, Father Brown,' said Vandam, earnestly. 'It seems so narrow; and you don't look narrow to me, though you are a parson. Don't you see, a miracle like this will knock all materialism endways? It will just tell the whole world in big print that spiritual powers can work and do work. You'll be serving religion as no parson ever served it yet.'

The priest had stiffened a little and seemed in some strange way clothed with unconscious and impersonal dignity, for all his stumpy figure. 'Well,' he said, 'you wouldn't suggest I should serve religion by what I know to be a lie? I don't know precisely what you mean by the phrase; and, to be quite candid, I'm not sure you do. Lying may be serving religion; I'm sure it's not serving God. And since you are harping so insistently on what I believe, wouldn't it be as well if you had some sort of notion of what it is?'

'I don't think I quite understand,' observed the millionaire, curiously.

'I don't think you do,' said Father Brown, with simplicity.

'You say this thing was done by spiritual powers. What spiritual powers? You don't think the holy angels took him and hung him on a garden tree, do you? And as for the unholy angels – no, no, no. The men who did this did a wicked thing, but they went no further than their own wickedness; they weren't wicked enough to be dealing with spiritual powers. I know something about Satanism, for my sins; I've been forced to know. I know what it is, what it practically always is. It's proud and it's sly. It likes to be superior; it loves to horrify the innocent with things half understood, to make children's flesh creep. That's why it's so fond of mysteries and initiations and secret societies and all the rest of it. Its eyes are turned inwards, and however grand and grave it may look, it's always hiding a small, mad smile.' He shuddered suddenly, as if caught in an icy draught of air. 'Never mind about them; they've got nothing to do with this, believe me. Do you think that poor, wild Irishman of mine, who ran raving down the street, who blurted out half of it when he first saw my face, and ran away for fear he should blurt out more, do you think Satan confides any secrets to him? I admit he joined in a plot, probably in a plot with two other men worse than himself; but for all that, he was just in an everlasting rage when he rushed down the lane and let off his pistol and his curse.'

'But what on earth does all this mean?' demanded Vandam. 'Letting off a toy pistol and a twopenny curse wouldn't do what was done, except by a miracle. It wouldn't make Wynd disappear like a fairy. It wouldn't make him reappear a quarter of a mile away with a rope round his neck.'

'No,' said Father Brown sharply; 'but what would it do?'

'And still I don't follow you,' said the millionaire gravely.

'I say, what would it do?' repeated the priest; showing, for the first time, a sort of animation verging on annoyance. 'You keep on repeating that a blank pistol-shot wouldn't do this and wouldn't do that; that if that was all, the murder wouldn't happen or the miracle wouldn't happen. It doesn't seem to occur to you to ask what would happen. What would happen to you if a lunatic let off a firearm without rhyme or reason right under your window? What's the very first thing that would happen?'

Vandam looked thoughtful. 'I guess I should look out of the window,' he said.

'Yes,' said Father Brown, 'you'd look out of the window. That's the whole story. It's a sad story, but it's finished now; and there were extenuating circumstances.'

'Why should looking out of the window hurt him?' asked Alboin. 'He didn't fall out, or he'd have been found in the lane.'

'No,' said Father Brown, in a low voice. 'He didn't fall. He rose.'

There was something in his voice like the groan of a gong, a note of doom, but otherwise he went on steadily:

'He rose, but not on wings; not on the wings of any holy or unholy angels. He rose at the end of a rope, exactly as you saw him in the garden; a noose dropped over his head the moment it was poked out of the window. Don't you remember Wilson, that big servant of his, a man of huge strength, while Wynd was the lightest of little shrimps? Didn't Wilson go to the floor above to get a pamphlet, to a room full of luggage corded in coils and coils of rope? Has Wilson been seen since that day? I fancy not.'

'Do you mean,' asked the secretary, 'that Wilson whisked him clean out of his own window like a trout on a line?'

'Yes,' said the other, 'and let him down again out of the other window into the park, where the third accomplice hooked him on to a tree. Remember the lane was always empty; remember the wall opposite was quite blank; remember it was all over in five minutes after the Irishman gave the signal with the pistol. There were three of them in it of course; and I wonder whether you can all guess who they were.'

They were all three staring at the plain, square window and the blank, white wall beyond; and nobody answered.

'By the way,' went on Father Brown, 'don't think I blame you for jumping to preternatural conclusions. The reason's very simple, really. You all swore you were hard-shelled materialists; and as a matter of fact you were all balanced on the very edge of belief – of belief in almost anything. There are thousands balanced on it today; but it's a sharp, uncomfortable edge to sit on. You won't rest till you believe something; that's why Mr Vandam went through new religions with a tooth-comb, and Mr Alboin quotes Scripture for his religion of breathing exercises, and Mr Fenner grumbles at the very God he denies. That's where you all split; it's natural to believe in the supernatural. It never feels natural to accept only natural things. But though it wanted only a touch to tip you into preternaturalism about these things, these things really were only natural things. They were not only natural, they were almost unnaturally simple. I suppose there never was quite so simple a story as this.'

Fenner laughed and then looked puzzled. 'I don't understand one thing,' he said. 'If it was Wilson, how did Wynd come to have a man like that on such intimate terms? How did he come to be killed by a man he'd seen every day for years? He was famous as being a judge of men.'

Father Brown thumped his umbrella on the ground with an emphasis he rarely showed.

'Yes,' he said, almost fiercely; 'that was how he came to be killed. He was killed for just that. He was killed for being a judge of men.'

They all stared at him, but he went on, almost as if they were not there.

'What is any man that he should be a judge of men?' he demanded. 'These three were the tramps that once stood before him and were dismissed rapidly right and left to one place or another; as if for them there were no cloak of courtesy, no stages of intimacy, no free-will in friendship. And twenty years has not exhausted the indignation born of that unfathomable insult in that moment when he dared to know them at a glance.'

'Yes,' said the secretary; 'I understand . . . and I understand how it is that you understand – all sorts of things.'

'Well, I'm blamed if I understand,' cried the breezy Western gentleman boisterously. 'Your Wilson and your Irishman seem to be just a couple of cut-throat murderers who killed their benefactor. I've no use for a black and bloody assassin of that sort in my morality, whether it's religion or not.'

'He was a black and bloody assassin, no doubt,' said Fenner, quietly. 'I'm not defending him; but I suppose it's Father Brown's business to pray for all men, even for a man like –'

'Yes,' assented Father Brown, 'it's my business to pray for all men, even for a man like Warren Wynd.'

FIVE

The Curse of the Golden Cross

SIX people sat around a small table, seeming almost as incongruous and accidental as if they had been shipwrecked separately on the same small desert island. At least the sea surrounded them; for in one sense their island was enclosed in another island, a large and flying island like Laputa. For the little table was one of many little tables dotted about in the dining saloon of that monstrous ship the *Moravia*, speeding through the night and the everlasting emptiness of the Atlantic. The little company had nothing in common except that all were travelling from America to England. Two of them at least might be called celebrities; others might be called obscure, and in one or two cases even dubious.

The first was the famous Professor Smaill, an authority on certain archaeological studies touching the later Byzantine Empire. His lectures, delivered in an American University, were accepted as of the first authority even in the most authoritative seats of learning in Europe. His literary works were so steeped in a mellow and imaginative sympathy with the European past, that it often gave strangers a start to hear him speak with an American accent. Yet he was, in his way, very American; he had long fair hair brushed back from a big square forehead, long straight features and a curious mixture of preoccupation with a poise of potential swiftness, like a lion pondering absent-mindedly on his next leap.

There was only one lady in the group; and she was (as the journalists often said of her) a host in herself; being quite prepared to play hostess, not to say empress, at that or any other table. She was Lady Diana Wales, the celebrated lady traveller in tropical and other countries; but there was nothing rugged or masculine about her appearance at dinner. She was herself handsome in an almost tropical fashion, with a mass of hot and heavy red hair; she was dressed in what the journalists call a daring fashion, but her face was intelligent and her eyes had that bright and rather prominent appearance which belongs to the eyes of ladies who ask questions at political meetings.

The other four figures seemed at first like shadows in this shining presence; but they showed differences on a close view. One of them was a young man entered on the ship's register as Paul T. Tarrant. He was an American type which might be more truly called an American antitype. Every nation probably has an antitype; a sort of extreme exception that proves the national rule. Americans really respect work, rather as Europeans respect war. There is a halo of heroism about it; and he who shrinks from it is less than a man. The antitype is evident through being exceedingly rare. He is the dandy or dude: the wealthy waster who makes a weak villain for so many American novels. Paul Tarrant seemed to have nothing whatever to do but change his clothes, which he did about six times a day; passing into paler or richer shades of his suit of exquisite light grey, like the delicate silver changes of the twilight. Unlike most Americans, he cultivated very carefully a short, curly beard; and unlike most dandies, even of his own type, he seemed rather sulky than showy. Perhaps there was something almost Byronic about his silence and his gloom.

The next two travellers were naturally classed together; merely because they were both English lecturers returning from an American tour. One of them was described as Leonard Smyth, apparently a minor poet, but something of a major journalist; long-headed, light-haired, perfectly dressed, and perfectly capable of looking after himself. The other was a rather comic contrast, being short and broad, with a black, walrus moustache, and as taciturn as the other was talkative. But as he had been both charged with robbing and praised for rescuing a Roumanian Princess threatened by a jaguar in his travelling menagerie, and had thus figured in a fashionable case, it was naturally felt that his views on God, progress, his own early life, and the future of Anglo-American relations would be of great interest and value to the inhabitants of Minneapolis and Omaha. The sixth and most insignificant figure was that of a little English priest going by the name of Brown. He listened to the conversation with respectful attention, and he was at that moment forming the impression that there was one rather curious thing about it.

'I suppose those Byzantine studies of yours, Professor,' Leonard Smyth was saying, 'would throw some light on this story of a tomb found somewhere on the south coast; near Brighton, isn't it? Brighton's a long way from Byzantium, of course. But I read something about the style of burying or embalming or something being supposed to be Byzantine.'

'Byzantine studies certainly have to reach a long way,' replied the Professor dryly. 'They talk about specialists; but I think the hardest thing on earth is to specialize. In this case, for instance: how can a man know anything about Byzantium till he knows everything about Rome before it and about Islam after it? Most Arab arts were old Byzantine arts. Why, take algebra –'

'But I won't take algebra,' cried the lady decisively. 'I never did, and I never do. But I'm awfully interested in embalming. I was with Gatton, you know, when he opened the Babylonian tombs. Ever since then I found mummies and preserved bodies and all that perfectly thrilling. Do tell us about this one.'

'Gatton was an interesting man,' said the Professor. 'They were an interesting family. That brother of his who went into Parliament was much more than an ordinary politician. I never understood the Fascisti till he made that speech about Italy.'

'Well, we're not going to Italy on this trip,' said Lady Diana persistently, 'and I believe you're going to that little place where they've found the tomb. In Sussex, isn't it?'

'Sussex is pretty large, as these little English sections go,' replied the Professor. 'One might wander about in it for a goodish time; and it's a good place to wander in. It's wonderful how large those low hills seem when you're on them.'

There was an abrupt accidental silence; and then the lady said, 'Oh, I'm going on deck,' and rose, the men rising with her. But the Professor lingered and the little priest was the last to leave the table, carefully folding up his napkin. And as they were thus left alone together the Professor said suddenly to his companion:

'What would you say was the point of that little talk?'

'Well,' said Father Brown, smiling, 'since you ask me, there was something that amused me a little. I may be wrong; but it seemed to me that the company made three attempts to get you to talk about an embalmed body said to be found in Sussex. And you, on your side, very courteously offered to talk – first about algebra, and then about the Fascisti, and then about the landscape of the Downs.'

'In short,' replied the Professor, 'you thought I was ready to talk about any subject but that one. You were quite right.'

The Professor was silent for a little time, looking down at the tablecloth; then he looked up and spoke with that swift impulsiveness that suggested the lion's leap.

'See here, Father Brown,' he said, 'I consider you about the wisest and whitest man I ever met.'

Father Brown was very English. He had all the normal national helplessness about what to do with a serious and sincere compliment suddenly handed to him to his face in the American manner. His reply was a meaningless murmur; and it was the Professor who proceeded, with the same staccato earnestness:

'You see, up to a point it's all simple enough. A Christian tomb of the Dark Ages, apparently that of a bishop, has been found under a little church at Dulham on the Sussex coast. The Vicar happens to be a good bit of an archaeologist himself and has been able to find a good deal more than I know yet. There was a rumour of the corpse being embalmed in a way peculiar to Greeks and Egyptians but unknown in the West, especially at that date. So Mr Walters (that is the Vicar) naturally wonders about Byzantine influences. But he also mentions something else, that is of even more personal interest to me.'

His long grave face seemed to grow even longer and graver as he frowned down at the tablecloth. His long finger seemed to be tracing patterns on it like the plans of dead cities and their temples and tombs.

'So I'm going to tell you, and nobody else, why it is I have to be careful about mentioning that matter in mixed company; and why, the more eager they are to talk about it, the more cautious I have to be. It is also stated that in the coffin is a chain with a cross, common enough to look at, but with a certain secret symbol on the back found on only one other cross in the world. It is from the arcana of the very earliest Church, and is suppposed to indicate St Peter setting up his See at Antioch before he came to Rome. Anyhow, I believe there is but one other like it, and it belongs to me. I hear there is some story about a curse on it; but I take no notice of that. But whether or no there is a curse, there really is, in one sense, a conspiracy; though the conspiracy should only consist of one man.'

'Of one man?' repeated Father Brown almost mechanically.

'Of one madman, for all I know,' said Professor Smaill. 'It's a long story and in some ways a silly one.'

He paused again, tracing plans like architectural drawings with his finger on the cloth, and then resumed:

'Perhaps I had better tell you about it from the beginning, in case you see some little point in the story that is meaningless to me. It began years and years ago, when I was conducting some investigations on my own account in the antiquities of Crete and the Greek islands. I did a great deal of it practically single-handed; sometimes with the most rude and temporary help from the inhabitants of the place, and sometimes literally alone. It was under the latter circumstances that I found a maze of subterranean passages which led at last to a heap of rich refuse, broken ornaments and scattered gems which I took to be the ruins of some sunken altar, and in which I found the curious gold cross. I turned it over, and on the back of it I saw the Ichthus or fish, which was an early Christian symbol, but of a shape and pattern rather different from that commonly found; and, as it seemed to me, more realistic – more as if the archaic designer had meant it to be not merely a conventional enclosure or nimbus, but to look a little more like a real fish. It seemed to me that there was a flattening towards one end of it that was not like mere mathematical decoration, but rather like a sort of rude or even savage zoology.

'In order to explain very briefly why I thought this find important, I must tell you the point of the excavation. For one thing, it had something of the nature of an excavation of an excavation.

We were on the track not only of antiquities, but of the antiquarians of antiquity. We had reason to believe, or some of us thought we had reason to believe, that these underground passages, mostly of the Minoan period, like that famous one which is actually identified with the labyrinth of the Minotaur, had not really been lost and left undisturbed for all the ages between the Minotaur and the modern explorer. We believed that these underground places, I might almost say these underground towns and villages, had already been penetrated during the intervening period by some persons prompted by some motive. About the motive there were different schools of thought: some holding that the Emperors had ordered an official exploration out of mere scientific curiosity; others that the furious fashion in the later Roman Empire for all sorts of lurid Asiatic superstitions had started some nameless Manichaean sect or other rioting in the caverns in orgies that had to be hidden from the face of the sun. I belong to the group which believed that these caverns had been used in the same way as the catacombs. That is, we believed that, during some of the persecutions which spread like a fire over the whole Empire, the Christians had concealed themselves in these ancient pagan labyrinths of stone. It was therefore with a thrill as sharp as a thunderclap that I found and picked up the fallen golden cross and saw the design upon it; and it was with still more of a shock of felicity that, on turning to make my way once more outwards and upwards into the light of day, I looked up at the walls of bare rock that extended endlessly along the low passages, and saw scratched in yet ruder outline, but if possible more unmistakable, the shape of the Fish.

'Something about it made it seem as if it might be a fossil fish or some rudimentary organism fixed for ever in a frozen sea. I could not analyse this analogy, otherwise unconnected with a mere drawing scratched upon the stone, till I realized that I was saying in my sub-conscious mind that the first Christians must have seemed something like fish, dumb and dwelling in a fallen world of twilight and silence, dropped far below the feet of men and moving in dark and twilight and a soundless world.

'Everyone walking along stone passages knows what it is to be followed by phantom feet. The echo follows flapping or clapping behind or in front, so that it is almost impossible for the man who is really lonely to believe in his loneliness. I had got used to the effects of this echo and had not noticed it much for some time past, when I caught sight of the symbolical shape scrawled on the wall of rock. I stopped, and at the same instant it seemed as if my heart stopped, too; for my own feet had halted, but the echo went marching on.

'I ran forward, and it seemed as if the ghostly footsteps ran also, but not with that exact imitation which marks the material reverberation of a sound. I stopped again, and the steps stopped also; but I could have sworn they stopped an instant too late; I called out a question; and my cry was answered; but the voice was not my own.

'It came round the corner of a rock just in front of me; and throughout that uncanny chase I noticed that it was always at some such angle of the crooked path that it paused and spoke. The little space in front of me that could be illuminated by my small electric torch was always as empty as an empty room. Under these conditions I had a conversation with I know not whom, which lasted all the way to the first white gleam of daylight, and even there I could not see in what fashion he vanished into the light of day. But the mouth of the labyrinth was full of many openings and cracks and chasms, and it would not have been difficult for him to have somehow darted back and disappeared again into the underworld of the caves. I only know that I came out on the lonely steps of a great mountain like a marble terrace, varied only with a green vegetation that seemed somehow more tropical than the purity of the rock, like the Oriental invasion that has spread sporadically over the fall of classic Hellas. I looked out on a sea of stainless blue, and the sun shone steadily on utter loneliness and silence; and there was not a blade of grass stirred with a whisper of flight nor the shadow of a shadow of man.

'It had been a terrible conversation; so intimate and so individual and in a sense so casual. This being, bodiless, faceless, nameless and yet calling me by my name, had talked to me in those crypts and cracks where we were buried alive with no more passion or melodrama than if we had been sitting in two arm-chairs at a club. But he had told me also that he would unquestionably kill me or any other man who came into the possession of the cross with the mark of the fish. He told me frankly he was not fool enough to attack me there in the labyrinth, knowing I had a loaded revolver, and that he ran as much risk as I. But he told me, equally calmly, that he would plan my murder with the certainty of success, with every detail developed and every danger warded off, with the sort of artistic perfection that a Chinese craftsman or an Indian embroiderer gives to the artistic work of a life-time. Yet he was no Oriental; I am certain he was a white man. I suspect that he was a countryman of my own.

'Since then I have received from time to time signs and symbols and queer impersonal messages that have made me certain, at least, that if the man is a maniac he is a monomaniac. He is always telling me, in this airy and detached way, that the preparations for my death and burial are proceeding satisfactorily; and that the only way in which I can prevent their being crowned with a comfortable success is to give up the relic in my possession – the unique cross that I found in the cavern. He does not seem to have any religious sentiment or fanaticism on the point; he seems to have no passion but the passion of a collector of curiosities. That is one of the things that makes me feel sure he is a man of the West and not of the East. But this particular curiosity seems to have driven him quite crazy.

'And then came this report, as yet unsubstantiated, about the duplicate relic found on an embalmed body in a Sussex tomb. If he had been a maniac before, this news turned him into a demon-iac possessed of seven devils. That there should be one of them belonging to another man was bad enough, but that there should be two of them and neither belonging to him was a torture not to be borne. His mad messages began to come thick and fast like showers of poisoned arrows; and each cried out more confidently than the last that death would strike me at the moment when I stretched out my unworthy hand towards the cross in the tomb.

'"You will never know me," he wrote, "you will never say my name; you will never see my face; you will die, and never know who has killed you. I may be in any form among those about you; but I shall be in that alone at which you have forgotten to look."

'From those threats I deduce that he is quite likely to shadow me on this expedition; and try to steal the relic or do me some mischief for possessing it. But as I never saw the man in my life, he may be almost any man I meet. Logically speaking, he may be any of the waiters who wait on me at table. He may be any of the passengers who sit with me at table.'

'He may be me,' said Father Brown, with cheerful contempt for grammar.

'He may be anybody else,' answered Smaill seriously. 'That is what I meant by what I said just now. You are the only man I feel sure is not the enemy.'

Father Brown again looked embarrassed; then he smiled and said: 'Well, oddly enough, I'm not. What we have to consider is any chance of finding out if he really is here before he – before he makes himself unpleasant.'

'There is one chance of finding out, I think,' remarked the Professor rather grimly. 'When we get to Southampton I shall take a car at once along the coast ; I should be glad if you would come with me, but in the ordinary sense, of course, our little party will break up. If any one of them turns up again in that little churchyard on the Sussex coast, we shall know who he really is.'

The Professor's programme was duly carried out, at least to the extent of the car and its cargo in the form of Father Brown. They coasted along the road with the sea on one side and the hills of Hampshire and Sussex on the other; nor was there visible to the eye any shadow of pursuit. As they approached the village of Dulham only one man crossed their path who had any connexion with the matter in hand; a journalist who had just visited the church and been courteously escorted by the vicar through the new excavated chapel; but his remarks and notes seemed to be of the ordinary newspaper sort. But Professor Smaill was perhaps a little fanciful, and could not dismiss the sense of something odd and discouraging in the attitude and appearance of the man, who was tall and shabby, hook-nosed and hollow-eyed, with moustaches that drooped with depression. He seemed anything but enlivened by his late experiment as a sightseer; indeed, he seemed to be striding as fast as possible from the sight, when they stopped him with a question.

'It's all about a curse,' he said; 'a curse on the place, according to the guide-book or the parson, or the oldest inhabitant or whoever is the authority; and really, it feels jolly like it. Curse or no curse, I'm glad to have got out of it.'

'Do you believe in curses?' asked Smaill curiously.

'I don't believe in anything; I'm a journalist,' answered the melancholy being – 'Boon, of the *Daily Wire*. But there's a something creepy about that crypt; and I'll never deny I felt a chill.' And he strode on towards the railway station with a further accelerated pace.

'Looks like a raven or a crow, that fellow,' observed Smaill as they turned towards the churchyard. 'What is it they say about a bird of ill omen?'

They entered the churchyard slowly, the eyes of the American antiquary lingering luxuriantly over the isolated roof of the lynch-gate and the large unfathomable black growth of the yew looking like night itself defying the broad daylight. The path climbed up amid heaving levels of turf in which the gravestones were tilted at all angles like stone rafts tossed on a green sea, till it came to the ridge beyond which the great sea itself ran like an iron bar, with pale lights in it like steel. Almost at their feet the tough rank grass turned into a tuft of sea-holly and ended in grey and yellow sand; and a foot or two from the holly, and outlined darkly against the steely sea, stood a motionless figure. But for its dark-grey clothing it might almost have been the statue on some sepulchral monument. But Father Brown instantly recognized something in the elegant stoop of the shoulders and the rather sullen outward thrust of the short beard.

'Gee!' exclaimed the professor of archaeology; 'it's that man Tarrant, if you call him a man. Did you think, when I spoke on the boat, that I should ever get so quick an answer to my question?'

'I thought you might get too many answers to it,' answered Father Brown.

'Why, how do you mean?' inquired the Professor, darting a look at him over his shoulder.

'I mean,' answered the other mildly, 'that I thought I heard voices behind the yew-tree. I don't think Mr Tarrant is so solitary as he looks; I might even venture to say, so solitary as he likes to look.'

Even as Tarrant turned slowly round in his moody manner, the confirmation came. Another voice, high and rather hard, but none the less feminine, was saying with experienced raillery:

'And how was I to know he would be here?'

It was borne in upon Professor Smaill that this gay observation was not addressed to him; so he was forced to conclude in some bewilderment, that yet a third person was present. As Lady Diana Wales came out, radiant and resolute as ever, from the shadow of the yew, he noted grimly that she had a living shadow of her own. The lean dapper figure of Leonard Smyth, that insinuating man of letters, appeared immediately behind her own flamboyant form, smiling, his head a little on one side like a dog's.

'Snakes!' muttered Smaill; 'why, they're all here! Or all except that little showman with the walrus whiskers.'

He heard Father Brown laughing softly beside him; and indeed the situation was becoming something more than laughable. It seemed to be turning topsy-turvy and tumbling about their ears like a pantomime trick; for even while the Professor had been speaking, his words had received the most comical contradiction. The round head with the grotesque black crescent of moustache had appeared suddenly and seemingly out of a hole in the ground. An instant afterwards they realized that the hole was in fact a very large hole, leading to a ladder which descended into the bowels of the earth; that it was in fact the entrance to the subterranean scene they had come to visit. The little man had been the first to find the entrance and had already descended a rung or two of the ladder before he put his head out again to address his fellow-travellers. He looked like some particularly preposterous Grave-digger in a burlesque of *Hamlet*. He only said thickly behind his thick moustaches, 'It is down here.' But it came to the rest of the company with a start of realization that, though they had sat opposite him at meal-times for a week, they had hardly ever heard him speak before; and that though he was supposed to be an English lecturer, he spoke with a rather occult foreign accent.

'You see, my dear Professor,' cried Lady Diana with trenchant cheerfulness, 'your Byzantine mummy was simply too exciting to be missed. I simply had to come along and see it; and I'm sure the gentlemen felt just the same. Now you must tell us all about it.'

'I do not know all about it,' said the Professor gravely, not to say grimly. 'In some respects I don't even know what it's all about. It certainly seems odd that we should have all met again so soon; but I suppose there are no limits to the modern thirst for information. But if we are all to visit the place it must be done in a responsible way and, if you will forgive me, under responsible leadership. We must notify whoever is in charge of the excavations; we shall probably at least have to put our names in a book.'

Something rather like a wrangle followed on this collision between the impatience of the lady and the suspicions of the archaeologist; but the latter's insistence on the official rights of the Vicar and the local investigation ultimately prevailed; the little man with the moustaches came reluctantly out of his grave again and silently acquiesced in a less impetuous descent. Fortunately, the clergyman himself appeared at this stage – a grey-haired, good-looking gentleman with a droop accentuated by double eyeglasses; and while rapidly establishing sympathetic relations with the Professor as a fellow-antiquarian, he did not seem to regard his rather motley group of companions with anything more hostile than amusement.

'I hope you are none of you superstitious,' he said pleasantly. 'I ought to tell you, to start with, that there are supposed to be all sorts of bad omens and curses hanging over our devoted heads in this business. I have just been deciphering a Latin inscription which was found over the entrance to the chapel; and it would seem that there are no less than three curses involved; a curse for entering the sealed chamber, a double curse for opening the coffin, and a triple and most terrible curse for touching the gold relic found inside it. The two first maledictions I have already incurred myself,' he added with a smile; 'but I fear that even you will have to incur the first and mildest of them if you are to see anything at all. According to the story, the curses descend in a rather lingering fashion, at long intervals and on later occasions. I don't know whether that is any comfort to you.' And the Reverend Mr Walters smiled once more in his drooping and benevolent manner.

'Story,' repeated Professor Smaill, 'why, what story is that?'

'It is rather a long story and varies, like other local legends,' answered the Vicar. 'But it is undoubtedly contemporary with the time of the tomb; and the substance of it is embodied in the inscription and is roughly this: Guy de Gisors, a lord of the manor here early in the thirteenth century, had set his heart on a beautiful black horse in the possession of an envoy from Genoa, which that practical merchant prince would not sell except for a huge price. Guy was driven by avarice to the crime of pillaging the shrine and, according to one story, even killing the bishop, who was then resident there. Anyhow, the bishop uttered a curse which was to fall on anybody who should continue to withhold the gold cross from its resting-pace in his tomb, or should take steps to disturb it when it had returned there. The feudal lord raised the money for the horse by selling the gold relic to a goldsmith in the town; but on the first day he mounted the horse the animal reared and threw him in front of the church porch, breaking his neck. Meanwhile the goldsmith, hitherto wealthy and prosperous, was ruined by a series of inexplicable accidents, and fell into the power of a Jew money-lender living in the manor. Eventually the unfortunate goldsmith, faced with nothing but starvation, hanged himself on an apple-tree. The gold cross with all his other goods, his house, shop, and tools, had long ago passed into the possession of the money-lender. Meanwhile, the son and heir of the feudal lord, shocked by the judgement on his blasphemous sire, had become a religious devotee in the dark and stern spirit of those times, and conceived it his duty to persecute all heresy and unbelief among his vassals. Thus the Jew, in his turn, who had been cynically tolerated by the father, was ruthlessly burnt by order of the son; so that he, in his turn, suffered for the possession of the relic; and after these three judgements, it was returned to the bishop's tomb; since when no eye has seen and no hand has touched it.'

Lady Diana Wales seemed to be more impressed than might have been expected.

'It really gives one rather a shiver,' she said, 'to think that we are going to be the first, except the vicar.'

The pioneer with the big moustaches and the broken English did not descend after all by his favourite ladder, which indeed had only been used by some of the workmen conducting the excavation; for the clergyman led them round to a larger and more convenient entrance about a hundred yards away, out of which he himself had just emerged from his investigations underground. Here the descent was by a fairly gradual slope with no difficulties save the increasing darkness; for they soon found themselves moving in single file down a tunnel as black as pitch, and it was some little time before they saw a glimmer of light ahead of them. Once during that silent march there was a sound like a catch in somebody's breath, it was impossible to say whose; and once there was an oath like a dull exposion, and it was in an unknown tongue.

They came out in a circular chamber like a basilica in a ring of round arches; for that chapel had been built before the first pointed arch of the Gothic had pierced our civilization like a spear. A glimmer of greenish light between some of the pillars marked the place of the other opening into the world above, and gave a vague sense of being under the sea, which was intensified by one or two other incidental and perhaps fanciful resemblances. For the dog-tooth pattern of the Norman was faintly traceable round all the arches, giving them, above the cavernous darkness, something of the look of the mouths of monstrous sharks. And in the centre the dark bulk of the tomb itself, with its lifted lid of stone, might almost have been the jaws of some such leviathan.

Whether out of the sense of fitness or from the lack of more modern appliances, the clerical antiquary had arranged for the illumination of the chapel only by four tall candles in big wooden candlesticks standing on the floor. Of these only one was alight when they entered, casting a faint glimmer over the mighty architectural forms. When they had all assembled, the clergyman proceeded to light the three others, and the appearance and contents of the great sarcophagus came more clearly into view.

All eyes went first to the face of the dead, preserved across all those ages in the lines of life by some secret Eastern process, it was said, inherited from heathen antiquity and unknown to the simple graveyards of our own island. The Professor could hardly repress an exclamation of wonder; for, though the face was as pale as a mask of wax, it looked otherwise like a sleeping man, who had but that moment closed his eyes. The face was of the ascetic, perhaps even the fanatical type, with a high framework of bones; the figure was clad in a golden cope and gorgeous vestments, and high up on the breast, at the base of the throat, glittered the famous gold cross upon a short gold chain, or rather necklace. The stone coffin had been opened by lifting the lid of it at the head and propping it aloft upon two strong wooden shafts or poles, hitched above under the edge of the upper slab and wedged below into the corners of the coffin behind the head of the corpse. Less could therefore be seen of the feet or the lower part of the figure, but the candle-light shone full on the face; and in contrast with its tones of dead ivory the cross of gold seemed to stir and sparkle like a fire.

Professor Smaill's big forehead had carried a big furrow of reflection, or possibly of worry, ever since the clergyman had told the story of the curse. But feminine intuition, not untouched by feminine hysteria, understood the meaning of his brooding immobility better than did the men around him. In the silence of that candle-lit cavern Lady Diana cried out suddenly:

'Don't touch it, I tell you!'

But the man had already made one of his swift leonine movements, leaning forward over the body. The next instant they all darted, some forward and some backward, but all with a dreadful ducking motion as if the sky were falling.

As the Professor laid a finger on the gold cross, the wooden props, that bent very slightly in supporting the lifted lid of stone, seemed to jump and straighten themselves with a jerk. The lip of the stone slab slipped from its wooden perch; and in all their souls and stomachs came a sickening sense of down-rushing ruin, as if they had all been flung off a precipice. Smaill had withdrawn his head swiftly, but not in time; and he lay senseless beside the coffin, in a red puddle of blood from scalp or skull. And the old stone coffin was once more closed as it had been for centuries; save that one or two sticks or splinters stuck in the crevice, horribly suggestive of bones crunched by an ogre. The leviathan had snapped its jaws of stone.

Lady Diana was looking at the wreck with eyes that had an electric glare as of lunacy; her red hair looked scarlet against the pallor of her face in the greenish twilight. Smyth was looking at her, still with something dog-like in the turn of his head; but it was the expression of a god who looks at a master whose catastrophe he can only partly understand. Tarrant and the foreigner had stiffened in their usual sullen attitudes, but their faces had turned the colour of clay. The Vicar seemed to have fainted. Father Brown was kneeling beside the fallen figure, trying to test its condition.

Rather to the general surprise, the Byronic lounger, Paul Tarrant, came forward to help him.

'He'd better be carried up into the air,' he said. 'I suppose there's just a chance for him.'

'He isn't dead,' said Father Brown in a low voice, 'but I think it's pretty bad; you aren't a doctor by any chance?'

'No; but I've had to pick up a good many things in my time,' said the other. 'But never mind about me just now. My real profession would probably surprise you.'

'I don't think so,' replied Father Brown, with a slight smile. 'I thought of it about halfway through the voyage. You are a detective shadowing somebody. Well, the cross is safe from thieves now, anyhow.'

While they were speaking Tarrant had lifted the frail figure of the fallen man with easy strength and dexterity, and was carefully carrying him towards the exit. He answered over his shoulder: 'Yes, the cross is safe enough.'

'You mean that nobody else is,' replied Brown. 'Are you thinking of the curse, too?'

Father Brown went about for the next hour or two under a burden of frowning perplexity that was something beyond the shock of the tragic accident. He assisted in carrying the victim to the little inn opposite the church, interviewed the doctor, who reported the injury as serious and threatening, though not certainly fatal, and carried the news to the little group of travellers who had gathered round the table in the inn parlour. But wherever he went the cloud of mystification rested on him and seemed to grow darker the more deeply he pondered. For the central mystery was growing more and more mysterious, actually in proportion as many of the minor mysteries began to clear themselves up in his mind. Exactly in proportion as the meaning of individual figures in that motley group began to explain itself, the thing that had happened grew more and more difficult to explain. Leonard Smyth had come merely because Lady Diana had come; and Lady Diana had come merely because she chose. They were engaged in one of those floating Society flirtations that are all the more silly for being semi-intellectual. But the lady's romanticism had a superstitious side to it; and she was pretty well prostrated by the terrible end of her adventure. Paul Tarrant was a private detective, possibly watching the flirtation, for some wife or husband; possibly shadowing the foreign lecturer with the moustaches, who had much the air of an undesirable alien. But if he or anybody else had intended to steal the relic, the intention had been finally frustrated. And to all mortal appearance, what had frustrated it was either an incredible coincidence or the intervention of the ancient curse.

As he stood in unusual perplexity in the middle of the village street, between the inn and the church, he felt a mild shock of surprise at seeing a recently familiar but rather unexpected figure advancing up the street. Mr Boon, the journalist, looking very haggard in the sunshine, which showed up his shabby raiment like that of a scarecrow, had his dark and deep-set eyes (rather close together on either side of the long drooping nose) fixed on the priest. The latter looked twice before he realized that the heavy dark moustache hid something like a grin or at least a grim smile.

'I thought you were going away,' said Father Brown a little sharply. 'I thought you left by that train two hours ago.'

'Well, you see I didn't,' said Boon.

'Why have you come back?' asked the priest almost sternly.

'This is not the sort of little rural paradise for a journalist to leave in a hurry,' replied the other. 'Things happen too fast here to make it worth while to go back to a dull place like London. Besides, they can't keep me out of the affair – I mean this second affair. It was I that found the body, or at any rate the clothes. Quite suspicious conduct on my part, wasn't it? Perhaps you think I wanted to dress up in his clothes. Shouldn't I make a lovely parson?'

And the lean and long-nosed mountebank suddenly made an extravagant gesture in the middle of the market-place, stretching out his arms and spreading out his dark-gloved hands in a sort of burlesque benediction and saying: 'Oh, my dear brethren and sisters, for I would embrace you all. . . .'

'What on earth are you talking about?' cried Father Brown, and rapped the stones slightly with his stumpy umbrella, for he was a little less patient than usual.

'Oh, you'll find out all about it if you ask that picnic party of yours at the inn,' replied Boon scornfully. 'That man Tarrant seems to suspect me merely because I found the clothes; though he only came up a minute too late to find them himself. But there are all sorts of mysteries in this business. The little man with the big moustaches may have more in him than meets the eye. For that matter I don't see why you shouldn't have killed the poor fellow yourself.'

Father Brown did not seem in the least annoyed at the

suggestion, but he seemed exceedingly bothered and bewildered by the remark.

'Do you mean,' he asked with simplicity, 'that it was I who tried to kill Professor Smaill?'

'Not at all,' said the other, waving his hand with the air of one making a handsome concession. 'Plenty of dead people for you to choose among. Not limited to Professor Smaill. Why, didn't you know somebody else had turned up, a good deal deader than Professor Smaill? And I don't see why you shouldn't have done him in, in a quiet way. Religious differences, you know ... lamentable disunion of Christendom. . . . I suppose you've always wanted to get the English parishes back.'

'I'm going back to the inn,' said the priest quietly; 'you say the people there know what you mean, and perhaps *they* may be able to say it.'

In truth, just afterwards his private perplexities suffered a momentary dispersal at the news of a new calamity. The moment he entered the little parlour where the rest of the company were collected, something in their pale faces told him they were shaken by something yet more recent than the accident at the tomb. Even as he entered, Leonard Smyth was saying: 'Where is all this going to end?'

'It will never end, I tell you,' repeated Lady Diana, gazing into vacancy with glassy eyes; 'it will never end till we all end. One after another the curse will take us; perhaps slowly, as the poor vicar said; but it will take us all as it has taken him.'

'What in the world has happened now?' asked Father Brown.

There was a silence, and then Tarrant said in a voice that sounded a little hollow:

'Mr Walters, the Vicar, has committed suicide. I suppose it was the shock unhinged him. But I fear there can be no doubt about it. We've just found his black hat and clothes on a rock jutting out from the shore. He seems to have jumped into the sea. I thought he looked as if it had knocked him half-witted, and perhaps we ought to have looked after him; but there was so much to look after.'

'You could have done nothing,' said the lady. 'Don't you see the thing is dealing doom in a sort of dreadful order? The Professor touched the cross, and he went first; the Vicar had opened the tomb, and he went second; we only entered the chapel, and we –'

'Hold on,' said Father Brown, in a sharp voice he very seldom used; 'this has got to stop.'

He still wore a heavy though unconscious frown, but in his eyes was no longer the cloud of mystification, but a light of almost terrible understanding.

'What a fool I am!' he muttered. 'I ought to have seen it long ago. The tale of the curse ought to have told me.'

'Do you mean to say,' demanded Tarrant, 'that we can really be killed now by something that happened in the thirteenth century?'

Father Brown shook his head and answered with quiet emphasis:

'I won't discuss whether we can be killed by something that happened in the thirteenth century; but I'm jolly certain that we we can't be killed by something that *never* happened in the thirteenth century, something that never happened at all.'

'Well,' said Tarrant, 'it's refreshing to find a priest so sceptical of the supernatural as all that.'

'Not at all,' replied the priest calmly; 'it's not the supernatural part I doubt. It's the natural part. I'm exactly in the position of the man who said, "I can believe the impossible, but not the improbable."'

'That's what you call a paradox, isn't it?' asked the other.

'It's what I call common sense, properly understood,' replied Father Brown. 'It really is more natural to believe a preternatural story, that deals with things we don't understand, than a natural story that contradicts things we do understand. Tell me that the great Mr Gladstone, in his last hours, was haunted by the ghost of Parnell, and I will be agnostic about it. But tell me that Mr Gladstone, when first presented to Queen Victoria, wore his hat in her drawing-room and slapped her on the back and offered her a cigar, and I am not agnostic at all. That is not impossible; it's only incredible. But I'm much more certain it didn't happen than that Parnell's ghost didn't appear; because it violates the laws of the world I do understand. So it is with that tale of the curse. It isn't the legend that I disbelieve – it's the history.'

Lady Diana had recovered a little from her trance of Cassandra, and her perennial curiosity about new things began to peer once more out of her bright and prominent eyes.

'What a curious man you are!' she said. 'Why should you disbelieve the history?'

'I disbelieve the history because it isn't history,' answered Father Brown. 'To anybody who happens to know a little about the Middle Ages, the whole story was about as probable as Gladstone offering Queen Victoria a cigar. But does anybody know anything about the Middle Ages? Do you know what a Guild was? Have you ever heard of *salvo managio suo*? Do you know what sort of people were *Servi Regis*?'

'No, of course I don't,' said the lady, rather crossly. 'What a lot of Latin words!'

'No, of course,' said Father Brown. 'If it had been Tutankhamen and a set of dried-up Africans preserved, Heaven knows why, at the other end of the world; if it had been Babylonia or China; if it had been some race as remote and mysterious as the Man in the Moon, your newspapers would have told you all about it, down to the last discovery of a tooth-brush or a collar-stud. But the men who built your own parish churches, and gave the names to your own towns and trades, and the very roads you walk on – it has never occurred to you to know anything about them. I don't claim to know a lot myself; but I know enough to see that story is stuff and nonsense from beginning to end. It was illegal for a money-lender to distrain on a man's shop and tools. It's exceedingly unlikely that the Guild would not have saved a man from such utter ruin, especially if he were ruined by a Jew. Those people had vices and tragedies of their own; they sometimes tortured and burned people. But that idea of a man, without God or hope in the world, crawling away to die because nobody cared whether he lived – that isn't a medieval idea. That's a product of our economic science and progress. The Jew wouldn't have been a vassal of the feudal lord. The Jews normally had a special position as servants of the King. Above all, the Jew couldn't possibly have been burned for his religion.'

'The paradoxes are multiplying,' observed Tarrant; 'but surely you won't deny that Jews were persecuted in the Middle Ages?'

'It would be nearer the truth,' said Father Brown, 'to say they were the only people who weren't persecuted in the Middle Ages. If you want to satirize medievalism, you could make a good case by saying that some poor Christian might be burned alive for making a mistake about the Homoousion, while a rich Jew might walk down the street openly sneering at Christ and the Mother of God. Well, that's what the story is like. It was never a story of the Middle Ages; it was never even a legend about the Middle Ages. It was made up by somebody whose notions came from novels and newspapers, and probably made up on the spur of the moment.'

The others seemed a little dazed by the historical digression, and seemed to wonder vaguely why the priest emphasized it and made it so important a part of the puzzle. But Tarrant, whose trade it was to pick the practical detail out of many tangles of digression, had suddenly become alert. His bearded chin was thrust forward farther than ever, but his sullen eyes were wide awake.

'Ah,' he said; 'made up on the spur of the moment!'

'Perhaps that is an exaggeration,' admitted Father Brown calmly. 'I should rather say made up more casually and carelessly than the rest of an uncommonly careful plot. But the plotter did not think the details of medieval history would matter much to anybody. And his calculation in a general way was pretty nearly right, like most of his other calculations.'

'Whose calculations? Who was right?' demanded the lady with a sudden passion of impatience. 'Who is this person you are talking about? Haven't we gone through enough, without your making our flesh creep with your he's and him's?'

'I am talking about the murderer,' said Father Brown.

'What murderer?' she asked sharply. 'Do you mean that the poor Professor was murdered?'

'Well,' said the staring Tarrant gruffly into his beard, 'we can't say "murdered", for we don't know he's killed.'

'The murderer killed somebody else, who was not Professor Smaill,' said the priest gravely.

'Why, whom else could he kill?' asked the other.

'He killed the Reverend John Walters, the Vicar of Dulham,' replied Father Brown with precision. 'He only wanted to kill those two, because they both had got hold of relics of one rare pattern. The murderer was a sort of monomaniac on the point.'

'It all sounds very strange,' muttered Tarrant. 'Of course we can't swear that the Vicar's really dead either. We haven't seen his body.'

'Oh yes, you have,' said Father Brown.

There was a silence as sudden as the stroke of a gong; a silence in which that sub-conscious guesswork that was so active and accurate in the woman moved her almost to a shriek.

'That is exactly what you have seen,' went on the priest. 'You have seen his body. You haven't seen him – the real living man; but you have seen his body all right. You have stared at it hard by the light of four great candles; and it was not tossing suicidally in the sea but lying in state like a Prince of the Church in a shrine built before the Crusade.'

'In plain words,' said Tarrant, 'you actually ask us to believe that the embalmed body was really the corpse of a murdered man.'

Father Brown was silent for a moment; then he said almost with an air of irrelevance:

'The first thing I noticed about it was the cross; or rather the string suspending the cross. Naturally, for most of you, it was only a string of beads and nothing else in particular; but, naturally also, it was rather more in my line than yours. You remember it lay close up to the chin, with only a few beads showing, as if the whole necklet were quite short. But the beads that showed were arranged in a special way, first one and then three, and so on; in fact, I knew at a glance that it was a rosary, an ordinary rosary with a cross at the end of it. But a rosary has at least five decades and additional beads as well; and I naturally wondered where all the rest of it was. It would go much more than once round the old man's neck. I couldn't understand it at the time; and it was only afterwards I guessed where the extra length had gone to. It was coiled round and round the foot of the wooden prop that was fixed in the corner of the coffin, holding up the lid. So that when poor Smaill merely plucked at the cross it jerked the prop out of its place and the lid fell on his skull like a club of stone.'

'By George!' said Tarrant; 'I'm beginning to think there's something in what you say. This is a queer story if it's true.'

'When I realized that,' went on Father Brown, 'I could manage more or less to guess the rest. Remember, first of all, that there never was any responsible archaeological authority for anything more than investigation. Poor old Walters was an honest antiquary, who was engaged in opening the tomb to *find out* if there was any truth in the legend about embalmed bodies. The rest was all rumour, of the sort that often anticipates or exaggerates such finds. As a fact, he found the body had not been embalmed, but had fallen into dust long ago. Only while he was working there by the light of his lonely candle in that sunken chapel, the candle-light threw another shadow that was not his own.'

'Ah!' cried Lady Diana with a catch in her breath; 'and I know what you mean now. You mean to tell us we have met the murderer, talked and joked with the murderer, let him tell us a romantic tale, and let him depart untouched.'

'Leaving his clerical disguise on a rock,' assented Brown. 'It is all dreadfully simple. This man got ahead of the Professor in the race to the churchyard and chapel, possibly while the Professor was talking to that lugubrious journalist. He came on the old clergyman beside the empty coffin and killed him. Then he dressed himself in the black clothes from the corpse, wrapped it in an old cope which had been among the real finds of the exploration, and put it in the coffin, arranging the rosary and the wooden support as I have described. Then, having thus set the trap for his second enemy, he went up into the daylight and greeted us all with the most amiable politeness of a country clergyman.'

'He ran a considerable risk,' objected Tarrant, 'of somebody knowing Walters by sight.'

'I admit he was half-mad,' agreed Father Brown; 'and I think you will admit that the risk was worth taking, for he has got off, after all.'

'I'll admit he was very lucky,' growled Tarrant. 'And who the devil was he?'

'As you say, he was very lucky,' answered Father Brown, 'and not least in that respect. For that is the one thing we may never know.'

He frowned at the table for a moment and then went on: 'This fellow has been hovering round and threatening for years, but the one thing he was careful of was to keep the secret of who he was; and he has kept it still. But if poor Smaill recovers, as I think he will, it is pretty safe to say that you will hear more of it.'

'Why, what will Professor Smaill do, do you think?' asked Lady Diana.

'I should think the first thing he would do,' said Tarrant, 'would be to put the detectives on like dogs after this murdering devil. I should like to have a go at him myself.'

'Well,' said Father Brown, smiling suddenly after his long fit of frowning perplexity, 'I think I know the very first thing he ought to do.'

'And what is that?' asked Lady Diana with graceful eagerness.

'He ought to apologize to all of you,' said Father Brown.

It was not upon this point, however, that Father Brown found himself talking to Professor Smaill as he sat by the bedside during the slow convalescence of that eminent archaeologist. Nor, indeed, was it chiefly Father Brown who did the talking; for though the Professor was limited to small doses of the stimulant of conversation, he concentrated most of it upon these interviews with his clerical friend. Father Brown had a talent for being silent in an encouraging way and Smaill was encouraged by it to talk about many strange things not always easy to talk about; such as the morbid phases of recovery and the monstrous dreams that often accompany delirium. It is often rather an unbalancing business to recover slowly from a bad knock on the head; and when the head is as interesting a head as that of Professor Smaill even its disturbances and distortions are apt to be original and curious. His dreams were like bold and big designs rather out of drawing, as they can be seen in the strong but stiff archaic arts that he had studied; they were full of strange saints with square and triangular haloes, of golden out-standing crowns and glories round dark and flattened faces, of eagles out of the east and the high head-dresses of bearded men with their hair bound like women. Only, as he told his friend, there was one much simpler and less entangled type, that continually recurred to his imaginative memory. Again and again all these Byzantine patterns would fade away like the fading gold on which they were traced as upon fire; and nothing remained but the dark bare wall of rock on which the shining shape of the fish was traced as with a finger dipped in the phosphorescence of fishes. For that was the sign which he once looked up and saw, in the moment when he first heard round the corner of the dark passage the voice of his enemy.

'And at last,' he said, 'I think I have seen a meaning in the picture and the voice; and one that I never understood before. Why should I worry because one madman among a million of sane men, leagued in a great society against him, chooses to brag of persecuting me or pursuing me to death? The man who drew in the dark catacomb the secret symbol of Christ was persecuted in a very different fashion. He was the solitary madman; the whole sane society was leagued together not to save but to slay him. I have sometimes fussed and fidgeted and wondered whether this or that man was my persecutor; whether it was Tarrant; whether it was Leonard Smyth; whether it was any one of them. Suppose it had been all of them? Suppose it had been all the men on the boat and the men on the train and the men in the village. Suppose, so far as I was concerned, they were all murderers. I thought I had a right to be alarmed because I was creeping through the bowels of the earth in the dark and there was a man who would destroy me. What would it have been like, if the destroyer had been up in the daylight and had owned all the earth and commanded all the armies and the crowds? How if he had been able to stop all the earths or smoke me out of my hole, or kill me the moment I put my nose out in the daylight? What was it like to deal with murder on that scale? The world has forgotten these things, as until a little while ago it had forgotten war.'

'Yes,' said Father Brown, 'but the war came. The fish may be driven underground again, but it will come up into the daylight once more. As St Antony of Padua humorously remarked, "It is only fishes who survive the Deluge." '

SIX

The Dagger with Wings

FATHER BROWN, at one period of his life, found it difficult to hang his hat on a hat-peg without repressing a slight shudder. The origin of this idiosyncrasy was indeed a mere detail in much more complicated events; but it was perhaps the only detail that remained to him in his busy life to remind him of the whole business. Its remote origin was to be found in the facts which led Dr Boyne, the medical officer attached to the police force, to send for the priest on a particular frosty morning in December.

Dr Boyne was a big dark Irishman, one of those rather baffling Irishmen to be found all over the world, who will talk scientific scepticism, materialism, and cynicism at length and at large, but who never dream of referring anything touching the ritual of religion to anything except the traditional religion of their native land. It would be hard to say whether their creed is a very superficial varnish or a very fundamental substratum; but most probably it is both, with a mass of materialism in between. Anyhow, when he thought that matters of that sort might be involved, he asked Father Brown to call, though he made no pretence of preference for that aspect of them.

'I'm not sure I want you, you know,' was his greeting. 'I'm not sure about anything yet. I'm hanged if I can make out whether it's a case for a doctor, or a policeman, or a priest.'

'Well,' said Father Brown with a smile, 'as I suppose you're both a policeman and a doctor, I seem to be rather in a minority.'

'I admit you're what politicians call an instructed minority,' replied the doctor. 'I mean, I know you've had to do a little in our line as well as your own. But it's precious hard to say whether this business is in your line or ours, or merely in the line of the Commissioners in Lunacy. We've just had a message from a man living near here, in that white house on the hill, asking for protection against a murderous persecution. We've gone into the facts as far as we could, and perhaps I'd better tell you the story, as it is supposed to have happened, from the beginning.

'It seems that a man named Aylmer, who was a wealthy land-owner in the West Country, married rather late in life and had three sons, Philip, Stephen, and Arnold. But in his bachelor days, when he thought he would have no heir, he had adopted a boy whom he thought very brilliant and promising, who went by the name of John Strake. His origin seems to be vague; they say he was a foundling; some say he was a gipsy. I think the last notion is mixed up with the fact that Aylmer in his old age dabbled in all sorts of dingy occultism, including palmistry and astrology, and his three sons say that Strake encouraged him in it. But they said a great many other things besides that. They said Strake was an amazing scoundrel, and especially an amazing liar; a genius in inventing lies on the spur of the moment, and telling them so as to deceive a detective. But that might very well be a natural prejudice, in the light of what happened. Perhaps you can more or less imagine what happened. The old man left practically every-thing to the adopted son; and when he died the three real sons disputed the will. They said their father had been frightened into surrender and, not to put too fine a point on it, into gibbering idiocy. They said Strake had the strangest and most cunning ways of getting at him, in spite of the nurses and the family, and terrorizing him on his death-bed. Anyhow, they seemed to have proved something about the dead man's mental condition, for the courts set aside the will and the sons inherited. Strake is said to have broken out in the most dreadful fashion, and sworn he would kill all three of them, one after another, and that nothing could hide them from his vengeance. It is the third or last of the brothers, Arnold Aylmer, who is asking for police protection.'

'Third and last,' said the priest, looking at him gravely.

'Yes,' said Boyne. 'The other two are dead.'

There was a silence before he continued. 'That is where the doubt comes in. There is no proof they were murdered, but they might possibly have been. The eldest, who took up his position as squire, was supposed to have committed suicide in his garden. The second, who went into trade as a manufacturer, was knocked on the head by the machinery in his factory; he might very well have taken a false step and fallen. But if Strake did kill them, he is certainly very cunning in his way of getting to work and getting away. On the other hand, it's more than likely that the whole thing is a mania of conspiracy founded on a coincidence. Look here, what I want is this. I want somebody of sense, who isn't an official, to go up and have a talk with this Mr Arnold Aylmer and form an impression of him. You know what a man with a delusion is like, and how a man looks when he is telling the truth. I want you to be the advance guard, before we take the matter up.'

'It seems rather odd,' said Father Brown, 'that you haven't had to take it up before. If there is anything in this business, it seems to have been going on for a good time. Is there any particular reason why he should send for you just now, any more than any other time?'

'That had occurred to me, as you may imagine,' answered Dr Boyne. 'He does give a reason, but I confess it is one of the things that make me wonder whether the whole thing isn't only the whim of some half-witted crank. He declared that all his servants have suddenly gone on strike and left him, so that he is obliged to call on the police to look after his house. And on making inquiries, I certainly do find that there has been a general exodus of servants from that house on the hill; and of course the town is full of tales, very one-sided tales I dare say. Their account of it seems to be that their employer had become quite impossible in his fidgets and fears and exactions; that he wanted them to guard the house like sentries, or sit up like night nurses in a hospital; that they could never be left alone because he must never be left alone. So they all announced in a loud voice that he was a lunatic, and left. Of course that does not prove he is a lunatic; but it seems rather rum nowadays for a man to expect his valet or his parlour-maid to act as an armed guard.'

'And so,' said the priest with a smile, 'he wants a policeman to act as his parlour-maid because his parlour-maid won't act as a policeman.'

'I thought that rather thick, too,' agreed the doctor; 'but I can't take the responsibility of a flat refusal till I've tried a compromise. You are the compromise.'

'Very well,' said Father Brown simply. 'I'll go and call on him now if you like.'

The rolling country round the little town was sealed and bound with frost, and the sky was as clear and cold as steel, except in the north-east where clouds with lurid haloes were beginning to climb up the sky. It was against these darker and more sinister colours that the house on the hill gleamed with a row of pale pillars, forming a short colonnade of the classical sort. A winding road led up to it across the curve of the down, and plunged into a mass of dark bushes. Just before it reached the bushes the air seemed to grow colder and colder, as if he were approaching an ice-house or the North Pole. But he was a highly practical person, never entertaining such fancies except as fancies. And he merely cocked his eye at the great livid cloud crawling up over the house, and remarked cheerfully:

'It's going to snow.'

Through a low ornamental iron gateway of the Italianate pattern he entered a garden having something of that desolation which only belongs to the disorder of orderly things. Deep-green growths were grey with the faint powder of the frost, large weeds had fringed the fading pattern of the flower-beds as if in a ragged frame; and the house stood as if waist-high in a stunted forest of shrubs and bushes. The vegetation consisted largely of evergreens or very hardy plants; and though it was thus thick and heavy, it was too northern to be called luxuriant. It might be described as an Arctic jungle. So it was in some sense with the house itself, which had a row of columns and a classical façade, which might have looked out on the Mediterranean; but which seemed now to be withering in the wind of the North Sea. Classical ornament here and there accentuated the contrast; caryatides and carved masks of comedy or tragedy looked down from corners of the building upon the grey confusion of the garden paths; but the faces seemed to be frost-bitten. The very volutes of the capitals might have curled up with the cold.

Father Brown went up the grassy steps to a square porch flanked by big pillars and knocked at the door. About four minutes afterwards he knocked again. Then he stood still patiently waiting with his back to the door and looked out on the slowly darkening landscape. It was darkening under the shadow of that one great continent of cloud that had come flying out of the north; and even as he looked out beyond the pillars of the porch, which seemed huge and black above him in the twilight, he saw the opalescent crawling rim of the great cloud as it sailed over the roof and bowed over the porch like a canopy. The grey canopy with its faintly coloured fringes seemed to sink lower and lower upon the garden beyond, until what had recently been a clear and pale-hued winter sky was left in a few silver ribbons and rags like a sickly sunset. Father Brown waited, and there was no sound within.

Then he betook himself briskly down the steps and round the house to look for another entrance. He eventually found one, a side door in the flat wall, and on this also he hammered and outside this also he waited. Then he tried the handle and found the door apparently bolted or fastened in some fashion; and then he moved along that side of the house, musing on the possibilities of the position, and wondering whether the eccentric Mr Aylmer had barricaded himself too deep in the house to hear any kind of summons; or whether perhaps he would barricade himself all the more, on the assumption that any summons must be the challenge of the avenging Strake. It might be that the decamping servants had only unlocked one door when they left in the morning, and that their master had locked that; but whatever he might have done it was unlikely that they, in the mood of that moment, had looked so carefully to the defences. He continued his prowl round the place; it was not really a large place, though perhaps a little pretentious; and in a few moments he found he had made the complete circuit. A moment after he found what he suspected and sought. The french window of one room, curtained and shadowed with creeper, stood open by a crack, doubtless accidentally left ajar, and he found himself in a central room, comfortably upholstered in a rather old-fashioned way, with a staircase leading up from it on one side and a door leading out of it on the other. Immediately opposite him was another door with red glass let into it, a little gaudily for later tastes; something that looked like a red-robed figure in cheap stained glass. On a round table to the right stood a sort of acquarium – a great bowl full of greenish water, in which fishes and similar things moved about as in a tank; and just opposite it a plant of the palm variety with very large green leaves. All this looked so very dusty and Early Victorian that the telephone, visible in the curtained alcove, was almost a surprise.

'Who is that?' a voice called out sharply and rather suspiciously from behind the stained-glass door.

'Could I see Mr Aylmer?' asked the priest apologetically.

The door opened and a gentleman in a peacock-green dressing-gown came out with an inquiring look. His hair was rather rough and untidy, as if he had been in bed or lived in a state of slowly getting up, but his eyes were not only awake but alert, and some would have said alarmed. Father Brown knew that the contradiction was likely enough in a man who had rather run to seed under the shadow either of a delusion or a danger. He had a fine aquiline face when seen in profile, but when seen full face the first impression was that of the untidiness and even the wilderness of his loose brown beard.

'I am Mr Aylmer,' he said, 'but I've got out of the way of expecting visitors.'

Something about Mr Aylmer's unrestful eye prompted the priest to go straight to the point. If the man's persecution was only a monomania, he would be the less likely to resent it.

'I was wondering,' said Father Brown softly, 'whether it is quite true that you never expect visitors.'

'You are right,' replied his host steadily. 'I always expect one visitor. And he may be the last.'

'I hope not,' said Father Brown, 'but at least I am relieved to infer that I do not look very like him.'

Mr Aylmer shook himself with a sort of savage laugh. 'You certainly do not,' he said.

'Mr Aylmer,' said Father Brown frankly, 'I apologize for the liberty, but some friends of mine have told me about your trouble, and asked me to see if I could do anything for you. The truth is, I have some little experience in affairs like this.'

'There are no affairs like this,' said Aylmer.

'You mean,' observed Father Brown, 'that the tragedies in your unfortunate family were not normal deaths?'

'I mean they were not even normal murders,' answered the other. 'The man who is hounding us all to death is a hell-hound, and his power is from hell.'

'All evil has one origin,' said the priest gravely. 'But how do you know they were not normal murders?'

Aylmer answered with a gesture which offered his guest a chair; then he seated himself slowly in another, frowning, with his hands on his knees; but when he looked up his expression had grown milder and more thoughtful, and his voice was quite cordial and composed.

'Sir,' he said, 'I don't want you to imagine that I'm in the least an unreasonable person. I have come to these conclusions by reason, because unfortunately reason really leads there. I have read a great deal on these subjects; for I was the only one who inherited my father's scholarship in somewhat obscure matters, and I have since inherited his library. But what I tell you does not rest on what I have read but on what I have seen.'

Father Brown nodded, and the other proceeded, as if picking his words:

'In my elder brother's case I was not certain at first. There were no marks or footprints where he was found shot, and the pistol was left beside him. But he had just received a threatening letter certainly from our enemy, for it was marked with a sign like a winged dagger, which was one of his infernal cabalistic tricks. And a servant said she had seen something moving along the garden wall in the twilight that was much too large to be a cat. I leave it there; all I can say is that if the murderer came, he managed to leave no traces of his coming. But when my brother Stephen died it was different; and since then I have known. A machine was working in an open scaffolding under the factory tower; I scaled the platform a moment after he had fallen under the iron hammer that struck him; I did not see anything else strike him, but I saw what I saw.

'A great drift of factory smoke was rolling between me and the factory tower; but through a rift of it I saw on the top of it a dark human figure wrapped in what looked like a black cloak. Then the sulphurous smoke drove between us again; and when it cleared I looked up at the distant chimney – there was nobody there. I am a rational man, and I will ask all rational men how he had reached that dizzy unapproachable turret, and how he left it.'

He stared across at the priest with a sphinx-like challenge; then after a silence he said abruptly:

'My brother's brains were knocked out, but his body was not much damaged. And in his pocket we found one of those warning messages dated the day before and stamped with the flying dagger.

'I am sure,' he went on gravely, 'that the symbol of the winged dagger is not merely arbitrary or accidental. Nothing about that abominable man is accidental. He is all design; though it is indeed a most dark and intricate design. His mind is woven not only out of elaborate schemes but out of all sorts of secret languages and signs, and dumb signals and wordless pictures which are the names of nameless things. He is the worst sort of man that the world knows: he is the wicked mystic. Now, I don't pretend to penetrate all that is conveyed by this symbol; but it seems surely that it must have a relation to all that was most remarkable, or even incredible, in his movements as he had hovered round my unfortunate family. Is there no connexion between the idea of a winged weapon and the mystery by which Philip was struck dead on his own lawn without the lightest touch of any footprint having disturbed the dust or grass? Is there no connexion between the plumed poignard flying like a feathered arrow and that figure which hung on the far top of the toppling chimney, clad in a cloak for pinions?'

'You mean,' said Father Brown thoughtfully, 'that he is in a perpetual state of levitation.'

'Simon Magus did it,' replied Aylmer, 'and it was one of the commonest predictions of the Dark Ages that Antichrist would be able to fly. Anyhow, there was the flying dagger on the document; and whether or no it could fly, it could certainly strike.'

'Did you notice what sort of paper it was on?' asked Father Brown. 'Common paper?'

The sphinx-like face broke abruptly into a harsh laugh.

'You can see what they're like,' said Aylmer grimly, 'for I got one myself this morning.'

He was leaning back in his chair now, with his long legs thrust out from under the green dressing-gown, which was a little short for him, and his bearded chin pillowed on his chest. Without moving otherwise, he thrust his hand deep in the dressing-gown pocket and held out a fluttering scrap of paper at the end of a rigid arm. His whole attitude was suggestive of a sort of paralysis, that was both rigidity and collapse. But the next remark of the priest had a curious effect of rousing him.

Father Brown was blinking in his short-sighted way at the paper presented to him. It was a singular sort of paper, rough without being common, as from an artist's sketch-book; and on it was drawn boldly in red ink a dagger decorated with wings like the rod of Hermes, with the written words, 'Death comes the day after this, as it came to your brothers.'

Father Brown tossed the paper on the floor and sat bolt upright in his chair.

'You mustn't let that sort of stuff stupefy you,' he said sharply. 'These devils always try to make us helpless by making us hopeless.'

Rather to his surprise, an awakening wave went over the prostrate figure, which sprang from its chair as if startled out of a dream.

'You're right, you're right!' cried Aylmer with a rather uncanny animation; 'and the devils shall find that I'm not so hopeless after all, nor so helpless either. Perhaps I have more hope and better help than you fancy.'

He stood with his hands in his pockets, frowning down at the priest, who had a momentary doubt, during that strained silence, about whether the man's long peril had not touched his brain. But when he spoke it was quite soberly.

'I believe my unfortunate brothers failed because they used the wrong weapons. Philip carried a revolver, and that was how his death came to be called suicide. Stephen had police protection, but he also had a sense of what made him ridiculous; and he could not allow a policeman to climb up a ladder after him to a scaffolding where he stood only a moment. They were both scoffers, reacting into scepticism from the strange mysticism of my father's last days. But I always knew there was more in my father than they understood. It is true that by studying magic he fell at last under the blight of black magic; the black magic of this scoundrel Strake. But my brothers were wrong about the antidote. The antidote to black magic is not brute materialism or worldly wisdom. The antidote to black magic is white magic.'

'It rather depends,' said Father Brown, 'what you mean by white magic.'

'I mean silver magic,' said the other, in a low voice, like one speaking of a secret revelation. Then after a silence he said: 'Do you know what I mean by silver magic? Excuse me a moment.'

He turned and opened the central door with the red glass and went into a passage beyond it. The house had less depth than Brown had supposed; instead of the door opening into interior rooms, the corridor it revealed ended in another door on the garden. The door of one room was on one side of the passage; doubtless, the priest told himself, the proprietor's bedroom whence he had rushed out in his dressing-gown. There was nothing else on that side but an ordinary hat-stand with the ordinary dingy cluster of old hats and overcoats; but on the other side was something more interesting: a very dark old oak sideboard laid out with some old silver, and overhung by a trophy or ornament of old weapons. It was by that that Arnold Aylmer halted, looking up at a long antiquated pistol with a bell-shaped mouth.

The door at the end of the passage was barely open, and through the crack came a streak of white daylight. The priest had very quick instincts about natural things, and something in the unusual brilliancy of that white line told him what had happened outside. It was indeed what he had prophesied when he was approaching the house. He ran past his rather startled host and opened the door, to face something that was at once a blank and a blaze. What he had seen shining through the crack was not only the most negative whiteness of daylight but the positive whiteness of snow. All round, the sweeping fall of the country was covered with that shining pallor that seems at once hoary and innocent.

'Here is white magic anyhow,' said Father Brown in his cheerful voice. Then, as he turned back into the hall, he murmured, 'And silver magic too, I suppose,' for the white lustre touched the silver with splendour and lit up the old steel here and there in the darkling armoury. The shaggy head of the brooding Aylmer seemed to have a halo of silver fire, as he turned with his face in shadow and the outlandish pistol in his hand.

'Do you know why I chose this sort of old blunderbuss?' he asked. 'Because I can load it with this sort of bullet.'

He had picked up a small apostle spoon from the sideboard and by sheer violence broke off the small figure at the top. 'Let us go back into the other room,' he added.

'Did you ever read about the death of Dundee?' he asked when they had reseated themselves. He had recovered from his momentary annoyance at the priest's restlessness. 'Graham of Claverhouse, you know, who persecuted the Covenanters and had a black horse that could ride straight up a precipice. Don't you know he could only be shot with a silver bullet, because he had sold himself to the Devil? That's one comfort about you; at least you know enough to believe in the Devil.'

'Oh, yes,' replied Father Brown, 'I believe in the Devil. What I don't believe in is the Dundee. I mean the Dundee of Covenanting legends, with his nightmare of a horse. John Graham was simply a seventeenth-century professional soldier, rather better than most. If he dragooned them it was because he was a dragoon, but not a dragon. Now my experience is that it's not that sort of swaggering blade who sells himself to the Devil. The devil-worshippers I've known were quite different. Not to mention names, which might cause a social flutter, I'll take a man in

Dundee's own day. Have you ever heard of Dalrymple of Stair?'

'No,' replied the other gruffly.

'You've heard of what he did,' said Father Brown, 'and it was worse than anything Dundee ever did; yet he escapes the infamy by oblivion. He was the man who made the Massacre of Glencoe. He was a very learned man and lucid lawyer, a statesman with very serious and enlarged ideas of statesmanship, a quiet man with a very refined and intellectual face. That's the sort of man who sells himself to the Devil.'

Aylmer half started from his chair with an enthusiasm of eager assent.

'By God! you are right,' he cried. 'A refined intellectual face! That is the face of John Strake.'

Then he raised himself and stood looking at the priest with a curious concentration. 'If you will wait here a little while,' he said, 'I will show you something.'

He went back through the central door, closing it after him; going, the priest presumed, to the old sideboard or possibly to his bedroom. Father Brown remained seated, gazing abstractedly at the carpet, where a faint red glimmer shone from the glass in the doorway. Once it seemed to brighten like a ruby and then darkened again, as if the sun of that stormy day had passed from cloud to cloud. Nothing moved except the aquatic creatures which floated to and fro in the dim green bowl. Father Brown was thinking hard.

A minute or two afterwards he got up and slipped quietly to the alcove of the telephone, where he rang up his friend Dr Boyne, at the official headquarters. 'I wanted to tell you about Aylmer and his affairs,' he said quietly. 'It's a queer story, but I rather think there's something in it. If I were you I'd send some men up here straight away; four or five men, I think, and surround the house. If anything does happen there'll probably be something startling in the way of an escape.'

Then he went back and sat down again, staring at the dark carpet, which again glowed blood-red with the light from the glass door. Something in the filtered light set his mind drifting on certain borderlands of thought, with the first white daybreak before the coming of colour, and all that mystery which is alternately veiled and revealed in the symbol of windows and of doors.

An inhuman howl in a human voice came from beyond the closed doors, almost simultaneously with the noise of firing. Before the echoes of the shot had died away the door was violently flung open and his host staggered into the room, the dressing-gown half torn from his shoulder and the long pistol smoking in his hand. He seemed to be shaking in every limb, yet he was shaken in part with an unnatural laughter.

'Glory be to the White Magic!' he cried. 'Glory be to the silver bullet! The hell-hound had hunted once too often, and my brothers are avenged at last.'

He sank into a chair and the pistol slid from his hand and fell on the floor. Father Brown darted past him, slipped through the glass door and went down the passage. As he did so he put his hand on the handle of the bedroom door, as if half intending to enter; then he stooped a moment, as if examining something – and then he ran to the outer door and opened it.

On the field of snow, which had been so blank a little while before, lay one black object. At the first glance it looked a little like an enormous bat. A second glance showed that it was, after all, a human figure; fallen on its face, the whole head covered by a broad black hat having something of a Latin-American look; while the appearance of black-wings came from the two flaps or loose sleeves of a very vast black cloak spread out, perhaps by accident, to their utmost length on either side. Both the hands were hidden, though Father Brown thought he could detect the position of one of them, and saw close to it, under the edge of the cloak, the glimmer of some metallic weapon. The main effect, however, was curiously like that of the simple extravagances of heraldry; like a black eagle displayed on a white ground. But by walking round it and peering under the hat the priest got a glimpse of the face, which was indeed what his host had called refined and intellectual; even sceptical and austere: the face of John Strake.

'Well, I'm jiggered,' muttered Father Brown. 'It really does look like some vast vampire that has swooped down like a bird.'

'How else could he have come?' came a voice from the doorway, and Father Brown looked up to see Aylmer once more standing there.

'Couldn't he have walked?' replied Father Brown evasively.

Aylmer stretched out his arm and swept the white landscape with a gesture.

'Look at the snow,' he said in a deep voice that had a sort of roll and thrill in it. 'Is not the snow unspotted – pure as the white magic you yourself called it? Is there a speck on it for miles, save that one foul black blot that has fallen there? There are no footprints, but a few of yours and mine; there are none approaching the house from anywhere.'

Then he looked at the little priest for a moment with a concentrated and curious expression, and said:

'I will tell you something else. That cloak he flies with is too long to walk with. He was not a very tall man, and it would trail behind him like a royal train. Stretch it out over his body, if you like, and see.'

'What happened to you both?' asked Father Brown abruptly.

'It was too swift to describe,' answered Aylmer. 'I had looked out of the door and was turning back when there came a kind of rushing of wind all around me, as if I were being buffeted by a wheel revolving in mid-air. I spun round somehow and fired blindly; and then I saw nothing but what you see now. But I am morally certain that you wouldn't see it if I had not had a silver shot in my gun. It would have been a different body lying there in the snow.'

'By the way,' remarked Father Brown, 'shall we leave it lying there in the snow? Or would you like it taken into your room – I suppose that's your bedroom in the passage?'

'No, no,' replied Aylmer hastily, 'we must leave it here till the police have seen it. Besides, I've had as much of such things as I can stand for the moment. Whatever else happens, I'm going to have a drink. After that, they can hang me if they like.'

Inside the central apartment, between the palm plant and the bowl of fishes, Aylmer tumbled into a chair. He had nearly knocked the bowl over as he lurched into the room, but he had managed to find the decanter of brandy after plunging his hand rather blindly into several cupboards and corners. He did not at any time look like a methodical person, but at this moment his distraction must have been extreme. He drank with a long gulp and began to talk rather feverishly, as if to fill up a silence.

'I see you are still doubtful,' he said, 'though you have seen the thing with your own eyes. Believe me, there was something more behind the quarrel between the spirit of Strake and the spirit of the house of Aylmer. Besides, you have no business to be an unbeliever. You ought to stand for all the things these stupid people call superstitions. Come now, don't you think there's a lot in those old wives' tales about luck and charms and so on, silver bullets included? What do you say about them as a Catholic?'

'I say I'm an agnostic,' replied Father Brown, smiling.

'Nonsense,' said Aylmer impatiently. 'It's your business to believe things.'

'Well, I do believe some things, of course,' conceded Father Brown; 'and therefore, of course, I don't believe other things.'

Aylmer was leaning forward, and looking at him with a strange intensity that was almost like that of a mesmerist.

'You do believe it,' he said. 'You do believe everything. We all believe everything, even when we deny everything. The denyers believe. The unbelievers believe. Don't you feel in your heart that these contradictions do not really contradict: that there is a cosmos that contains them all? The soul goes round upon a wheel of stars and all things return; perhaps Strake and I have striven in many shapes, beast against beast and bird against bird, and perhaps we shall strive for ever. But since we seek and need each other, even that eternal hatred is an eternal love. Good and evil go round in a wheel that is one thing and not many. Do you not realize in your heart, do you not believe behind all your beliefs, that there is but one reality and we are its shadows; and that all things are but aspects of one thing: a centre where men melt into Man and Man into God?'

138

'No,' said Father Brown.

Outside, twilight had begun to fall, in that phase of such a snow-laden evening when the land looks brighter than the sky. In the porch of the main entrance, visible through a half-curtained window, Father Brown could dimly see a bulky figure standing. He glanced casually at the french windows through which he had originally entered, and saw they were darkened with two equally motionless figures. The inner door with the coloured glass stood slightly ajar; and he could see in the short corridor beyond, the ends of two long shadows, exaggerated and distorted by the level light of evening, but still like grey caricatures of the figures of men. Dr Boyne had already obeyed the telephone message. The house was surrounded.

'What is the good of saying no?' insisted his host, still with the same hypnotic stare. 'You have seen part of that eternal drama with your own eyes. You have seen the threat of John Strake to slay Arnold Aylmer by black magic. You have seen Arnold Aylmer slay John Strake by white magic. You see Arnold Aylmer alive and talking to you now. And yet you don't believe it.'

'No, I do not believe it,' said Father Brown, and rose from his chair like one terminating a visit.

'Why not?' asked the other.

The priest only lifted his voice a little, but it sounded in every corner of the room like a bell.

'Because you are not Arnold Aylmer,' he said. 'I know who you are. Your name is John Strake; and you have murdered the last of the brothers, who is lying outside in the snow.'

A ring of white showed round the iris of the other man's eyes; he seemed to be making, with bursting eyeballs, a last effort to mesmerize and master his companion. Then he made a sudden movement sideways; and even as he did so the door behind him opened and a big detective in plain clothes put one hand quietly on his shoulder. The other hand hung down, but it held a revolver. The man looked wildly round, and saw plain-clothes men in all corners of the quiet room.

That evening Father Brown had another and longer conversation with Dr Boyne about the tragedy of the Aylmer family.

By that time there was no longer any doubt of the central fact of the case, for John Strake had confessed his identity and even confessed his crimes; only it would be truer to say that he boasted of his victories. Compared to the fact that he had rounded off his life's work with the last Aylmer lying dead, everything else, including existence itself, seemed to be indifferent to him.

'The man is a sort of monomaniac,' said Father Brown. 'He is not interested in any other matter; not even in any other murder. I owe him something for that; for I had to comfort myself with the reflection a good many times this afternoon. As has doubtless occurred to you, instead of weaving all that wild but ingenious romance about winged vampires and silver bullets, he might have put an ordinary leaden bullet into me, and walked out of the house. I assure you it occurred quite frequently to me.'

'I wonder why he didn't,' observed Boyne. 'I don't understand it; but I don't understand anything yet. How on earth did you discover it, and what in the world did you discover?'

'Oh, you provided me with very valuable information,' replied Father Brown modestly, 'especially the one piece of information that really counted. I mean the statement that Strake was a very inventive and imaginative liar, with great presence of mind in producing his lies. This afternoon he needed it; but he rose to the occasion. Perhaps his only mistake was in choosing a preternatural story; he had the notion that because I am a clergyman I should believe anything. Many people have little notions of that kind.'

'But I can't make head or tail of it,' said the doctor. 'You must really begin at the beginning.'

'The beginning of it was a dressing-gown,' said Father Brown simply. 'It was the one really good disguise I've ever known. When you meet a man in a house with a dressing-gown on, you assume quite automatically that he's in his own house. I assumed it myself; but afterwards queer little things began to happen. When he took the pistol down he clicked it at arm's length, as a man does to make sure a strange weapon isn't loaded; of course he would know whether the pistols in his own hall were loaded or not. I didn't like the way he looked for the brandy, or the way he nearly barged into the bowl of fishes. For a man who has a fragile thing of that sort as a fixture in his rooms gets a quite mechanical habit of avoiding it. But these things might possibly have been fancies; the first real point was this. He came out from the little passage between the two doors; and in that passage there's only one other door leading to a room; so I assumed it was the bedroom he had just come from. I tried the handle; but it was locked. I thought this odd; and looked through the keyhole. It was an utterly bare room, obviously deserted; no bed, no anything. Therefore he had not come from inside any room, but from outside the house. And when I saw that, I think I saw the whole picture.

'Poor Arnold Aylmer doubtless slept and perhaps lived upstairs, and came down in his dressing-gown and passed through the red glass door. At the end of the passage, black against the winter daylight, he saw the enemy of his house. He saw a tall bearded man in a broad-brimmed black hat and a large flapping black cloak. He did not see much more in this world. Strake sprang at him, throttling or stabbing him; we cannot be sure till the inquest. Then Strake, standing in the narrow passage between the hat-stand and the old sideboard, and looking down in triumph on the last of his foes heard something he had not expected. He heard footsteps in the parlour beyond. It was myself entering by the french windows.

'His masquerade was a miracle of promptitude. It involved not only a disguise but a romance – an impromptu romance. He took off his big black hat and cloak and put on the dead man's dressing-gown. Then he did a rather grisly thing; at least a thing that affects my fancy as more grisly than the rest. He hung the corpse like a coat on one of the hat pegs. He draped it in his own long cloak, and found it hung well below the heels; he covered the head entirely with his own wide hat. It was the only possible way of hiding it in that little passage with the locked door; but it was really a very clever one. I myself walked past the hat-stand once without knowing it was anything but a hat-stand. I think that unconsciousness of mine will always give me a shiver.

'He might perhaps have left it at that; but I might have

discovered the corpse at any minute; and, hung where it was, it was a corpse calling for what you might call an explanation. He adopted the bolder stroke of discovering it himself and explaining it himself.

'Then there dawned on this strange and frightfully fertile mind the conception of a story of substitution; the reversal of the parts. He had already assumed the part of Arnold Aylmer. Why should not his dead enemy assume the part of John Strake? There must have been something in that topsy-turvydom to take the fancy of that darkly fanciful man. It was like some frightful fancy-dress ball to which the two mortal enemies were to go dressed up as each other. Only, the fancy-dress ball was to be a dance of death: and one of the dancers would be dead. That is why I can imagine that man putting it in his own mind, and I can imagine him smiling.'

Father Brown was gazing into vacancy with his large grey eyes, which, when not blurred by his trick of blinking, were the one notable thing in his face. He went on speaking simply and seriously:

'All things are from God; and above all, reason and imagination and the great gifts of the mind. They are good in themselves; and we must not altogether forget their origin even in their perversion. Now this man had in him a very noble power to be perverted; the power of telling stories. He was a great novelist; only he had twisted his fictive power to practical and to evil ends; to deceiving men with false fact instead of with true fiction. It began with his deceiving old Aylmer with elaborate excuses and ingeniously detailed lies; but even that may have been, at the beginning, little more than the tall stories and tarradiddles of the child who may say equally he has seen the King of England or the King of the Fairies. It grew strong in him through the vice that perpetuates all vices, pride; he grew more and more vain of his promptitude in producing stories of his originality, and subtlety in developing them. That is what the young Aylmers meant by saying that he could always cast a spell over their father; and it was true. It was the sort of spell that the storyteller cast over the tyrant in the Arabian Nights. And to the last he walked the world with the pride of a poet, and with the false yet unfathomable courage of a great liar. He could always produce more Arabian Nights if ever his neck was in danger. And today his neck was in danger.

'But I am sure, as I say, that he enjoyed it as a fantasy as well as a conspiracy. He set about the task of telling the true story the wrong way round: of treating the dead man as living and the live man as dead. He had already got into Aylmer's dressing-gown; he proceeded to get into Aylmer's body and soul. He looked at the corpse as if it were his own corpse lying cold in the snow. Then he spread-eagled it in that strange fashion to suggest the sweeping descent of a bird of prey, and decked it out not only in his own dark and flying garments but in a whole dark fairy-tale about the black bird that could only fall by the silver bullet. I do not know whether it was the silver glittering on the sideboard or the snow shining beyond the door that suggested to his intensely artistic temperament the theme of white magic and the white metal used against magicians. But whatever its origin, he made it his own like a poet; and did it very promptly, like a practical man. He completed the exchange and reversal of parts by flinging the corpse out on to the snow as the corpse of Strake. He did his best to work up a creepy conception of Strake as something hovering in the air everywhere, a harpy with wings of speed and claws of death; to explain the absence of footprints and other things. For one piece of artistic impudence I hugely admire him. He actually turned one of the contradictions in his case into an argument for it; and said that the man's cloak being too long for him proved that he never walked on the ground like an ordinary mortal. But he looked at me very hard while he said that; and something told me that he was at that moment trying a very big bluff.'

Dr Boyne looked thoughtful. 'Had you discovered the truth by then?' he asked. 'There is something very queer and close to the nerves, I think, about notions affecting identity. I don't know whether it would be more weird to get a guess like that swiftly or slowly. I wonder when you suspected and when you were sure.'

'I think I really suspected when I telephoned to you,' replied his friend. 'And it was nothing more than the red light from the closed door brightening and darkening on the carpet. It looked like a splash of blood that grew vivid as it cried for vegeance. Why should it change like that? I knew the sun had not come out; it could only be because the second door behind it had been opened and shut on the garden. But if he had gone out and seen his enemy then, he would have raised the alarm then; and it was some time afterwards that the fracas occurred. I began to feel he had gone out to do something . . . to prepare something . . . but as to when I was certain, that is a different matter. I knew that right at the end he was trying to hypnotize me, to master me by the black art of eyes like talismans and a voice like an incantation. That's what he used to do with old Aylmer, no doubt. But it wasn't only the way he said it, it was what he said. It was the religion and philosophy of it.'

'I'm afraid I'm a practical man,' said the doctor with gruff humour, 'and I don't bother much about religion and philosophy.'

'You'll never be a practical man till you do,' said Father Brown. 'Look here, doctor; you know me pretty well; I think you know I'm not a bigot. You know I know there are all sorts in all religions; good men in bad ones and bad men in good ones. But there's just one little fact I've learned simply as a practical man, an entirely practical point, that I've picked up by experience, like the tricks of an animal or the trade-mark of a good wine. I've scarcely ever met a criminal who philosophized at all, who didn't philosophize along those lines of orientalism and recurrence and reincarnation, and the wheel of destiny and the serpent biting its own tail. I have found merely in practice that there is a curse on the servants of that serpent; on their belly shall they go and the dust shall they eat; and there was never a blackguard or a profligate born who could not talk that sort of spirituality. It may not be like that in its real religious origins; but here in our working world it is the religion of rascals; and I knew it was a rascal who was speaking.'

'Why,' said Boyne, 'I should have thought that a rascal could pretty well profess any religion he chose.'

'Yes,' assented the other; 'he could profess any religion; that is he could pretend to any religion, if it was all a pretence. If it was mere mechanical hypocrisy and nothing else, no doubt it could be done by a mere mechanical hypocrite. Any sort of mask can be put on any sort of face. Anybody can learn certain phrases or state verbally that he holds certain views. I can go out into the street and state that I am a Wesleyan Methodist or a Sandemanian, though I fear in no very convincing accent. But we are talking about an artist; and for the enjoyment of the artist the mask must be to some extent moulded on the face. What he makes outside him must correspond to something inside him; he can only make his effects out of some of the materials of his soul. I suppose he could have said he was a Wesleyan Methodist; but he could never be an eloquent Methodist as he can be an eloquent mystic and fatalist. I am talking of the sort of ideal such a man thinks of if he really tries to be idealistic. It was his whole game with me to be as idealistic as possible; and whenever that is attempted by that sort of man, you will generally find it is that sort of ideal. That sort of man may be dripping with gore; but he will always be able to tell you quite sincerely that Buddhism is better than Christianity. Nay, he will tell you quite sincerely that Buddhism is more Christian than Christianity. That alone is enough to throw a hideous and ghastly ray of light on his notion of Christianity.'

'Upon my soul,' said the doctor, laughing, 'I can't make out whether you're denouncing or defending him.'

'It isn't defending a man to say he is a genius,' said Father Brown. 'Far from it. And it is simply a psychological fact that an artist will betray himself by some sort of sincerity. Leonardo da Vinci cannot draw as if he couldn't draw. Even if he tried, it will always be a strong parody of a weak thing. This man would have made something much too fearful and wonderful out of the Wesleyan Methodist.'

When the priest went forth again and set his face homeward, the cold had grown more intense and yet was somehow intoxicating. The trees stood up like silver candelabra of some incredible cold candlemas of purification. It was a piercing cold, like that silver sword of pure pain that once pierced the very heart of purity. But it was not a killing cold, save in the sense of seeming to kill all the mortal obstructions to our immortal and immeasurable vitality. The pale green sky of twilight, with one star like the star of Bethlehem, seemed by some strange contradiction to be a cavern of clarity. It was as if there could be a green furnace of cold which wakened all things to life like warmth, and that the deeper they went into those cold crystalline colours the more were they light like winged creatures and clear like coloured glass. It tingled with truth and it divided truth from error with a blade like ice; but all that was left had never felt so much alive. It was as if all joy were a jewel in the heart of an iceberg. The priest hardly understood his own mood as he advanced deeper and deeper into the green gloaming, drinking deeper and deeper draughts of that virginal vivacity of the air. Some forgotten muddle and morbidity seemed to be left behind, or wiped out as the snow had painted out the footprints of the man of blood. As he shuffled homewards through the snow, he muttered to himself: 'And yet he is right enough about there being a white magic, if he only knows where to look for it.'

SEVEN

The Doom of the Darnaways

Two landscape-painters stood looking at one landscape, which was was also a seascape, and both were curiously impressed by it, though their impressions were not exactly the same. To one of them, who was a rising artist from London, it was new as well as strange. To the other, who was a local artist but with something more than a local celebrity, it was better known; but perhaps all the more strange for what he knew of it.

In terms of tone and form, as these men saw it, it was a stretch of sands against a stretch of sunset, the whole scene lying in strips of sombre colour, dead green and bronze and brown and a drab that was not merely dull but in that gloaming in some way more mysterious than gold. All that broke these level lines was a long building which ran out from the fields into the sands of the sea, so that its fringe of dreary weeds and rushes seemed almost to meet the seaweed. But its most singular feature was that the upper part of it had the ragged outlines of a ruin, pierced by so many wide windows and large rents as to be a mere dark skeleton against the dying light; while the lower bulk of the building had hardly any windows at all, most of them being blind and bricked up and their outlines only faintly traceable in the twilight. But one window at least was still a window; and it seemed strangest of all that it showed a light.

'Who on earth can live in that old shell?' exclaimed the Londoner, who was a big, bohemian-looking man, young but with a shaggy red beard that made him look older; Chelsea knew him familiarly as Harry Payne.

'Ghosts, you might suppose,' replied his friend Martin Wood. 'Well, the people who live there really are rather like ghosts.'

It was perhaps rather a paradox that the London artist seemed almost bucolic in his boisterous freshness and wonder, while the local artist seemed a more shrewd and experienced person, regarding him with mature and amiable amusement; indeed, the latter was altogether a quieter and more conventional figure, wearing darker clothes and with his square and stolid face clean-shaven.

'It is only a sign of the times, of course,' he went on, 'or of the passing of old times and old families with them. The last of the great Darnaways live in that house, and not many of the new poor are as poor as they are. They can't even afford to make their own top-storey habitable; but have to live in the lower rooms of a ruin, like bats and owls. Yet they have family portraits that go back to the Wars of the Roses and the first portrait-painting in England, and very fine some of them are; I happen to know, because they asked for my professional advice in overhauling them. There's one of them especially, and one of the earliest, but it's so good that it gives you the creeps.'

'The whole place gives you the creeps, I should think by the look of it,' replied Payne.

'Well,' said his friend, 'to tell you the truth, it does.'

The silence that followed was stirred by a faint rustle among the rushes by the moat; and it gave them, rationally enough, a slight nervous start when a dark figure brushed along the bank, moving rapidly and almost like a startled bird. But it was only a man walking briskly with a black bag in his hand: a man with a long sallow face and sharp eyes that glanced at the London stranger in a slightly darkling and suspicious manner.

'It's only Dr Barnet,' said Wood with a sort of relief. 'Good evening, Doctor. Are you going up to the house? I hope nobody's ill.'

'Everybody's always ill in a place like that,' growled the doctor; 'only sometimes they're too ill to know it. The very air of the place is a blight and a pestilence. I don't envy the young man from Australia.'

'And who,' asked Payne abruptly and rather absently, 'may the young man from Australia be?'

'Ah!' snorted the doctor; 'hasn't your friend told you about him? As a matter of fact I believe he is arriving today. Quite a romance in the old style of melodrama: the heir back from the colonies to his ruined castle, all complete even down to an old family compact for his marrying the lady watching in the ivied tower. Queer old stuff, isn't it? but it really happens sometimes. He's even got a little money, which is the only bright spot there ever was in this business.'

'What does Miss Darnaway herself, in her ivied tower, think of the business?' asked Martin Wood dryly.

'What she thinks of everything else by this time,' replied the doctor. 'They don't think in this weedy old den of superstitions, they only dream and drift. I think she accepts the family contract and the colonial husband as part of the Doom of the Darnaways, don't you know. I really think that if he turned out to be a hump-backed Negro with one eye and a homicidal mania, she would only think it added a finishing touch and fitted in with the twilight scenery.'

'You're not giving my friend from London a very lively picture of my friends in the country,' said Wood, laughing. 'I had intended taking him there to call; no artist ought to miss those Darnaway portraits if he gets the chance. But perhaps I'd better postpone it if they're in the middle of the Australian invasion.'

'Oh, do go in and see them, for the Lord's sake,' said Dr Barnet warmly. 'Anything that will brighten their blighted lives will make my task easier. It will need a good many colonial cousins to cheer things up, I should think; and the more the merrier. Come, I'll take you in myself.'

As they drew nearer to the house it was seen to be isolated like an island in a moat of brackish water which they crossed by a bridge. On the other side spread a fairly wide stony floor or embankment with great cracks across it, in which little tufts of weed and thorn sprouted here and there. This rock platform looked large and bare in the grey twilight, and Payne could hardly have believed that such a corner of space could have contained so much of the soul of a wilderness. This platform only jutted out on one side, like a giant door-step and beyond it was the door; a very low-browed Tudor archway standing open, but dark like a cave.

When the brisk doctor led them inside without ceremony, Payne had, as it were, another shock of depression. He could have expected to find himself mounting to a very ruinous tower, by very narrow winding staircases; but in this case the first steps into the house were actually steps downwards. They went down several short and broken stairways into large twilit rooms which, but for their lines of dark pictures and dusty bookshelves, might have been the traditional dungeons beneath the castle moat. Here and there a candle in an old candlestick lit up some dusty accidental detail of a dead elegance; but the visitor was not so much impressed or depressed by this artificial light as by the one pale gleam of natural light. As he passed down the long room he saw the only window in that wall – a curious low oval window of a late-seventeenth-century fashion. But the strange thing about it was that it did not look out directly on any space of sky but only on a reflection of sky; a pale strip of daylight merely mirrored in the moat, under the hanging shadow of the bank. Payne had a memory of the Lady of Shallot who never saw the world outside except in a mirror. The lady of this Shallot not only in some sense saw the world in a mirror, but even saw the world upside-down.

'It's as if the house of Darnaway were falling literally as well as metaphorically,' said Wood in a low voice; 'as if it were sinking slowly into a swamp or a quicksand, until the sea goes over it like a green roof.'

Even the sturdy Dr Barnet started a little at the silent approach of the figure that came to receive them. Indeed, the room was so silent that they were all startled to realize that it was not empty. There were three people in it when they entered: three dim figures motionless in the dim room; all three dressed in black and looking like dark shadows. As the foremost figure drew nearer the grey light from the window, he showed a face that looked almost as grey as its frame of hair. This was old Vine, the steward, long left *in loco parentis* since the death of that eccentric parent, the last Lord Darnaway. He would have been a handsome old man if he had had no teeth. As it was, he had one which showed every now and then and gave him a rather sinister appearance. He received the doctor and his friends with a fine courtesy and escorted them to where the other two figures in black were seated. One of them seemed to Payne to give another appropriate touch

of gloomy antiquity to the castle by the mere fact of being a
Roman Catholic priest, who might have come out of a priest's
hole in the dark old days. Payne could imagine him muttering
prayers or telling beads, or tolling bells or doing a number of
indistinct and melancholy things in that melancholy place. Just
then he might be supposed to have been giving religious consolation to the lady; but it could hardly be supposed that the
consolation was very consoling, or at any rate that it was very
cheering. For the rest, the priest was personally insignificant
enough, with plain and rather expressionless features; but the
lady was a very different matter. Her face was very far from being
plain or insignificant; it stood out from the darkness of her dress
and hair and background with a pallor that was almost awful,
but a beauty that was almost awfully alive. Payne looked at it
as long as he dared; and he was to look at it a good deal longer
before he died.

Wood merely exchanged with his friends such pleasant and
polite phrases as would lead up to his purpose of revisiting the
portraits. He apologized for calling on the day which he heard
was to be one of family welcome; but he was soon convinced
that the family was rather mildly relieved to have visitors to
distract them or break the shock. He did not hesitate, therefore,
to lead Payne through the central reception-room into the library
beyond, where hung the portrait, for there was one which he was
especially bent on showing, not only as a picture but almost as
a puzzle. The little priest trudged along with them; he seemed to
know something about old pictures as well as about old prayers.

'I'm rather proud of having spotted this,' said Wood. 'I believe
it's a Holbein. If it isn't, there was somebody living in Holbein's
time who was as great as Holbein.'

It was a portrait in the hard but sincere and living fashion of
the period, representing a man clad in black trimmed with gold
and fur, with a heavy, full, rather pale face but watchful eyes.

'What a pity art couldn't have stopped for ever at just that
transition stage,' cried Wood, 'and never transitioned any more.
Don't you see it's just realistic enough to be real? Don't you see
the face speaks all the more because it stands out from a rather

stiffer framework of less essential things? And the eyes are even more real than the face. On my soul, I think the eyes are too real for the face! It's just as if those sly, quick eyeballs were protruding out of a great pale mask.'

'The stiffness extends to the figure a little, I think,' said Payne. 'They hadn't quite mastered anatomy when medievalism ended, at least in the north. That left leg looks to me a good deal out of drawing.'

'I'm not so sure,' replied Wood quietly. 'Those fellows who painted just when realism began to be done, and before it began to be overdone, were often more realistic than we think. They put real details of portraiture into things that are thought merely conventional. You might say this fellow's eyebrows or eye-sockets are a little lop-sided; but I bet if you knew him you'd find that one of his eyebrows did really stick up more than the other. And I shouldn't wonder if he was lame or something, and that black leg was meant to be crooked.'

'What an old devil he looks!' burst out Payne suddenly. 'I trust his reverence will excuse my language.'

'I believe in the devil, thank you,' said the priest with an inscrutable face. 'Curiously enough there was a legend that the devil was lame.'

'I say,' protested Payne, 'you can't really mean that he was the devil; but who the devil was he?'

'He was the Lord Darnaway under Henry VII and Henry VIII,' replied his companion. 'But there are curious legends about him, too; one of them is referred to in that inscription round the frame, and further developed in some notes left by somebody in a book I found here. They are both rather curious reading.'

Payne leaned forward, craning his head so as to follow the archaic inscription round the frame. Leaving out the antiquated lettering and spelling, it seemed to be a sort of rhyme running somewhat thus:

> *In the seventh heir I shall return:*
> *In the seventh hour I shall depart:*
> *None in that hour shall hold my hand:*
> *And woe to her that holds my heart.*

'It sounds creepy somehow,' said Payne, 'but that may be partly because I don't understand a word of it.'

'It's pretty creepy even when you do,' said Wood in a low voice. 'The record made at a later date, in the old book I found, is all about how this beauty deliberately killed himself in such a way that his wife was executed for his murder. Another note commemorates a later tragedy, seven successions later – under the Georges – in which another Darnaway committed suicide, having first thoughtfully left poison in his wife's wine. It's said that both suicides took place at seven in the evening. I suppose the inference is that he does really return with every seventh inheritor and makes things unpleasant, as the rhyme suggests, for any lady unwise enough to marry him.'

'On that argument,' replied Payne, 'it would be a trifle uncomfortable for the next seventh gentleman.'

Wood's voice was lower still as he said:

'The new heir will be the seventh.'

Harry Payne suddenly heaved up his great chest and shoulders like a man flinging off a burden.

'What crazy stuff are we all talking?' he cried. 'We're all educated men in an enlightened age, I suppose. Before I came into this damned dank atmosphere I'd never have believed I should be talking of such things, except to laugh at them.'

'You are right,' said Wood. 'If you lived long enough in this underground palace you'd begin to feel differently about things. I've begun to feel very curiously about that picture, having had so much to do with handling and hanging it. It sometimes seems to me that the painted face is more alive than the dead faces of the people living here; that it is a sort of talisman or magnet: that it commands the elements and draws out the destinies of men and things. I suppose you would call it very fanciful.'

'What is that noise?' cried Payne suddenly.

They all listened, and there seemed to be no noise except the dull boom of the distant sea; then they began to have the sense of something mingling with it; something like a voice calling through the sound of the surf, dulled by it at first, but coming nearer and nearer. The next moment they were certain: someone was shouting outside in the dusk.

Payne turned to the low window behind him and bent to look out. It was the window from which nothing could be seen except the moat with its reflection of bank and sky. But that inverted vision was not the same that he had seen before. From the hanging shadow of the bank in the water depended two dark shadows reflected from the feet and legs of a figure standing above upon the bank. Through that limited aperture they could see nothing but the two legs black against the reflection of a pale and livid sunset. But somehow that very fact of the head being invisible, as if in the clouds, gave something dreadful to the sound that followed; the voice of a man crying aloud what they could not properly hear or understand. Payne especially was peering out of the little window with an altered face, and he spoke with an altered voice:

'How queerly he's standing!'

'No, no,' said Wood, in a sort of soothing whisper. 'Things often look like that in reflection. It's the wavering of the water that makes you think that.'

'Think what?' asked the priest shortly.

'That his left leg is crooked,' said Wood.

Payne had thought of the oval window as a sort of mystical mirror; and it seemed to him that there were in it other inscrutable images of doom. There was something else beside the figure that he did not understand; three thinner legs showing in dark lines against the light, as if some monstrous three-legged spider or bird were standing beside the stranger. Then he had the less crazy thought of a tripod like that of the heathen oracles; and the next moment the thing had vanished and the legs of the human figure passed out of the picture.

He turned to meet the pale face of old Vine, the steward, with his mouth open, eager to speak, and his single tooth showing.

'He has come,' he said. 'The boat arrived from Australia this morning.'

Even as they went back out of the library into the central salon they heard the footsteps of the newcomer clattering down the

entrance steps, with various items of light luggage trailed behind
him. When Payne saw one of them, he laughed with a reaction
of relief. His tripod was nothing but the telescopic legs of a
portable camera, easily packed and unpacked; and the man who
was carrying it seemed so far to take on equally solid and normal
qualities. He was dressed in dark clothes, but of a careless and
holiday sort; his shirt was of grey flannel, and his boots echoed
uncompromisingly enough in those still chambers. As he strode
forward to greet his new circle his stride had scarcely more
than the suggestion of a limp. But Payne and his companions
were looking at his face, and could scarcely take their eyes
from it.

He evidently felt there was something curious and uncomfortable about his reception; but they could have sworn that he did
not himself know the cause of it. The lady, supposed to be in some
sense already betrothed to him, was certainly beautiful enough to
attract him; but she evidently also frightened him. The old
steward brought him a sort of feudal homage, yet treated him as
if he were the family ghost. The priest still looked at him with a
face which was quite indecipherable, and therefore perhaps all the
more unnerving. A new sort of irony, more like the Greek irony,
began to pass over Payne's mind. He had dreamed of the stranger
as a devil, but it seemed almost worse that he was an unconscious
destiny. He seemed to march towards crime with the monstrous
innocence of Oedipus. He had approached the family mansion
in so blindly buoyant a spirit as to have set up his camera to
photograph his first sight of it; and even the camera had taken
on the semblance of the tripod of a tragic pythoness.

Payne was surprised, when taking his leave a little while after,
at something which showed that the Australian was already less
unconscious of his surroundings. He said in a low voice:

'Don't go . . . or come again soon. You look like a human
being. This place fairly gives me the jumps.'

When Payne emerged out of those almost subterranean halls
and came into the night air and the smell of the sea, he felt as if
he had come out of that underworld of dreams in which events
tumble on top of each other in a way at once unrestful and unreal.

The arrival of the strange relative had been somehow unsatisfying and, as it were, unconvincing. The doubling of the same face in the old portrait and the new arrival troubled him like a two-headed monster. And yet it was not altogether a nightmare; nor was it that face, perhaps, that he saw most vividly.

'Did you say?' he asked of the doctor, as they strode together across the striped dark sands by the darkening sea; 'did you say that young man was betrothed to Miss Darnaway by a family compact or something? Sounds rather like a novel.'

'But an historical novel,' answered Dr Barnet. 'The Darnaways all went to sleep a few centuries ago, when things were really done that we only read of in romances. Yes; I believe there's some family tradition by which second or third cousins always marry when they stand in a certain relation of age, in order to unite the property. A damned silly tradition, I should say; and if they often married in and in, in that fashion, it may account on principles of heredity for their having gone so rotten.'

'I should hardly say,' answered Payne a little stiffly, 'that they had all gone rotten.'

'Well,' replied the doctor, 'the young man doesn't look rotten, of course, though he's certainly lame.'

'The young man!' cried Payne, who was suddenly and unreasonably angry. 'Well, if you think the young lady looks rotten, I think it's you who have rotten taste.'

The doctor's face grew dark and bitter. 'I fancy I know more about it than you do,' he snapped.

They completed the walk in silence, each feeling that he had been irrationally rude and had suffered equally irrational rudeness; and Payne was left to brood alone on the matter, for his friend Wood had remained behind to attend to some of his business in connexion with the pictures.

Payne took very full advantage of the invitation extended by the colonial cousin, who wanted somebody to cheer him up. During the next few weeks he saw a good deal of the dark interior of the Darnaway home; though it might be said that he did not confine himself entirely to cheering up the colonial cousin. The lady's melancholy was of longer standing and perhaps needed more lifting; anyhow, he showed a laborious readiness to lift it. He was not without a conscience, however, and the situation made him doubtful and uncomfortable. Weeks went by and nobody could discover from the demeanour of the new Darnaway whether he considered himself engaged according to the old compact or no. He went mooning about the dark galleries and stood staring vacantly at the dark and sinister picture. The shades of that prison-house were certainly beginning to close on him, and there was little of his Australian assurance left. But Payne could discover nothing upon the point that concerned him most. Once he attempted to confide in his friend Martin Wood, as he was pottering about in his capacity of picture-hanger; but even out of him he got very little satisfaction.

'It seems to me you can't butt in,' said Wood shortly, 'because of the engagement.'

'Of course I shan't butt in if there is an engagement,' retorted his friend; 'but is there? I haven't said a word to her of course; but I've seen enough of her to be pretty certain she doesn't think there is, even if she thinks there may be. He doesn't say there is, or even hint that there ought to be. It seems to me this shilly-shallying is rather unfair on everybody.'

'Especially on you, I suppose,' said Wood a little harshly. 'But if you ask me, I'll tell you what I think – I think he's afraid.'

'Afraid of being refused?' asked Payne.

'No; afraid of being accepted,' answered the other. 'Don't bite my head off – I don't mean afraid of the lady. I mean afraid of the picture.'

'Afraid of the picture!' repeated Payne.

'I mean afraid of the curse,' said Wood. 'Don't you remember the rhyme about the Darnaway doom falling on him and her.'

'Yes, but look here,' cried Payne; 'even the Darnaway doom can't have it both ways. You tell me first that I mustn't have my own way because of the compact, and then that the compact mustn't have its own way because of the curse. But if the curse can destroy the compact, why should she be tied to the compact?

If they're frightened of marrying each other, they're free to marry anybody else, and there's an end of it. Why should I suffer for the observance of something they don't propose to observe? It seems to me your position is very unreasonable.'

'Of course it's all a tangle,' said Wood rather crossly, and went on hammering at the frame of a canvas.

Suddenly, one morning, the new heir broke his long and baffling silence. He did it in a curious fashion, a little crude, as was his way, but with an obvious anxiety to do the right thing. He asked frankly for advice, not of this or that individual as Payne had done, but collectively as of a crowd. When he did speak he threw himself on the whole company like a statesman going to the country. He called it 'a show-down'. Fortunately the lady was not included in this large gesture; and Payne shuddered when he thought of her feelings. But the Australian was quite honest; he thought the natural thing was to ask for help and for information, calling a sort of family council at which he put his cards on the table. It might be said that he flung down his cards on the table, for he did it with a rather desperate air, like one who had been harassed for days and nights by the increasing pressure of a problem. In that short time the shadows of that place of low windows and sinking pavements had curiously changed him, and increased a certain resemblance that crept through all their memories.

The five men, including the doctor, were sitting round a table; and Payne was idly reflecting that his own light tweeds and red hair must be the only colours in the room, for the priest and the steward were in black, and Wood and Darnaway habitually wore dark grey suits that looked almost like black. Perhaps this incongruity had been what the young man had meant by calling him a human being. At that moment the young man himself turned abruptly in his chair and began to talk. A moment after the dazed artist knew that he was talking about the most tremendous thing in the world.

'Is there anything in it?' he was saying. 'That is what I've come to asking myself till I'm nearly crazy. I'd never have believed I should come to thinking of such things; but I think of the portrait and the rhyme and the coincidences or whatever you call them, and I go cold. Is there anything in it? Is there any Doom of the Darnaways or only a damned queer accident? Have I got a right to marry, or shall I bring something big and black out of the sky, that I know nothing about, on myself and somebody else?'

His rolling eye had roamed round the table and rested on the plain face of the priest, to whom he now seemed to be speaking. Payne's submerged practicality rose in protest against the problem of superstition being brought before that supremely superstitious tribunal. He was sitting next to Darnaway and struck in before the priest could answer.

'Well, the coincidences are curious, I admit,' he said, rather forcing a note of cheerfulness; 'but surely we –' and then he stopped as if he had been struck by lightning. For Darnaway had turned his head sharply over his shoulder at the interruption, and with the movement, his left eyebrow jerked up far above its fellow and for an instant the face of the portrait glared at him with a ghastly exaggeration of exactitude. The rest saw it; and all had the air of having been dazzled by an instant of light. The old steward gave a hollow groan.

'It is no good,' he said hoarsely; 'we are dealing with something too terrible.'

'Yes,' assented the priest in a low voice, 'we are dealing with something terrible; with the most terrible thing I know, and the name of it is nonsense.'

'What did you say?' said Darnaway, still looking towards him.

'I said nonsense,' repeated the priest. 'I have not said anything in particular up to now, for it was none of my business; I was only taking temporary duty in the neighbourhood and Miss Darnaway wanted to see me. But since you're asking me personally and point-blank, why, it's easy enough to answer. Of course there's no Doom of the Darnaways to prevent your marrying anybody you have any decent reason for marrying. A man isn't fated to fall into the smallest venial sin, let alone into crimes like suicide and murder. You can't be made to do wicked things against your will because your name is Darnaway, any more than I can because my name is Brown. The Doom of the Browns,' he added with relish – 'the Weird of the Browns would sound even better.'

'And you of all people,' repeated the Australian, staring, 'tell me to think like that about it.'

'I tell you to think about something else,' replied the priest cheerfully. 'What has become of the rising art of photography? How is the camera getting on? I know it's rather dark downstairs, but those hollow arches on the floor above could easily be turned into a first-rate photographic studio. A few workmen could fit it out with a glass roof in no time.'

'Really,' protested Martin Wood, 'I do think you should be the last man in the world to tinker about with those beautiful Gothic arches, which are about the best work your own religion has ever done in the world. I should have thought you'd have had some feeling for that sort of art; but I can't see why you should be so uncommonly keen on photography.'

'I'm uncommonly keen on daylight,' answered Father Brown, 'especially in this dingy business; and photography has the virtue of depending on daylight. And if you don't know that I would grind all the Gothic arches in the world to powder to save the sanity of a single human soul, you don't know so much about my religion as you think you do.'

The young Australian had sprung to his feet like a man rejuvenated. 'By George! that's the talk,' he cried; 'though I never thought to hear it from that quarter. I'll tell you what, reverend sir, I'll do something that will show I haven't lost my courage after all.'

The old steward was still looking at him with quaking watchfulness, as if he felt something fey about the young man's defiance. 'Oh,' he cried, 'what are you going to do now?'

'I am going to photograph the portrait,' replied Darnaway.

Yet it was barely a week afterwards that the storm of the catastrophe seemed to stoop out of the sky, darkening that sun of sanity to which the priest had appealed in vain, and plunging the mansion once more in the darkness of the Darnaway doom. It had been easy enough to fit up the new studio; and seen from inside it looked very like any other such studio, empty except for the fullness of the white light. A man coming from the gloomy rooms below had more than normally the sense of stepping into a more than modern brilliancy, as blank as the future. At the suggestion of Wood, who knew the castle well and had got over his first aesthetic grumblings, a small room remaining intact in the upper ruins was easily turned into a dark room, into which Darnaway went out of the white daylight to grope by the crimson gleams of a red lamp. Wood said, laughing, that the red lamp had reconciled him to the vandalism; as that bloodshot darkness was as romantic as an alchemist's cave.

Darnaway had risen at daybreak on the day that he meant to photograph the mysterious portrait, and had it carried up from the library by the single corkscrew staircase that connected the two floors. There he had set it up in the wide white daylight on a sort of easel and planted his photographic tripod in front of it. He said he was anxious to send a reproduction of it to a great antiquary who had written on the antiquities of the house; but the others knew that this was an excuse covering much deeper things. It was, if not exactly a spiritual duel between Darnaway and the demoniac picture, at least a duel between Darnaway and his own doubts. He wanted to bring the daylight of photography face to face with that dark masterpiece of painting; and to see whether the sunshine of the new art would not drive out the shadows of the old.

Perhaps this was why he preferred to do it by himself, even if some of the details seemed to take longer and involve more than normal delay. Anyhow, he rather discouraged the few who visited his studio during the day of the experiment, and who found him focusing and fussing about in a very isolated and impenetrable fashion. The steward had left a meal for him, as he refused to come down; the old gentleman also returned some hours afterwards and found the meal more or less normally disposed of; but when he brought it he got no more gratitude than a grunt. Payne went up once to see how he was getting on, but finding the photographer disinclined for conversation came down again. Father Brown had wandered that way in an unobtrusive style to take Darnaway a letter from the expert to whom the photograph was to be sent. But he left the letter on a tray, and whatever he thought of that great glasshouse full of daylight and devotion to a hobby, a world he had himself in some sense created, he kept it to himself and came down. He had reason to remember very soon that he was the last to come down the solitary staircase connecting the floors, leaving a lonely man and an empty room behind him. The others were standing in the salon that led into the library, just under the great black ebony clock that looked like a titanic coffin.

'How was Darnaway getting on,' asked Payne, a little later, 'when you last went up?'

The priest passed a hand over his forehead. 'Don't tell me I'm getting psychic,' he said with a sad smile. 'I believe I'm quite dazzled with daylight up in that room and couldn't see things straight. Honestly, I felt for a flash as if there were something uncanny about Darnaway's figure standing before that portrait.'

'Oh, that's the lame leg,' said Barnet promptly. 'We know all about that.'

'Do you know,' said Payne abruptly, but lowering his voice, 'I don't think we do know all about it or anything about it. What's the matter with his leg? What was the matter with his ancestor's leg?'

'Oh, there's something about that in the book I was reading in there, in the family archives,' said Wood; 'I'll fetch it for you.' And he stepped into the library just beyond.

'I think,' said Father Brown quietly, 'Mr Payne must have some particular reason for asking that.'

'I may as well blurt it out once and for all,' said Payne, but in a yet lower voice. 'After all, there is a rational explanation. A man from anywhere might have made up to look like the portrait. What do we know about Darnaway? He is behaving rather oddly –'

The others were staring at him in a rather startled fashion; but the priest seemed to take it very calmly.

'I don't think the old portrait's ever been photographed,' he said. 'That's why he wants to do it. I don't think there's anything odd about that.'

'Quite an ordinary state of things, in fact,' said Wood with a smile; he had just returned with the book in his hand. And even as he spoke there was a stir in the clockwork of the great dark clock behind him and successive strokes thrilled through the room up to the number of seven. With the last stroke there came a crash from the floor above that shook the house like a thunderbolt; and Father Brown was already two steps up the winding staircase before the sound had ceased.

'My God!' cried Payne involuntarily; 'he is alone up there.'

'Yes,' said Father Brown without turning, as he vanished up the stairway. 'We shall find him alone.'

When the rest recovered from their first paralysis and ran helter-skelter up the stone steps and found their way to the new studio, it was true in that sense that they found him alone. They found him lying in a wreck of his tall camera, with its long splintered legs standing out grotesquely at three different angles; and Darnaway had fallen on top of it with one black crooked leg lying at a fourth angle along the floor. For the moment the dark heap looked as if he were entangled with some huge and horrible spider. Little more than a glance and a touch were needed to tell them that he was dead. Only the portrait stood untouched upon the easel, and one could fancy the smiling eyes shone.

An hour afterwards Father Brown in helping to calm the confusion of the stricken household, came upon the old steward muttering almost as mechanically as the clock had ticked and struck the terrible hour. Almost without hearing them, he knew what the muttered words must be.

> *In the seventh heir I shall return*
> *In the seventh hour I shall depart.*

As he was about to say something soothing, the old man seemed suddenly to start awake and stiffen into anger; his mutterings changed to a fierce cry.

'You!' he cried; 'you and your daylight! Even you won't say now there is no Doom for the Darnaways.'

'My opinion about that is unchanged,' said Father Brown mildly.

163

Then after a pause he added: 'I hope you will observe poor Darnaway's last wish, and see the photograph is sent off.'

'The photograph!' cried the doctor sharply. 'What's the good of that? As a matter of fact, it's rather curious; but there isn't any photograph. It seems he never took it after all, after pottering about all day.'

Father Brown swung round sharply. 'Then take it yourselves,' he said. 'Poor Darnaway was perfectly right. It's most important that the photograph should be taken.'

As all the visitors, the doctor, the priest, and the two artists trailed away in a black and dismal procession across the brown and yellow sands, they were at first more or less silent, rather as if they had been stunned. And certainly there had been something like a crack of thunder in a clear sky about the fulfilment of that forgotten superstition at the very time when they had most forgotten it; when the doctor and the priest had both filled their minds with rationalism as the photographer had filled his rooms with daylight. They might be as rationalistic as they liked; but in broad daylight the seventh heir had returned, and in broad daylight at the seventh hour he had perished.

'I'm afraid everybody will always believe in the Darnaway superstition now,' said Martin Wood.

''I know one who won't,' said the doctor sharply. 'Why should I indulge in superstition because somebody else indulges in suicide?'

'You think poor Mr Darnaway committed suicide?' asked the priest.

'I'm sure he committed suicide,' replied the doctor.

'It is possible,' agreed the other.

'He was quite alone up there, and he had a whole drug-store of poisons in the dark room. Besides, it's just the sort of thing that Darnaways do.'

'You don't think there's anything in the fulfilment of the family curse?'

'Yes,' said the doctor; 'I believe in one family curse, and that is the family constitution. I told you it was heredity, and they are all half mad. If you stagnate and breed in and brood in your own swamp like that, you're bound to degenerate whether you like it or not. The laws of heredity can't be dodged; the truths of science can't be denied. The minds of the Darnaways are falling to pieces, as their blighted old sticks and stones are falling to pieces, eaten away by the sea and the salt air. Suicide – of course he committed suicide; I dare say all the rest will commit suicide. Perhaps the best thing they could do.'

As the man of science spoke there sprang suddenly and with startling clearness into Payne's memory the face of the daughter of the Darnaways, a tragic mask pale against an unfathomable blackness, but itself of a blinding and more than mortal beauty. He opened his mouth to speak and found himself speechless.

'I see,' said Father Brown to the doctor; 'so you do believe in the superstition after all?'

'What do you mean – believe in the superstition? I believe in the suicide as a matter of scientific necessity.'

'Well,' replied the priest, 'I don't see a pin to choose between your scientific superstition and the other magical superstition. They both seem to end in turning people into paralytics, who can't move their own legs or arms or save their own lives or souls. The rhyme said it was the Doom of the Darnaways to be killed, and the scientific textbook says it is the Doom of the Darnaways to kill themselves. Both ways they seem to be slaves.'

'But I thought you said you believed in rational views of these things,' said Dr Barnet. 'Don't you believe in heredity?'

'I said I believed in daylight,' replied the priest in a loud and clear voice, 'and I won't choose between two tunnels of subterranean superstition that both end in the dark. And the proof of it is this: that you are all entirely in the dark about what really happened in that house.'

'Do you mean about the suicide?' asked Payne.

'I mean about the murder,' said Father Brown; and his voice, though only slightly lifted to a louder note, seemed somehow to resound over the whole shore. 'It was murder; but murder is of the will, which God made free.'

What the other said at the moment in answer to it Payne never knew. For the word had a rather curious effect on him; stirring him like the blast of a trumpet and yet bringing him to a halt. He stood still in the middle of the sandy waste and let the others go on in front of him; he felt the blood crawling through all his veins and the sensation that is called the hair standing on end; and yet he felt a new and unnatural happiness. A psychological process too quick and too complicated for himself to follow had already reached a conclusion that he could not analyse; but the conclusion was one of relief. After standing still for a moment he turned and went back slowly across the sands to the house of the Darnaways.

He crossed the moat with a stride that shook the bridge, descended the stairs and traversed the long rooms with a resounding tread, till he came to the place where Adelaide Darnaway sat haloed with the low light of the oval window, almost like some forgotten saint left behind in the land of death. She looked up, and an expression of wonder made her face yet more wonderful.

'What is it?' she said. 'Why have you come back?'

'I have come for the Sleeping Beauty,' he said in a tone that had the resonance of a laugh. 'This old house went to sleep long ago, as the doctor said; but it is silly for you to pretend to be old. Come up into the daylight and hear the truth. I have brought you a word; it is a terrible word, but it breaks the spell of your captivity.'

She did not understand a word he said, but something made her rise and let him lead her down the long hall and up the stairs and out under the evening sky. The ruins of a dead garden stretched towards the sea, and an old fountain with the figure of a triton, green with rust, remained poised there, pouring nothing out of a dried horn into an empty basin. He had often seen that desolate outline against the evening sky as he passed, and it had seemed to him a type of fallen fortunes in more ways than one. Before long, doubtless, those hollow fonts would be filled, but it would be with the pale green bitter waters of the sea and the flowers would be drowned and strangled in seaweed. So, he had told himself, the daughter of the Darnaways might indeed be wedded; but she would be wedded to death and a doom as deaf and ruthless as the sea. But now he laid a hand on the bronze triton that was like the hand of a giant, and shook it as if he meant to hurl it over like an idol or an evil god of the garden.

'What do you mean?' she asked steadily. 'What is this word that will set us free?'

'The word is murder,' he said, 'and the freedom it brings is as fresh as the flowers of spring. No; I do not mean I have murdered anybody. But the fact that anybody can be murdered is itself good news, after the evil dreams you have been living in. Don't you understand? In that dream of yours everything that happened to you came from inside you; the Doom of the Darnaways was stored up in the Darnaways; it unfolded itself like a horrible flower. There was no escape even by happy accident; it was all inevitable; whether it was Vine and his old-wives' tales, or Barnet and his new-fangled heredity. But this man who died was not the victim of a magic curse or an inherited madness. He was murdered; and for us that murder is simply an accident; yes, *requiescat in pace:* but a happy accident. It is a ray of daylight, because it comes from outside.'

She suddenly smiled. 'Yes, I believe I understand. I suppose you are talking like a lunatic, but I understand. But who murdered him?'

'I do not know,' he answered calmly, 'but Father Brown knows. And as Father Brown says, murder is at least done by the will, free as that wind from the sea.'

'Father Brown is a wonderful person,' she said after a pause; 'he was the only person who ever brightened my existence in any way at all until –'

'Until what?' asked Payne, and made a movement almost impetuous, leaning towards her and thrusting away the bronze monster so that it seemed to rock on its pedestal.

'Well, until you did,' she said and smiled again.

So was the sleeping palace awakened, and it is no part of this story to describe the stages of its awakening, though much of it had come to pass before the dark of that evening had fallen upon the shore. As Harry Payne strode homewards once more, across those dark sands that he had crossed in so many moods, he was at the highest turn of happiness that is given in this mortal life, and the whole red sea within him was at the top of its tide. He would have had no difficulty in picturing all that place again in flower, and the bronze triton bright as a golden god and the fountain flowing with water or with wine. But all this brightness and blossoming had been unfolded for him by the one word 'murder', and it was still a word that he did not understand. He had taken it on trust, and he was not unwise; for he was one of those who have a sense of the sound of truth.

It was more than a month later that Payne returned to his London house to keep an appointment with Father Brown, taking the required photograph with him. His personal romance had prospered as well as was fitting under the shadow of such a tragedy, and the shadow itself therefore lay rather more lightly on him; but it was hard to view it as anything but the shadow of a family fatality. In many ways he had been much occupied; and it was not until the Darnaway household had resumed its somewhat stern routine, and the portrait had long been restored to its place in the library, that he had managed to photograph it with a magnesium flare. Before sending it to the antiquary, as originally arranged, he brought it to the priest who had so pressingly demanded it.

'I can't understand your attitude about all this, Father Brown,' he said. 'You act as if you had already solved the problem in some way of your own.'

The priest shook his head mournfully. 'Not a bit of it,' he answered. 'I must be very stupid, but I'm quite stuck; stuck about the most practical point of all. It's a queer business; so simple up to a point and then – Let me have a look at that photograph, will you?'

He held it close to his screwed, short-sighted eyes for a moment, and then said: 'Have you got a magnifying glass?'

Payne produced one, and the priest looked through it intently for some time and then said: 'Look at the title of that book at the the edge of the bookshelf beside the frame; it's "The History of Pope Joan". Now, I wonder ... yes, by George; and the one

168

above is something or other of Iceland. Lord! what a queer way to find it out! What a dolt and donkey I was not to notice it when I was there!'

'But what have you found out?' asked Payne impatiently.

'The last link,' said Father Brown, 'and I'm not stuck any longer. Yes; I think I know how that unhappy story went from first to last now.'

'But why?' insisted the other.

'Why, because,' said the priest with a smile, 'the Darnaway library contained books about Pope Joan and Iceland, not to mention another I see with the title beginning "The Religion of Frederick", which is not so very hard to fill up.' Then, seeing the other's annoyance, his smile faded and he said more earnestly:

'As a matter of fact, this last point, though it is the last link, is not the main business. There were much more curious things in the case than that. One of them is rather a curiosity of evidence. Let me begin by saying something that may surprise you. Darnaway did not die at seven o'clock that evening. He had been already dead for a whole day.'

'Surprise is rather a mild word,' said Payne grimly, 'since you and I both saw him walking about afterwards.'

'No, we did not,' replied Father Brown quietly. 'I think we both saw him, or thought we saw him, fussing about with the focusing of his camera. Wasn't his head under that black cloak when you passed through the room? It was when I did. And that's why I felt there was something queer about the room and the figure. It wasn't that the leg was crooked, but rather that it wasn't crooked. It was dressed in the same sort of dark clothes; but if you see what you believe to be one man standing in the way that another man stands, you will think he's in a strange and strained attitude.'

'Do you really mean,' cried Payne with something like a shudder, 'that it was some unknown man?'

'It was the murderer,' said Father Brown. 'He had already killed Darnaway at daybreak and hid the corpse and himself in the dark room – an excellent hiding-place, because nobody normally goes into it or can see much if he does. But he let it fall out on the floor at seven o'clock, of course, that the whole thing might be explained by the curse.'

'But I don't understand' observed Payne. 'Why didn't he kill him at seven o'clock then, instead of loading himself with a corpse for fourteen hours?'

'Let me ask you another question,' said the priest. 'Why was there no photograph taken? Because the murderer made sure of killing him when he first got up, and before he could take it. It was essential to the murderer to prevent that photograph reaching the expert on the Darnaway antiquities.'

There was a sudden silence for a moment, and then the priest went on in a lower tone:

'Don't you see how simple it is? Why, you yourself saw one side of the possibility; but it's simpler even than you thought. You said a man might be faked to resemble an old picture. Surely it's simpler that a picture should be faked to resemble a man. In plain words, it's true in a rather special way that there was no Doom of the Darnaways. There was no old picture; there was no old rhyme; there was no legend of a man who caused his wife's death. But there was a very wicked and a very clever man who was willing to cause another man's death in order to rob him of his promised wife.'

The priest suddenly gave Payne a sad smile, as if in reassurance. 'For the moment I believe you thought I meant you,' he said, 'but you were not the only person who haunted that house for sentimental reasons. You know the man, or rather you think you do. But there were depths in the man called Martin Wood, artist and antiquary, which none of his mere artistic acquaintances were likely to guess. Remember that he was called in to criticize and catalogue the pictures; in an aristocratic dustbin of that sort that practically means simply to tell the Darnaways what art treasures they had got. They would not be surprised at things turning up they had never noticed before. It had to be done well, and it was; perhaps he was right when he said that if it wasn't Holbein it was somebody of the same genius.'

'I feel rather stunned,' said Payne; 'and there are twenty things

I don't see yet. How did he know what Darnaway looked like? How did he actually kill him? The doctors seem rather puzzled at present.'

'I saw a photograph the lady had which the Australian sent on before him,' said the priest, 'and there are several ways in which he could have learned things when the new heir was once recognized. We may not know these details; but they are not difficulties. You remember he used to help in the dark room; it seems to me an ideal place, say, to prick a man with a poisoned pin, with the poisons all handy. No; I say these were not difficulties. The difficulty that stumped me was how Wood could be in two places at once. How could he take the corpse from the dark-room and prop it against the camera so that it would fall in a few seconds, without coming downstairs, when he was in the library looking out a book? And I was such a fool that I never looked at the books in the library; and it was only in this photograph, by very undeserved good luck, that I saw the simple fact of a book about Pope Joan.'

'You've kept your best riddle for the end,' said Payne grimly. 'What on earth can Pope Joan have to do with it?'

'Don't forget the book about the Something of Iceland,' advised the priest, 'or the religion of somebody called Frederick. It only remains to ask what sort of man was the late Lord Darnaway.'

'Oh, does it?' observed Payne heavily.

'He was a cultivated, humorous sort of eccentric, I believe,' went on Father Brown. 'Being cultivated, he knew there was no such person as Pope Joan. Being humorous, he was very likely to have thought of the title of "The Snakes of Iceland" or something else that didn't exist. I venture to reconstruct the third title as "The Religion of Frederick the Great" – which also doesn't exist. Now, doesn't it strike you that those would be just the titles to put on the backs of books that didn't exist; or in other words on a bookcase that wasn't a book-case?'

'Ah!' cried Payne; 'I see what you mean now. There was some hidden staircase – '

'Up to the room Wood himself selected as a dark room,' said

the priest nodding. 'I'm sorry. It couldn't be helped. It's dreadfully banal and stupid, as stupid as I have been on this pretty banal case. But we were mixed up in a real musty old romance of decayed gentility and a fallen family mansion; and it was too much to hope that we could escape having a secret passage. It was a priest's hole; and I deserve to be put in it.'

EIGHT

The Ghost of Gideon Wise

FATHER BROWN always regarded the case as the queerest example of the theory of an alibi: the theory by which it is maintained, in defiance of the mythological Irish bird, that it is impossible for anybody to be in two places at once. To begin with, James Byrne, being an Irish journalist, was perhaps the nearest approximation to the Irish bird. He came as near as anybody could to being in two places at once: for he was in two places at the opposite extremes of the social and political world within the the space of twenty minutes. The first was in the Babylonian halls of the big hotel, which was the meeting place of the three commercial magnates concerned with arranging for a coal lock-out and denouncing it as a coal-strike, the second was in a curious tavern, having the façade of a grocery store, where met the more subterranean triumvirate of those who would have been very glad to turn the lock-out into a strike – and the strike into a revolution. The reporter passed to and fro between the three millionaires and the three Bolshevist leaders with the immunity of the modern herald or the new ambassador.

He found the three mining magnates hidden in a jungle of flowering plants and a forest of fluted and florid columns of gilded plaster; gilded birdcages hung high under the painted domes amid the highest leaves of the palms; and in them were birds of motley colours and varied cries. No bird in the wilderness ever sang more unheeded, and no flower ever wasted its sweetness on the desert air more completely than the blossoms of those tall plants wasted theirs upon the brisk and breathless business men, mostly American, who talked and ran to and fro in that place. And there, amid a riot of rococo ornament that nobody ever looked at, and a chatter of expensive foreign birds that nobody ever heard, and a mass of gorgeous upholstery and a labyrinth of luxurious architecture, the three men sat and talked of how success was founded on the thought and thrift and a vigilance of economy and self-control.

One of them indeed did not talk so much as the others; but he watched with very bright and motionless eyes, which seemed to be pinched together by his pince-nez, and the permanent smile under his small black moustache was rather like a permanent sneer. This was the famous Jacob P. Stein, and he did not speak till he had something to say. But his companion, old Gallup the Pennsylvanian, a huge fat fellow with reverend grey hair but a face like a pugilist, talked a great deal. He was in a jovial mood and was half rallying, half bullying the third millionaire, Gideon Wise – a hard, dried, angular old bird of the type that his countrymen compare to hickory, with a stiff grey chin-beard and the manners and clothes of any old farmer from the central plains. There was an old argument between Wise and Gallup about combination and competition. For old Wise still retained, with the manners of the old backwoodsman, something of his opinions of the old individualist; he belonged, as we should say in England, to the Manchester School; and Gallup was always trying to persuade him to cut out competition and pool the resources of the world.

'You'll have to come in, old fellow, sooner or later,' Gallup was saying genially as Byrne entered. 'It's the way the world is going, and we can't go back to the one-man-business now. We've all got to stand together.'

'If I might say a word,' said Stein, in his tranquil way, 'I would say there is something a little more urgent even than standing together commercially. Anyhow, we must stand together politically; and that's why I've asked Mr Byrne to meet us here today. On the political issue we must combine; for the simple reason that all our most dangerous enemies are already combined.'

'Oh, I quite agree about political combination,' grumbled Gideon Wise.

'See here,' said Stein to the journalist; 'I know you have the run of these queer places, Mr Byrne, and I want you to do something for us unofficially. You know where these men meet; there are only two or three of them that count, John Elias and Jake Halket, who does all the spouting, and perhaps that poet fellow, Horne.'

'Why Horne used to be a friend of Gideon,' said the jeering Mr Gallup; 'used to be in his Sunday School class or something.'

'He was a Christian, then,' said old Gideon solemnly; 'but when a man takes up with atheists you never know. I still meet him now and then. I was quite ready to back him against war and conscription and all that, of course, but when it comes to all the goldarn bolshies in creation –'

'Excuse me,' interposed Stein, 'the matter is rather urgent, so I hope you will excuse me putting it before Mr Byrne at once. Mr Byrne, I may tell you in confidence that I hold information, or rather evidence that would land at least two of those men in prison for long terms, in connexion with conspiracies during the late war. I don't want to use that evidence. But I want you to go to them quietly and tell them that I shall use it, and use it tomorrow, unless they alter their attitude.'

'Well,' replied Byrne, 'what you propose would certainly be called compounding a felony and might be called blackmail. Don't you think it is rather dangerous?'

'I think it is rather dangerous for them,' said Stein with a snap; 'and I want you to go and tell them so.'

'Oh, very well,' said Byrne standing up, with a half humorous sigh. 'It's all in the day's work; but if I get into trouble, I warn you I shall try to drag you into it.'

'You will try, boy,' said old Gallup with a hearty laugh.

For so much still lingers of that great dream of Jefferson and the thing that men have called Democracy that in his country, while the rich rule like tyrants, the poor do not talk like slaves; but there is candour between the oppressor and the oppressed.

The meeting-place of the revolutionists was a queer, bare, white-washed place, on the walls of which were one or two distorted uncouth sketches in black and white, in the style of something that was supposed to be Proletarian Art, of which not one proletarian in a million could have made head or tail. Perhaps the one point in common to the two council chambers was that both violated the American Constitution by the display of strong drink. Cocktails of various colours had stood before the three millionaires. Halket, the most violent of the Bolshevists, thought it only appropriate to drink vodka. He was a long, hulking fellow with a menacing stoop, and his very profile was aggressive like a dog's, the nose and lips thrust out together, the latter carrying a ragged red moustache and the whole curling outwards with perpetual scorn. John Elias was a dark watchful man in spectacles, with a black pointed beard; and he had learnt in many European cafés a taste for absinthe. The journalist's first and last feeling was how very like each other, after all, were John Elias and Jacob P. Stein. They were so like in face and mind and manner, that the millionaire might have disappeared down a trap-door in the Babylon Hotel and come up again in the stronghold of the Bolshevists.

The third man also had a curious taste in drinks, and his drink was symbolic of him. For what stood in front of the poet Horne was a glass of milk, and its very mildness seemed in that setting to have something sinister about it, as if its opaque and colourless colour were of some leprous paste more poisonous than the dead sick green of absinthe. Yet in truth the mildness was so far genuine enough; for Henry Horne came to the camp of revolution along a very different road and from very different origins from those of Jake, the common tub-thumper, and Elias, the cosmopolitan wire-puller. He had·had what is called a careful upbringing, had gone to chapel in his childhood, and carried through life a teetotalism which he could not shake off when he cast away such trifles as Christianity and marriage. He had fair hair and a fine face that might have looked like Shelley, if he had not weakened the chin with a little foreign fringe of beard. Somehow the beard made him look more like a woman; it was as if those few golden hairs were all he could do.

When the journalist entered, the notorious Jake was talking, as he generally was. Horne had uttered some casual and conventional phrase about 'Heaven forbid' something or other, and this was quite enough to set Jake off with a torrent of profanity.

'Heaven forbid! and that's about all it bally well does do,' he said. 'Heaven never does anything but forbid this, that and the other; forbids us to strike, and forbids us to fight, and forbids us to shoot the damned usurers and blood-suckers where they sit. Why doesn't Heaven forbid *them* something for a bit? Why don't your damned priests and parsons stand up and tell the truth about these brutes for a change? Why doesn't their precious God –'

Elias allowed a gentle sigh, as of faint fatigue, to escape him.

'Priests,' he said, 'belonged, as Marx has shown, to the feudal stage of economic development and are therefore no longer really any part of the problem. The part once played by the priest is now played by the capitalist expert and –'

'Yes,' interrupted the journalist, with his grim and ironic impartiality, 'and it's about time you knew that some of them are pretty expert in playing it.' And without moving his own eyes from the bright but dead eyes of Elias, he told him of the threat of Stein.

'I was prepared for something of that sort,' said the smiling Elias without moving; 'I may say quite prepared.'

'Dirty dogs!' exploded Jake. 'If a poor man said a thing like that he'd go to penal servitude. But I reckon they'll go somewhere worse before they guess. If they don't go to hell, I don't know where the hell they'll go to –'

Horne made a movement of protest, perhaps not so much at what the man was saying as at what he was going to say, and Elias cut the speech short with cold exactitude.

'It is quite unnecessary for us,' he said, looking at Byrne steadily through his spectacles, 'to bandy threats with the other side. It is quite sufficient that their threats are quite ineffective so far as we are concerned. We also have made all our own arrangements, and some of them will not appear until they appear in action. So far as we are concerned, an immediate rupture and an extreme trial of strength will be quite according to plan.'

As he spoke in a quite quiet and dignified fashion, something in his motionless yellow face and his great goggles started a faint fear creeping up the journalist's spine. Halket's savage face might seem to have a snarl in its very silhouette when seen sideways; but when seen face to face, the smouldering rage in his eyes had also something of anxiety, as if the ethical and economic riddle were after all a little too much for him; and Horne seemed even more hung on wires of worry and self-criticism. But about this third man with the goggles, who spoke so sensibly and simply, there was something uncanny; it was like a dead man talking at the table.

As Byrne went out with his message of defiance, and passed along the very narrow passage beside the grocery store, he found the end of it blocked by a strange though strangely familiar figure: short and sturdy, and looking rather quaint when seen in dark outline with its round head and wide hat.

'Father Brown!' cried the astonished journalist. 'I think you must have come into the wrong door. You're not likely to be in this little conspiracy.'

'Mine is a rather older conspiracy,' replied Father Brown smiling, 'but it is quite a widespread conspiracy.'

'Well,' replied Byrne, 'you can't imagine any of the people here being within a thousand miles of your concern.'

'It is not always easy to tell,' replied the priest equably; 'but as a matter of fact, there is one person here who's within an inch of it.'

He disappeared into the dark entrance and the journalist went on his way very much puzzled. He was still more puzzled by a small incident that happened to him as he turned into the hotel to make his report to his capitalist clients. The bower of blossoms and bird-cages in which those crabbed old gentlemen were embosomed was approached by a flight of marble steps, flanked by gilded nymphs and tritons. Down these steps ran an active young man with black hair, a snub nose, and a flower in his button-hole, who seized him and drew him aside before he could ascend the stair.

'I say,' whispered the young man, 'I'm Potter – old Gid's secretary, you know; now, between ourselves, there is a sort of a thunderbolt being forged, isn't there, now?'

'I came to the conclusion,' replied Byrne cautiously, 'that the Cyclops had something on the anvil. But always remember that the Cyclops is a giant, but he has only one eye. I think Bolshevism is –'

While he was speaking the secretary listened with a face that had a certain almost Mongolian immobility, despite the liveliness of his legs and his attire. But when Byrne said the word 'Bolshevism', the young man's sharp eyes shifted and he said quickly: 'What has that – oh yes, that sort of thunderbolt; so sorry, my mistake. So easy to say anvil when you mean ice-box.'

With which the extraordinary young man disappeared down the steps and Byrne continued to mount them, more and more mystification clouding his mind.

He found the group of three augmented to four by the presence of a hatchet-faced person with very thin straw-coloured hair and a monocle, who appeared to be a sort of adviser to old Gallup, possibly his solicitor, though he was not definitely so called. His name was Nares, and the questions which he directed towards Byrne referred chiefly, for some reason or other, to the number of those probably enrolled in the revolutionary organization. Of this, as Byrne knew little, he said less; and the four men eventually rose from their seats, the last word being with the man who had been most silent.

'Thank you, Mr Byrne,' said Stein, folding up his eyeglasses. 'It only remains to say that everything is ready; on that point I quite agree with Mr Elias. Tomorrow, before noon, the police will have arrested Mr Elias, on evidence I shall by then have put before them, and those three at least will be in jail before night. As you know, I attempted to avoid this course. I think that is all, gentlemen.'

But Mr Jacob P. Stein did not lay his formal information next day, for a reason that has often interrupted the activities of such industrious characters. He did not do it because he happened to be dead; and none of the rest of the programme was carried out, for a reason which Byrne found displayed in gigantic letters when he opened his morning paper: 'Terrific Triple Murder: Three Millionaires Slain in One Night.' Other exclamatory phrases followed in smaller letters, only about four times the size of normal type, which insisted on the special feature of the mystery: the fact that the three men had been killed not only simultaneously but in three widely separated places – Stein in his artistic and luxurious country seat a hundred miles inland, Wise outside the little bungalow on the coast where he lived on sea breezes and the simple life, and old Gallup in a thicket just outside the lodge-gates of his great house at the other end of the county. In all three cases there could be no doubt about the scenes of violence that had preceded death, though the actual body of Gallup was not found till the second day, where it hung, huge and horrible, amid the broken forks and branches of the little wood into which its weight had crashed, like a bison rushing on the spears: while Wise had clearly been flung over the cliff into the sea, not without a struggle, for his scraping and slipping footprints could still be traced upon the very brink. But the first signal of the tragedy had been the sight of his large limp straw hat, floating far out upon the waves and conspicuous from the cliffs above. Stein's body also had at first eluded search, till a faint trail of blood led the investigators to a bath on the ancient Roman model he had been constructing in his garden; for he had been a man of an experimental turn of mind with a taste for antiquities.

Whatever he might think, Byrne was bound to admit that there was no legal evidence against anybody as things stood. A motive for murder was not enough. Even a moral aptitude for murder was not enough. And he could not conceive that pale young pacifist, Henry Horne, butchering another man by brutal violence, though he might imagine the blaspheming Jake and even the sneering Jew as capable of anything. The police, and the man who appeared to be assisting them (who was no other than the rather mysterious man with the monocle, who had been introduced as Mr Nares), realized the position quite as clearly as the journalist. They knew that at the moment the Bolshevist conspirators could not be prosecuted and convicted, and that it would be a highly sensational failure if they were prosecuted and acquitted. Nares started with an artful candour by calling them in some sense to the council, inviting them to a private conclave and asking them to give their opinions freely in the interests of humanity. He had started his investigations at the nearest scene of tragedy, the bungalow by the sea; and Byrne was permitted to be present at a curious scene, which was at once a peaceful parley of diplomatists and a veiled inquisition or putting of suspects to the question. Rather to Byrne's surprise the incongruous company, seated round the table in the seaside bungalow, included the dumpy figure and owlish head of Father Brown, though his connexion with the affair did not appear until some time afterwards. The presence of young Potter, the dead man's secretary, was more natural; yet somehow his demeanour was not quite so natural. He alone was quite familiar with their meeting-place, and was even in some grim sense their host; yet he offered little assistance or information. His round snub-nosed face wore an expression more like sulks than sorrow.

Jake Halket as usual talked most; and a man of his type could not be expected to keep up the polite fiction that he and his friends were not accused. Young Horne, in his more refined way, tried to restrain him when he began to abuse the men who had been murdered; but Jake was always quite as ready to roar down his friends as his foes. In a spout of blasphemies he relieved his soul of a very unofficial obituary notice of the late Gideon Wise. Elias sat quite still and apparently indifferent behind those spectacles that masked his eyes.

'It would be useless, I suppose,' said Nares coldly, 'to tell you' that your remarks are indecent. It may affect you more if I tell you they are imprudent. You practically admit that you hated the dead man.'

'Going to put me in quod for that, are you?' jeered the demagogue. 'All right. Only you'll have to build a prison for a million men if you're going to jail all the poor people who had reason to hate Gid Wise. And you know it's God truth as well as I do.'

Nares was silent; and nobody spoke until Elias interposed with his clear though faintly lisping drawl.

'This appears to me to be a highly unprofitable discussion on both sides,' he said. 'You have summoned us here either to ask us for information or to subject us to cross-examination. If you trust us, we tell you we have no information. If you distrust us, you must tell us of what we are accused, or have the politeness to keep the fact to yourselves. Nobody has been able to suggest the faintest trace of evidence connecting any one of us with these tragedies any more than with the murder of Julius Caesar. You dare not arrest us, and you will not believe us. What is the good of our remaining here?'

And he rose, calmly buttoning his coat, his friends following his example. As they went towards the door, young Horne turned back and faced the investigators for a moment with his pale fanatical face.

'I wish to say,' he said, 'that I went to a filthy jail during the whole war because I would not consent to kill a man.'

With that they passed out, and the members of the group remaining looked grimly at each other.

'I hardly think,' said Father Brown, 'that we remain entirely victorious, in spite of the retreat.'

'I don't mind anything,' said Nares, 'except being bullyragged by that blasphemous blackguard Halket. Horne is a gentleman, anyhow. But whatever they say, I am dead certain they know; they are in it, or most of them are. They almost admitted it. They taunted us with not being able to prove we're right, much more than with being wrong. What do you think, Father Brown?'

The person addressed looked across at Nares with a gaze almost disconcertingly mild and meditative.

'It is quite true,' he said, 'that I have formed an idea that one particular person knows more than he has told us. But I think it would be well if I did not mention his name just yet.'

Nare's eyeglass dropped from his eye, and he looked up sharply. 'This is unofficial so far,' he said. 'I suppose you know that at a later stage if you withhold information, your position may be serious.'

'My position is simple,' replied the priest. 'I am here to look after the legitimate interests of my friend Halket. I think it will be in his interest, under the circumstances, if I tell you I think he will before long sever his connexion with this organization, and cease to be a Socialist in that sense. I have every reason to believe he will probably end as a Catholic.'

'Halket!' exploded the other incredulously. 'Why he curses priests from morning till night!'

'I don't think you quite understand that kind of man,' said Father Brown mildly. 'He curses priests for failing (in his opinion) to defy the whole world for justice. Why should he expect them to defy the whole world for justice, unless he had already begun to assume they were – what they are? But we haven't met here to discuss the psychology of conversion. I only mention this because it may simplify your task – perhaps narrow your search.'

'If it is true, it would jolly well narrow it to that narrow-faced rascal Elias – and I shouldn't wonder, for a more creepy, cold-blooded, sneering devil I never saw.'

Father Brown sighed. 'He always reminded me of poor Stein,' he said, 'in fact I think he was some relation.'

'Oh, I say,' began Nares, when his protest was cut short by the door being flung open, revealing once more the long loose figure and pale face of young Horne; but it seemed as if he had not merely his natural, but a new and unnatural pallor.

'Hullo,' cried Nares, putting up his single eyeglass, 'why have you come back again?'

Horne crossed the room rather shakily without a word and sat down heavily in a chair. Then he said, as in a sort of daze: 'I missed the others ... I lost my way. I thought I'd better come back.'

The remains of evening refreshments were on the table, and Henry Horne, that lifelong Prohibitionist, poured himself out a wine-glassful of liqueur brandy and drank it at a gulp.

'You seem upset,' said Father Brown.

Horne had put his hands to his forehead and spoke as from under the shadow of it: he seemed to be speaking to the priest only, in a low voice.

'I may as well tell you. I have seen a ghost.'

'A ghost!' repeated Nares in astonishment. 'Whose ghost?'

'The ghost of Gideon Wise, the master of this house,' answered Horne more firmly, 'standing over the abyss into which he fell.'

'Oh, nonsense!' said Nares; 'no sensible person believes in ghosts.'

'That is hardly exact,' said Father Brown, smiling a little. 'There is really quite as good evidence for many ghosts as there is for most crimes.'

'Well, it's my business to run after the criminals,' said Nares rather roughly, 'and I will leave other people to run away from the ghosts. If anybody at this time of day chooses to be frightened of ghosts it's his affair.'

'I didn't say I was frightened of them, though I dare say I might be,' said Father Brown. 'Nobody knows till he tries. I said I believed in them, at any rate, enough to want to hear more about this one. What, exactly, did you see, Mr Horne?'

'It was over there on the brink of those crumbling cliffs; you know there is a sort of gap or crevice just about the spot where he was thrown over. The others had gone on ahead, and I was crossing the moor towards the path along the cliff. I often went that way, for I liked seeing the high seas dash up against the crags. I thought little of it to-night, beyond wondering that the sea should be so rough on this sort of clear moonlight night. I could see the pale crests of spray appear and disappear as the great waves leapt up at the headland. Thrice I saw the momentary flash of foam in the moonlight and then I saw something inscrutable. The fourth flash of the silver foam seemed to be fixed in the sky. It did not fall; I waited with insane intensity for it to fall. I fancied I was mad, and that time had been for me mysteriously arrested or prolonged. Then I drew nearer, and then I think I screamed aloud. For that suspended spray, like unfallen snowflakes, had fitted together into a face and a figure, white as the shining leper in a legend, and terrible as the fixed lightning.'

'And it was Gideon Wise, you say?'

Horne nodded without speech. There was a silence broken abruptly by Nares rising to his feet; so abruptly indeed that he knocked a chair over.

'Oh, this is all nonsense,' he said, 'but we'd better go out and see.'

'I won't go,' said Horne with sudden violence. 'I'll never walk by that path again.'

'I think we must all walk by that path tonight,' said the priest gravely; 'though I will never deny it has been a perilous path . . . to more people than one.'

'I will not . . . God, how you all goad me,' cried Horne, and his eyes began to roll in a strange fashion. He had risen with the rest, but he made no motion towards the door.

'Mr Horne,' said Nares firmly, 'I am a police-officer, and this house, though you may not know it, is surrounded by the police. I have tried to investigate in a friendly fashion, but I must investigate everything, even anything so silly as a ghost. I must ask you to take me to the spot you speak of.'

There was another silence while Horne stood heaving and panting as with indescribable fears. Then he suddenly sat down on his chair again and said with an entirely new and much more composed voice:

'I can't do it. You may just as well know why. You will know it sooner or later. I killed him.'

For an instant there was the stillness of a house struck by a thunderbolt and full of corpses. Then the voice of Father Brown sounded in that enormous silence strangely small like the squeak of a mouse.

'Did you kill him deliberately?' he asked.

'How can one answer such a question?' answered the man in the chair, moodily gnawing his finger. 'I was mad, I suppose. He was intolerable and insolent, I know. I was on his land and I believe he struck me; anyhow, we came to a grapple and he went over the cliff. When I was well away from the scene it burst upon me that I had done a crime that cut me off from men; the brand of Cain throbbed on my brow and my very brain; I realized for the first time that I had indeed killed a man. I knew I should have to confess it sooner or later.' He sat suddenly erect in his chair. 'But I will say nothing against anybody else. It is no use asking me about plots or accomplices – I will say nothing.'

'In the light of the other murders,' said Nares, 'it is difficult to believe that the quarrel was quite so unpremeditated. Surely somebody sent you there?'

'I will say nothing against anybody I worked with,' said Horne proudly. 'I am a murderer, but I will not be a traitor.'

Nares stepped between the man and the door and called out in an official fashion to someone outside.

'We will all go to the place, anyhow,' he said in a low voice to the secretary; 'but this man must go in custody.'

The company generally felt that to go spook-hunting on a

seacliff was a very silly anti-climax after the confession of the murderer. But Nares, though the most sceptical and scornful of all,
thought it his duty to leave no stone unturned; as one might say,
no gravestone unturned. For, after all, that crumbling cliff was
the only gravestone over the watery grave of poor Gideon Wise.
Nares locked the door, being the last out of the house, and
followed the rest across the moor to the cliff, when he was
astonished to see young Potter, the secretary, coming back quickly
towards them, his face in the moonlight looking white as a moon.

'By God, sir,' he said, speaking for the first time that night,
'there really is something there. It – it's just like him.'

'Why, you're raving,' gasped the detective. 'Everybody's raving.'

'Do you think I don't know him when I see him?' cried the
secretary with singular bitterness. 'I have reason to.'

'Perhaps,' said the detective sharply, 'you are one of those who
had reason to hate him, as Halket said.'

'Perhaps,' said the secretary; 'anyhow, I know him, and I tell
you I can see him standing there stark and staring under this
hellish moon.'

And he pointed towards the crack in the cliffs, where they could
already see something that might have been a moonbeam or a
streak of foam, but which was already beginning to look a little
more solid. They had crept a hundred yards nearer, and it was still
motionless; but it looked like a statue in silver.

Nares himself looked a little pale and seemed to stand debating
what to do. Potter was frankly as much frightened as Horne himself; and even Byrne, who was a hardened reporter, was rather
reluctant to go any nearer if he could help it. He could not help
considering it a little quaint, therefore, that the only man who did
not seem to be frightened of a ghost was the man who had said
openly that he might be. For Father Brown was advancing as
steadily, at his stumping pace, as if he were going to consult a
notice-board.

'It don't seem to bother you much,' said Byrne to the priest;
'and yet I thought you were the only one who believed in spooks.'

'If it comes to that,' replied Father Brown, 'I thought you

186

were one who didn't believe in them. But believing in ghosts is one thing, and believing in a ghost is quite another.'

Byrne looked rather ashamed of himself, and glanced almost covertly at the crumbling headlands in the cold moonlight which were the haunts of the vision or delusion.

'I didn't believe in it till I saw it,' he said.

'And I did believe in it till I saw it,' said Father Brown.

The journalist stared after him as he went stumping across the great waste ground that rose towards the cloven headland like the sloping side of a hill cut in two. Under the discolouring moon the grass looked like long grey hair all combed one way by the wind, and seeming to point towards the place where the breaking cliff showed pale gleams of chalk in the grey-green turf, and where stood the pale figure or shining shade that none could yet understand. As yet that pale figure dominated a desolate landscape that was empty except for the black square back and business-like figure of the priest advancing alone towards it. Then the prisoner Horne broke suddenly from his captors with a piercing cry and ran ahead of the priest, falling on his knees before the spectre.

'I have confessed,' they heard him crying. 'Why have you come to tell them I killed you?'

'I have come to tell them you did not,' said the ghost, and stretched forth a hand to him. Then the kneeling man sprang up with quite a new kind of scream; and they knew it was the hand of flesh.

It was the most remarkable escape from death in recent records, said the experienced detective and the no less experienced journalist. Yet, in a sense, it had been very simple after all. Flakes and shards of the cliff were continually falling away, and some had caught in the gigantic crevice, so as to form what was really a ledge or pocket in what was supposed to be a sheer drop through darkness to the sea. The old man, who was a very tough and wiry old man, had fallen on this lower shoulder of rock and had passed a pretty terrible twenty-four hours in trying to climb back by crags that constantly collapsed under him, but at length formed by their very ruins a sort of stairway of escape. This might be the explanation of Horne's optical illusion about a white wave that appeared and disappeared, and finally came to stay. But anyhow there was Gideon Wise, solid in bone and sinew, with his white hair and white dusty country clothes and harsh country features, which were, however, a great deal less harsh than usual. Perhaps it is good for millionaires to spend twenty-four hours on a ledge of rock within a foot of eternity. Anyhow, he not only disclaimed all malice against the criminal, but gave an account of the matter which considerably modified the crime. He declared that Horne had not thrown him over at all; that the continually breaking ground had given way under him, and that Horne had even made some movement as of attempted rescue.

'On that providential bit of rock down there,' he said solemnly, 'I promised the Lord to forgive my enemies; and the Lord would think it mighty mean if I didn't forgive a little accident like that.'

Horne had to depart under police supervision, of course, but the detective did not disguise from himself that the prisoner's detention would probably be short, and his punishment, if any, trifling. It is not every murderer who can put the murdered man in the witness-box to give him a testimonial.

'It's a strange case,' said Byrne, as the detective and the others hastened along the cliff path towards the town.

'It is,' said Father Brown. 'It's no business of ours; but I wish you'd stop with me and talk it over.'

There was a silence and then Byrne complied by saying suddenly: 'I suppose you were thinking of Horne already, when you said somebody wasn't telling all he knew.'

'When I said that,' replied his friend, 'I was thinking of the exceedingly silent Mr Potter, the secretary of the no longer late or (shall we say) lamented Mr Gideon Wise.'

'Well, the only time Potter ever spoke to me I thought he was a lunatic,' said Byrne, staring, 'but I never thought of his being a criminal. He said something about it all having to do with an ice-box.'

'Yes, I thought he knew something about it,' said Father Brown reflectively. 'I never said he had anything to do with it . . .

I suppose old Wise really is strong enough to have climbed out of that chasm.'

'What do you mean?' asked the astonished reporter. 'Why, of course he got out of that chasm; for there he is.'

The priest did not answer the question but asked abruptly:

'What do you think of Horne?'

'Well, one can't call him a criminal exactly,' answered Byrne. 'He never was at all like any criminal I ever knew, and I've had some experience; and, of course, Nares has had much more. I don't think we ever quite believed him a criminal.'

'And I never believed in him in another capacity,' said the priest quietly. 'You may know more about criminals. But there's one class of people I probably do know more about than you do, or even Nares for that matter. I've known quite a lot of them, and I know their little ways.'

'Another class of people,' repeated Byrne, mystified. 'Why what class do you know about?'

'Penitents,' said Father Brown.

'I don't quite understand,' objected Byrne. 'Do you mean you don't believe in his crime?'

'I don't believe in his confession,' said Father Brown. 'I've heard a good many confessions, and there was never a genuine one like that. It was romantic; it was all out of books. Look how he talked about having the brand of Cain. That's out of books. It's not what anyone would feel who had in his own person done a thing hitherto horrible to him. Suppose you were an honest clerk or shop-boy shocked to feel that for the first time you'd stolen money. Would you immediately reflect that your action was the same as that of Barabbas? Suppose you'd killed a child in some ghastly anger. Would you go back through history, till you could identify your action with that of an Idumean potentate named Herod? Believe me, our own crimes are far too hideously private and prosaic to make our first thoughts turn towards historical parallels, however apt. And why did he go out of his way to say he would not give his colleagues away? Even in saying so, he was giving them away. Nobody had asked him so far to give away anything or anybody. No; I don't think he was genuine, and I wouldn't give him absolution. A nice state of things, if people started getting absolved for what they hadn't done.' And Father Brown, his head turned away, looked steadily out to sea.

'But I don't understand what you're driving at,' cried Byrne. 'What's the good of buzzing round him with suspicions when he's pardoned? He's out of it anyhow. He's quite safe.'

Father Brown spun round like a teetotum and caught his friend by the coat with unexpected and inexplicable excitement.

'That's it,' he cried emphatically. 'Freeze on to that! He's quite safe. He's out of it. That's why he's the key of the whole puzzle.'

'Oh, help,' said Byrne feebly.

'I mean,' persisted the little priest, 'he's in it because he's out of it. That's the whole explanation.'

'And a very lucid explanation too,' said the journalist with feeling.

They stood looking out to sea for a time in silence, and then Father Brown said cheerfully:

'And so we come back to the ice-box. Where you have all gone wrong from the first in this business is where a good many of the papers and the public men do go wrong. It's because you assumed that there is nothing whatever in the modern world to fight about except Bolshevism. This story has nothing whatever to do with Bolshevism; except perhaps as a blind.'

'I don't see how that can be,' remonstrated Byrne. 'Here you have the three millionaires in that one business murdered –'

'No!' said the priest in a sharp ringing voice. 'You do not. That is just the point. You do not have three millionaires murdered. You have two millionaires murdered; and you have the third millionaire very much alive and kicking and quite ready to kick. And you have that third millionaire freed for ever from the threat that was thrown at his head before your very face, in playfully polite terms, and in that conversation you described as taking place in the hotel. Gallup and Stein threatened the more old-fashioned and independent old huckster that if he would not come into their combine they would freeze him out. Hence the ice-box, of course.'

After a pause he went on. 'There is undoubtedly a Bolshevist movement in the modern world, and it must undoubtedly be resisted, though I do not believe very much in your way of resisting it. But what nobody notices is that there is another movement equally modern and equally moving: the great movement towards monopoly or the turning of all trades into trusts. That also is a revolution. That also produces what all revolutions produce. Men will kill for that and against that, as they do for and against Bolshevism. It has its ultimatums and its invasions and its executions. These trust magnates have their courts like kings; they have their bodyguard and bravos; they have their spies in the enemy camp. Horne was one of old Gideon's spies in one of the enemy camps; but he was used here against another enemy: the rivals who were ruining him for standing out.'

'I still don't quite see how he was used,' said Byrne, 'or what was the good of it.'

'Don't you see,' cried Father Brown sharply, 'that they gave each other an alibi?'

Byrne still looked at him a little doubtfully, though understanding was dawning on his face.

'That's what I mean,' continued the other, 'when I say they were in it because they were out of it. Most people would say they must be out of the other two crimes, because they were in this one. As a fact, they were in the other two because they were out of this one; because this one never happened at all. A very queer, improbable sort of alibi, of course; improbable and therefore impenetrable. Most people would say a man who confesses a murder must be sincere; a man who forgives his murderer must be sincere. Nobody would think of the notion that the thing never happened, so that one man had nothing to forgive and the other nothing to fear. They were fixed here for that night by a story against themselves. But they were not here that night; for Horne was murdering old Gallup in the Wood, while Wise was strangling that little Jew in his Roman bath. That's why I ask whether Wise was really strong enough for the climbing adventure.'

'It was quite a good adventure,' said Byrne regretfully. 'It fitted into the landscape, and was really very convincing.'

'Too convincing to convince,' said Father Brown, shaking his head. 'How very vivid was that moonlit foam flung up and turning to a ghost. And how very literary! Horne is a sneak and a skunk, but do not forget that, like many other sneaks and skunks in history, he is also a poet.'